Advance praise for
When It All Syncs Up

"A bold, insightful debut that explores young artists experiencing trauma. Maya Ameyaw writes about the psychological tolls and triumphs of dancing with a captivating freshness that will pull readers into this intense, intimate story."
—MARIKO TURK, author of *The Other Side of Perfect*

"Maya Ameyaw's storytelling is as expressive and entrancing as the human form in dance. *When It All Syncs Up* is a stunning read—an emotionally complex tale of friendships and first loves that's simmering with tension and gripping to the final word."
—DEBBIE RIGAUD, *New York Times* bestselling author of *Simone Breaks All the Rules* and *A Girl's Guide to Love & Magic*

"Aisha is every teen who's struggled to separate their self-worth from the expectations of their parents. A touching story of healing and self-discovery."
—RYAN DOUGLASS, *New York Times* bestselling author of *The Taking of Jake Livingston*

"With storytelling that's beautifully dark and moving, Ameyaw crafts a captivating journey of healing and growth."

—JOYA GOFFNEY, author of *Excuse Me While I Ugly Cry* and *Confessions of an Alleged Good Girl*

"When It All Syncs Up is a powerful story of finding the light when the clouds roll in. Ameyaw crafts an emotional tale of journeying through mental health dilemmas while dealing with friendship, love, and starting over. A gorgeous narrative of new beginnings, fresh hope, and taking back control."

—JOY L. SMITH, author of *Turning*

"Ameyaw's debut is raw and real. It contextualizes Black girlhood through the lens of mental health and what it looks like to heal within community. Aisha is strong and soft, a perfect balance in a relatable heroine."

—LOUISA ONOMÉ, author of *Like Home* and *Twice as Perfect*

"At times hopeful and beautiful but also heartbreakingly devastating, *When It All Syncs Up* is a story of love in so many forms. But maybe most important of all, it is about the love we give ourselves, and allow ourselves to be given, even at our most broken."

—JONNY GARZA VILLA, author of the Pura Belpré Honor Book *Fifteen Hundred Miles from the Sun*

"Delicate and fervent, like any good ballet performance, *When It All Syncs Up* is honest, captivating, and fresh. It will stay with you long after you've finished the book."

—GABRIELA MARTINS, author of *Like a Love Song* and *Bad at Love*

"*When It All Syncs Up* is a journey that will pirouette into your hearts and leave you breathless. So much more than a story about dance, the pages are filled with depth, tackling heavy issues from a relatable point of view. Ameyaw reminds us throughout of the lengths one will go to for the love of friendship. And how sometimes, finding your own path along the way will offer the surprising self-discovery of courage and strength. I cannot wait to see what's next from this debut author because I am here for the ride."

—VANESSA L. TORRES, author of *The Turning Pointe*

"*When It All Syncs Up* is a powerful, needed story of healing. Aisha deals with racism, mental health issues, and bullying, as well as experiencing first love. It's a story that will resonate with so many teens and help others have more compassion. The honesty, vibrancy, and compelling writing make it an unputdownable book."

—CHERYL RAINFIELD, author of *Scars* and *Stained*

"Powerful, moving, and achingly personal, *When It All Syncs Up* is the perfect read for teens who need a book that feels like a friend who understands."

—KAYLA ANCRUM, author of *The Wicker King*, *The Weight of the Stars*, and *Darling*

WHEN IT ALL Syncs UP

MAYA AMEYAW

annick press
toronto + berkeley

Cover design by Zainab's Echo
Cover art by PeachPod
Interior design by Zainab's Echo

Edited by Claire Caldwell
Copy edited by Debbie Innes
Proofread by Mary Ann Blair

Special thanks to Ameerah Holliday for her contributions to this work.

Annick Press Ltd.

We acknowledge the support of the Canada Council for the Arts and the Ontario Arts Council, and the participation of the Government of Canada/la participation du gouvernement du Canada for our publishing activities.

Library and Archives Canada Cataloguing in Publication

Title: When it all syncs up / Maya Ameyaw.
Names: Ameyaw, Maya, author.
Identifiers: Canadiana (print) 20220412820 | Canadiana (ebook) 20220412871 | ISBN 9781773217819 (hardcover) | ISBN 9781773217833 (HTML) | ISBN 9781773217840 (PDF)
Classification: LCC PS8601.M49 W54 2023 | DDC jC813/.6—dc23

Published in the U.S.A. by Annick Press (U.S.) Ltd.
Distributed in Canada by University of Toronto Press.
Distributed in the U.S.A. by Publishers Group West.

Printed in Canada

annickpress.com
mayaameyaw.com

Also available as an e-book. Please visit annickpress.com/ebooks for more details.

For all the highly melanated girls—
You are beautiful and belong in the sun.

—M.A.

Author's Note

The ultimate intention of this story is to hold space for people, particularly young Black women, who have experienced trauma. This is a story centered around healing and support; however, there are a lot of dark places that are travelled along the way.

Those sensitive to issues of racial discrimination, mental health challenges, disordered eating, and verbal abuse, please be aware that these topics are covered at length throughout this story. There are also a lot of on-the-page descriptions of addiction issues in relation to a supporting character, as well as brief off-the-page mentions of physical and sexual assault of a supporting character. I advise those who find these topics potentially triggering to proceed carefully and at their own pace.

1

"Stop freaking out. You've got this, Aisha."

Michaela's voice cuts through the jittery, jumbled thoughts that have me pinned in place in front of my dresser mirror. When I glance at her across my tiny dorm room, her dark eyes are fixed on me, daring me to disagree.

Inhaling deeply, I sink to the floor. The faint chemical musk of carpet cleaner fills my nose. My heartbeat starts to slow down as I contort myself into a split, pressing down hard on my calves.

"You're right. I worked my ass off last week."

"Exactly." Michaela's still focused on me, looking as effortlessly confident as always. *"Warner had to have noticed. You're definitely scoring an apprenticeship spot."*

"We'll see. Wish me luck."

Jumping up, I cross my room in a few steps. I tap my chest once before tapping hers. My fingers glide off the glossy magazine poster of Michaela DePrince tacked to the wall above my desk next to my Misty

Copeland and Raven Wilkinson posters. I tap Misty and Raven next.

Michaela's airborne form, poised gracefully in a *grand jeté*, is physics-defying. A pattern of tiny vitiligo spots is a beautiful explosion of sparks across her deep brown skin. My own skin is a similar shade but slightly darker.

"Sweetie, remember what I said about staying out of the sun!" My mom calls out as I skip into the kitchen from the backyard. My shoulders stiffen, but I pretend not to hear her as I twirl my iridescent pink Sailor Moon wand, watching it glimmer in the sunlight.

Snapping out of the memory, I find myself still staring at the poster. Looking away, my face grows warm like someone is witnessing this, even though I'm alone.

It's pretty sad that I've had a variation of this same fake conversation every morning for the last three years. But being almost friendless forces you to get creative.

I would definitely be completely friendless if Neil knew about my little morning ritual.

"I get that you love Michaela. But it's just a stupid *poster,* Ish." I can almost hear his snorting laugh.

I'm somehow annoyed even imagining Neil saying that. Which is dumb. I should stick to being annoyed with him about something he actually did—missing our weekly virtual dance party last night. I stayed up way too late waiting for him to call, but he must have fallen asleep early.

All right, here we go. Time to stop zoning out and talking to myself like a freak.

I grab my hoodie off the back of my desk chair and wrap it securely around my waist over my leotard. Straightening my spine, I perfect my posture, arranging my face in a placid expression fit for public consumption. Wouldn't want to scare anyone faint of heart with my natural resting bitch face.

Taking a final deep breath, I step out of the warmth of my room into the cool, hushed hallway. The rubber soles of my knitted boots squeak against the sparkling floor.

I squint my eyes almost shut. The rising sun peeking out from the towering crop of evergreens behind the dorms is way too bright through the empty hall's floor-to-ceiling windows.

A door clicks open behind me, and I quickly rummage around in my dance bag for my headphones. Tchaikovsky drifts gently into my ears, and I focus on mentally running through today's choreo. I visualize myself doing my *chaîné* turns effortlessly, my turnout flawless as the music swells.

I'm brought back to the present by someone shouldering past me, bumping me off balance from behind. Gritting my teeth for a moment, I force my face back into its unbothered position as I look up from my phone. It's Stephanie, not even stopping to apologize as she books it toward the washroom, her toiletry basket swinging wildly behind her.

Oh, no worries, Steph. I'm all good. Containing a sharp glare, I keep moving toward the studio.

Almost everyone is gathered by the windows when I get there. Taking my usual spot close to the door, I don't look up from my phone even as I feel their eyes on me.

There's some faint whispering, followed by the familiar sharp peal of laughter from Noelle. It always reminds me of the sound a cat would make if someone mistakenly stepped on its tail. There are some quieter giggles from her friends, and I turn my music up, a fury of strings drowning them out. I concentrate on changing into my pointe shoes.

Usually, summer vacation is a much-needed break from Noelle and the rest of the girls but not this year. Everyone else in our level is gone for the summer; there are just ten of us here for the final intensive.

Only five of us are going to move forward to the apprenticeship program at the Western Canadian Ballet, the major company that's partnered with my school. The program starts next week, once the school year is back in session. We've been in the studio all of August— today's our very last day.

I'm trying not to freak out about it too much, but this is the biggest opportunity I've had since Neil and I placed in the Youth American Grand Prix.

But that was almost exactly three years ago—basically a lifetime in ballet. This apprenticeship is my last chance to get back on track with potentially scoring a contract with a respected company.

The Western Canadian Ballet is as good as it'll get for me now. I try not to think too much about what could have been—what *should* have been. I try not to picture what it would have been like if Neil and I won YAGP scholarships to the School of American Ballet, the number one ballet school in North America. SAB is where we always planned to go when we were kids. We worked endless hours preparing for that before—

Squeezing my eyes closed, I shake my head. I can't do anything about the past now. All I can do is focus on nailing today.

Madame Warner enters, and everyone scrambles to their feet to take their places at the barre. Stephanie bolts in a second afterward and takes her spot, flanking Noelle. Warner puckers her wrinkled face, and Stephanie mutters an apology.

Warner turns on the music, and we begin warming up at the barre, starting with our *pliés*. I settle into my usual rhythm, studying my form carefully in the mirror as I move through the positions, bending my knees so they're exactly over my toes. Warner's voice slowly transforms into the voice of my first dance teacher, Madame Dmitriyev. That always happens when I'm in the zone; her deep, throaty voice keeping me in perfect time, yelling out the eight-count in Russian.

Close to the end of class, I feel eyes on me again, and I realize Warner has paused right in front of me. Which she's never done before.

She claps twice, and we all freeze. Her gaze remains fixed on me, and my stomach drops straight to my bowels.

Biting the inside of my cheek, I prepare myself to be reamed out for my form.

Tuck your zadnitsa! Madame D.'s voice reverberates in my brain from beyond the grave. I can almost feel the light tap of her cane on my butt, and I resist the urge to flinch.

"Let's see you solo," Warner says, and I blink at her. It takes me a moment to register the meaning of her words.

Earth to Aisha. This is it. This is your shot.

I manage a nod and force my shaking legs to move toward the front of the room. Sweat drips down the back of my neck.

I start, keeping my arms graceful and light as I lift them into my first position. I kick my front foot forward and up, my extended toe soaring toward the ceiling.

There's no way in hell I'm going to mess this up—not after everything. I've imagined this moment thousands of times. And now my daydreams are somehow bleeding into reality.

Letting go, my body fully awakens, and muscle memory sets in. My *chaîné* turns are perfectly executed as I float across the room in perfect time with the music. For a moment, I wonder if this is just another vivid fantasy, but when the music and my body stop as one, my heart rams against my ribcage so hard I know I can't be making this up.

Warner's studying me. The room is so silent I can hear birds trilling to each other from the woods outside the window.

Turning to the rest of the class, she lifts a finger in my direction. "*That's* what I want to see."

I can't help the grin that takes over my face. She's been stingy with praise all summer. Warner turns and faces me again; her eyes run the length of my body. She takes in my pink tights and pointe shoes—a stark contrast to my deep complexion. She says nothing to me, but her thoughts are as clear as day in her eyes.

What a shame.

The realization hits me with a sickening thud, leaving me breathless. It doesn't matter how closely I followed the choreo. Even though my movements were cuttingly precise, even though my figure—besides my overgrown legs and hips—matches the rest of the girls, my skin never will.

Warner looks away and swivels on her heel as she heads toward the door. "The apprenticeship list is posted in the locker room."

I walk back to my spot by the door with my head held high, consciously keeping my face as expressionless as possible as the other girls shoot me side-eyed glances. I swallow down the acidic rage sprouting within me.

Stay cool. Just stay cool. Grabbing my headphones, I switch from calming Tchaikovsky to my loudest playlist, electric guitars wailing in relentless riffs. I shut my eyes and make myself focus on some winding down stretches.

When everyone else has headed into the locker room, I slowly get to my feet. The sickly-sweet strawberry flavored meal replacement shake I forced down first thing this morning sloshes violently in my stomach.

You don't know for sure what Warner was thinking. You can't *know for sure. You're being paranoid.*

I push open the locker room door and glance at the list on the bulletin board. My name isn't there.

Okay. So I definitely read Warner's face correctly.

A squeezing knot forms in my throat. I manage to take in a full breath, tinged with the classic locker room mix of mildew and body odor.

I want to throw myself on the floor and scream, but I keep perfectly still. This was my very last chance; this was the only way I would ever be able to get anywhere decent with my ballet career—

Keep it together.

I collapse onto a bench near my locker, facing away from the other girls. With a flick of my wrist, I sweep some stray braids back into my bun and start untying my pointe shoes.

The tip of my left shoe is a deep crimson. When I get it off, the bandage on my big toe is soaked through. I grab a new bandage and unwrap the old one, discovering what's left of my toenail barely hanging on. Bracing myself, I rip it off.

I think of pain in levels since I'm always in it, my muscles perpetually aching. Losing a toenail usually cuts through the background pain for a sharp moment, but the wince that crosses my face is only a reflex.

I feel absolutely nothing.

My pulse speeds up to a vibrating hum, and the fluorescent overhead lights start to weave and bob erratically. All sensation in my feet fades, but it's not like normal pins and needles. It's like my nerve endings have all been snipped at once.

A locker door slams, and the room comes back into focus. I run a hand over my sweaty face and rewrap my toe as tightly as I can, fresh blood seeping through the new dressing.

The girls' voices fade and then they're gone, leaving me alone in the locker room. The bone-deep numbness in my feet spreads up my ankles and then my legs before it races through me. Erasing me.

I untether from myself like a ghostly apparition. Somehow, I'm now staring into my own dark eyes, as lifeless as a propped-up doll's.

The utter strangeness of this jars me back into my body again. I bite my tongue to keep from yelling out.

What the hell is happening to me?

Trembling, I get to my feet and throw on my hoodie before I grab my bag. When I get out into the hallway, it's empty. Searing midday sun is unabashedly streaming in through the windows now. I should head to the cafeteria to grab lunch, but as if of their own accord, my feet move toward the dorms.

I stare at my phone's lock screen. It's a picture of me and Neil— we're both laughing so hard our faces are contorted, our grins slightly blurred as we throw our heads back. For the life of me, I can't remember what was so funny. It could've been anything. He never fails to crack me up with the dumbest shit.

Since I didn't get the apprenticeship, maybe I could visit Neil before the school year starts up again next week? Dad should be okay with it; he let me visit him last summer.

The cool surface of my phone is pressed up against my ear, and I become aware of it ringing.

When I hear Neil's voice, I let out a breath of relief.

"You know what to do."

"What?" There's a blaring beep, and I register it's just his voicemail.

This is the first time he hasn't picked up my call. Ever. I stare at my phone in disbelief for a moment before hanging up and calling my dad instead.

"Hey, honey. What's up?" he says through a yawn. "It's late over here."

I wince at myself for blanking on the fact that Tokyo is sixteen hours ahead. "Oh yeah, sorry."

"No worries. What's going on? Did you get into the program?" he asks, his voice perking up. "Congrats!"

I step back into my room. Now that I'm alone, I let my face fall and my shoulders droop.

"I didn't get in." I keep my voice as light as I can manage. "No big deal, though," I add quickly.

I really don't want him to start worrying about me again. Like when he sent me to that horrible clinic before I moved here. Shaking my head, I envision holding a match to the memory and setting it ablaze.

But whatever just happened in the locker room, it wasn't like before. As spaced out as I used to get sometimes, floating out of my own body is a brand-new development in terms of my general screwed-up-ness.

"I know how much this meant to you, honey. I'm so sorry. Are you all right?"

I kick off my boots and plop down on my bed, stomach first.

"I'll be okay. I can go to a dance college instead when I graduate." I say this like it's a perfectly feasible second option instead of the complete failure that it truly is. The most prestigious ballet companies in the world choose their new dancers through apprenticeships, not college programs.

"Are you sure you're all right?" His voice gets all syrupy with concern.

"Yeah, it's fine." Bitterness almost overwhelms me for a moment, but I push it back down. Stewing over this won't change the fact that my future of mediocrity is now sealed. "I was only calling to check in . . . Do you mind if I visit Neil in Toronto for a few days before school starts next week? I promise I won't book a super pricey flight or anything."

He's silent for a long moment.

I wonder if he's annoyed that I didn't ask to visit him in Tokyo instead. As much as I would really love to see him, he'd probably have to work the whole time I was there anyway. Biting my lip, I fight the urge to ask if he can visit me anytime soon. I know it'll just make him feel bad if he can't get time off before Christmas.

"Okay, that's fine. But I need to ask you something first." His voice is strangely grave.

"Uh, sure. What is it?"

"Are you and Neil dating?"

I screw up my face in confusion as I wrack my brain for anything that could have prompted this from him. Neil and I met when Madame D. put us together at her dance studio when we were eight.

Before my parents' divorce, he was over at our house almost every day. He's basically family.

"Yeah. We're dating." I snort as I roll over onto my back. "We've been keeping this from you for years. Congrats, you finally clocked us. You're kidding, right?"

I expect him to laugh but he doesn't. "If you're seeing each other now, I'm not comfortable with you staying over at his place like when you were kids."

I roll my eyes toward the ceiling. "You know we're just friends."

He's quiet again for a moment before responding. "I didn't expect you two to stay so close these last few years."

I'm guessing that's because the last time Dad saw him, I wasn't exactly thrilled with Neil. It was the day I left for the academy. We'd stopped at Neil's house to say goodbye on the way to the airport.

Neil stares down at his front steps, refusing to look at me.

My voice is almost gone from screaming. I'm completely beyond caring that Dad can hear me from the car a few feet away. "You promised you wouldn't—"

I sit up abruptly, suddenly short of breath. *Don't think about it.* Shaking my head, I make myself focus on his voice again.

"I thought you'd make some new friends in Alberta—"

"I thought you liked Neil." Neil and my dad used to be close too, to the point that it irritated me sometimes when they would talk for hours on end about boring-ass sports crap.

"I do. He's a great kid."

Thankfully, Dad has no idea that Neil isn't quite the same sweet little goody-two-shoes he used to be.

"Well, like I said, it isn't like that with us. So can I go?"

"All right. Just check in with Neil's dad. And one last thing—"

"I won't visit Mom while I'm in town," I say in a monotone.

God, why is he so obsessed with thinking I want to see her every chance I get? I've always been way closer with him than my mom—even before the divorce. But in the past couple years, I've only seen her for brief, awkward holiday dinners before my dad and I would go actually celebrate with Mexican takeout.

"Aisha," he says warningly. "I know you think I'm being ridiculous. But I don't feel comfortable with you seeing your mother on your own."

Why would I even want to see her? The idea of telling her I didn't get the apprenticeship makes my skin itch like I'm about to break out in hives.

"I promise, I won't," I say, keeping the annoyance out of my voice this time.

"Thank you. Let me know when you land safely. Love you."

"Okay. You too."

Once I'm off the phone with him, I try Neil again.

I let out a long breath when I get his answering machine. "How the hell are you *still* asleep? Look, sorry this is last minute, but I'm heading back to the city. I can crash at your place, right? Call me back."

I toss my phone on the mattress and look over at Michaela, Misty, and Raven. I wait for some reassuring words, but there's nothing. They're just stupid, silent posters.

That same consuming numbness from the locker room starts to creep up on me again. Before it can overtake me, I jump up from my bed and hastily untack the posters. Not able to bear the thought of crumpling them, I just release my hold, letting them float gently into the waste can. Turning away, I go to the dresser and empty its contents into my gym bag.

I try to convince myself that a break from this place is all I need. Once I see Neil, I'll for sure feel more like myself again.

2

When I get off the plane at Pearson, the continual conspicuousness of being one of the only Black people in a public space subsides. The back of my neck stops prickling from the sensation of being constantly watched.

The faces in the jam-packed terminal reflect a dizzying array of cultures from around the world. I sidestep a pair of zombified parents and their screeching twin toddlers before letting my agreeable veneer slip from my face. Navigating through the crowd toward the exit, I swear under my breath when Neil doesn't pick up my call for the thousandth time.

Humidity blasts me in the face as I step out of the terminal and head toward the taxi queue. I wipe my sweaty forehead, trying to come up with some explanation other than Neil not wanting to talk to me. Maybe he lost his phone charger. Maybe he lost his phone altogether. Neil's not the sort of person who loses track of his things often, though.

Is he upset with me for some reason? He's been a little weird recently, calling me at the oddest hours, but he hasn't said anything out of the ordinary. The last time we talked was two nights ago. I always sleep with my phone on vibrate next to my pillow to be ready if he calls. I'd been so dead asleep I didn't even remember waking up and grabbing my phone. I'd just found myself sitting up in bed, his groggy voice in my ear.

"Ish?"

"Yeah. I'm here." The pitch-dark window reflected my puffy eyes back at me. I rubbed a hand over my face and groaned internally.

Neil usually called me super late once a month, but in the week before that call it had turned into almost every night.

We talked and laughed about nothing like we always did—what teachers we hated, stupid drama at school—anything and everything except for the fact that it was three in the morning. It was getting more and more difficult not to ask him what was going on with him, but I held my tongue. I knew he'd just shut me down like always.

He lost his phone. He had to have lost his phone. I try to take a deep breath of hot, smoggy air as I shoot my dad a text to let him know I landed. Shuffling forward in the taxi line, I try Neil again, just to leave him another message that I'm on my way over. There's the click of the line being picked up after only one ring.

I let out a full exhale for the first time all day. "Thank God."

"Uh, hey, Aisha." It isn't Neil's voice.

My mind races for a moment before I realize it's his friend Ollie. We've only spoken on the phone a few times, but I distinctly remember the melodic way my name rolls off his tongue. He says it with two syllables instead of three, the way it's pronounced in Arabic. "This is—"

"Ollie, I'm headed to Neil's right now," I cut him off as I inch closer to the front of the taxi line. I plug my right ear and raise my voice above a honking cab. "Are you with him? Why do you have his phone?"

"Wait, you're in town?"

"Where's Neil?"

"He's, uh . . . We're—we're—at the . . ." I strain to hear his voice.

Bile scratches its way up my throat as I hazard a guess. "At the hospital?"

Ollie sighs. "Yeah. Mercy General."

I tighten my grip on my gym bag strap until it digs deep into my palm.

"What happened? Is he okay?"

Why am I only asking this now instead of any of the nights Neil called and things seemed off with him? My mind shuts down for a moment. Another car horn sounds, and I snap back into myself and realize it's my turn to grab a taxi.

Ollie still hasn't answered me.

"Is he okay?" My voice is half-strangled as I rush forward and open the cab's back door.

"You should get down here."

∗
∗

Outside my window, the sunset ignites the sky for a final moment before it's snuffed out by the night. All around me, endless dark windows in overgrown skyscrapers start to blink awake. I count the tiny rectangles of waking light instead of the price meter rocketing upward as the taxi inches its way through gridlocked traffic.

Once we're out of the downtown core, traffic eases up as we head toward the city's outer limits. Skyscrapers are replaced by social housing units and dated strip malls that sit only streets apart from lakefront mansions and sprawling golf courses. Neighborhoods filled with smaller mid-century houses are scattered across the divide. Eventually, the cab approaches Mercy General, and I grab my credit card out of my wallet. Thankfully, I found a deal on my flight earlier—the cost of the taxi would've maxed out my card otherwise.

I know I should call my dad and tell him Neil's in the hospital. But I also know he won't let me stay at his place anymore if he finds out.

Maybe he injured himself dancing. Neil quit ballet after I moved away because his dad couldn't afford to let him keep competing professionally or send him to a private academy like mine, without a scholarship. But I know he still does other styles like modern, jazz, and hip hop at his public school. Or maybe he was just messing around doing a stunt like a backflip and broke his arm or something. Hopefully it's not anything serious.

I've never been inside Mercy General before. When I developed tendinitis when I first started pointe work, my parents took me to a specialist at St. Paul's, which is a few miles closer to our old house by the lake. I remember its entrance was framed with an immaculately maintained garden. Mercy General's first level is covered in old construction siding painted with intricate street art.

The emergency room's AC turns my sweat into a wet chill that shoots shivers through me. The small waiting room is half-full and within a few seconds I spot Ollie sitting in one of the tiny plastic green chairs that line the room.

He's a tall, skinny kid in a faded band tee. His deep olive skin tone suggests that he might have a Middle Eastern background, but I don't actually know. I've never met him in person before. I only recognize him from the times he's been over at Neil's place while we were on FaceTime. He's half-stranger, half someone I know a weird amount of personal things about. Ollie is Neil's closest friend besides me, so his name has come up fairly often in the last couple of years.

Ollie's expression fills me with such dread that I can't move. After a moment, I force myself forward until I'm right in front of him. He's standing now, his gangly arms hanging limp at his sides. He avoids my gaze, staring past me at the sliding exit doors. I wrap my arms around myself to keep from visibly shaking.

"What happened?" My voice comes out too loud, but I don't care.

He sits down again, looking like he doesn't know what to do with himself. "I guess Neil got really wasted last night."

"By himself?"

His dad is often out of town for work and never locks up the liquor cabinet. Neil dips into his dad's supply sometimes for our weekly dance nights, and we had a few drinks last summer, but I didn't realize he did that alone.

Ollie nods. "When I dropped by his place earlier . . ." He stops short and hunches in on himself, digging his fingers into his eyelids. I take a slow breath to stop myself from yelling at him to finish his sentence. Eventually, he mumbles into his hands, but I still make out his words. "He wouldn't wake up, so I called 911."

"Fuck," I whisper as my legs give, and I thud into the chair next to him. "Is he all right?"

He shakes his head. "I don't know."

"What do you mean?" My pulse buzzes in my ears, and I can't catch my breath. "Why wouldn't he wake up?"

"When I found him, he was . . ." He stops short, taking a deep breath.

I manage a sympathetic nod and clamp down on my tongue since it looks like he's not processing anymore. He's obviously having a hard time.

From some stuff Neil's mentioned in passing, I know that Ollie's had a bit of a difficult time outside of all this. But I need him to tell me what happened to Neil right now.

After an excruciating minute, Ollie speaks again. He stares down at his hands, a mass of loose curls falling into his face and obscuring his eyes. "By the time the ambulance got to his place, he wasn't doing so hot."

That's all he says, but the weight of everything he's not telling me slams down on my chest. I blink against my swirling vision, still unable to catch my breath.

"How long ago was that?" I choke out. I grip my knees to keep my hands still.

"A few hours ago. They haven't told me anything yet. I tried calling his dad, but his voicemail is full. Do you know another way to reach him?"

Tightening my grip on my knees, I shake my head. Neil doesn't talk about it, but I've gathered over the years that his mom died when he was little, before we knew each other. Ollie doesn't ask about Neil's mom, so I guess he knows.

He finally focuses on my face for more than a second, studying me for a long moment. His dark brown eyes are rimmed in red. "You live out in Alberta, right? Neil didn't say you'd be visiting."

"It was last minute," I mutter, looking away from him.

Somehow, Ollie has never been around when I've been in town to visit Neil, even though he lives the next street over from him. Last summer, Neil said he was going to stop by, like, three times the week I was there, but he never ended up showing.

We fall into a silence that stretches into a painful chasm.

The quiet hum of the lights and the hushed conversations become muted and distant. All I can think is how I should have tried to talk to Neil about something other than all the dumb things that didn't matter.

I start losing feeling in my feet again, and the numbness slithers up my legs. Curling up in my chair, I hug my knees tight, like that'll somehow keep me from exiting my body.

"Aisha?"

I blink, jolting back into myself. From the way Ollie's staring at me, he must have said my name more than once.

"Are you feeling okay?"

The fact that he's asking me that—considering how messed up he is right now—alerts me that I must really look like I'm losing it. I mean to nod but shake my head instead.

"Here." He reaches into his pocket and holds an earbud out to me.

After staring at it for a moment, I put it in my ear, and he sticks the other in his own. He turns on an old folk song I've never heard before. I close my eyes, focusing on the gentle, calming chords.

After a few hours, I feel like I should give his earbud back to him and listen to my own music, but I don't. Everything he's put on has miraculously kept my mind from traveling to terrible places.

"This is really good," I find myself saying after a while.

Ollie starts out of his half-asleep daze, his head almost bumping mine. "What?"

I point at his phone on the armrest between us.

He hands it over and shuts his eyes again. I take my time flipping through his encyclopedic collection. Even though we've been waiting for hours at this point, I haven't looked through even a fraction of his library by the time we're called up to the front.

We're moved to a smaller waiting room. A nurse, a middle-aged man in scrubs with deep bags under his eyes, shows up and starts asking questions. I can't stop myself from interrupting him.

"Can you tell us where our friend is now?"

"I'll see what I can find out. And where are your parents?"

Ollie stares dully. "Sleeping, I'd guess?" It's a little after three in the morning.

"I'm from out of town," I say quickly when the nurse turns to me. "Can you please let us know if he's all right?" My voice cracks at the end.

The nurse sighs. "I'll be right back."

He heads for the door and closes it quietly behind him. Ollie watches him head toward reception and then turns to me. "Aren't you from here originally? Your parents don't live in town anymore?"

Neil's mentioned things about Ollie in the past couple years, so he's probably told Ollie lots of things about me too. The thought makes my face prickle with heat, wondering if Neil told him anything about my parents' divorce or what happened around the time I left for the academy.

I shrug noncommittally, and he gives me a long, unreadable look.

Guilt tugs at my gut. I tell myself for the millionth time that Neil's going to be all right and I shouldn't worry my dad about this. I can handle it. I don't need to call him yet. Neil has to be okay.

We both turn when we hear the door open and the nurse steps back in.

"Neil Roi's in room 136. He had a bad case of alcohol poisoning, but he's in stable condition now . . ." He says more but I can't concentrate, I'm so relieved. The invisible vice that's been squeezing my windpipe starts to loosen.

The nurse exits again, and as soon as he's gone my body betrays me, the sobs I've been choking down all night erupting. I wish the scuffed linoleum floor would crack open, dropping me into the earth's depths. Instead, I'm stuck here while Ollie witnesses this pathetic display.

"Aisha." Ollie's hand brushes my back for half a second. "He's okay."

I nod, but my face won't stop leaking. He grabs a tissue from the box on the table and crouches in front of me, handing it over. I can't meet his gaze, my face burning as I wipe it dry. Ollie's still crouched in front of me, like he's at a loss for what to do now.

I clear my stuffed-up throat before managing to focus on him. "Thanks."

Ollie opens his mouth, but no sound escapes him. He blinks at me with glazed eyes before the space between us is gone. My face is absolutely flaming now. It happened so fast that I don't know if it was him who moved to wrap his arms around me or if I leaned in first. His hand is on the back of my head, and I find myself pressing my face into his shirt. The harsh fluorescence of the room and every single one of my thoughts are completely blotted out.

The doorknob rattles, and I jerk away from Ollie at the sound, almost knocking him over.

An older nurse enters, hardly glancing at us as she focuses on her chart. "You can see"—she squints at the sheet—"Neil Roi now. Follow me."

3

Ollie and I are silent as the nurse leads us to Neil's room. I feel Ollie glance at me, but I'm unable to meet his eyes, so I focus on a small wet spot on the shoulder of his T-shirt instead. When it occurs to me that the stain is my gross doing, I quickly look over at the nurse again.

She stops in front of Neil's room and turns to us. "Visiting hours are over, but I'll give you a few minutes."

I nod before she walks off. Taking a deep breath, I open the door.

"Ish?" Neil's voice is a hoarse shadow of itself as he sits up in his cramped bed. "What're you doing here?"

Crossing the tiny room in a second flat, I wrap my arms around him. He hugs back for a moment before detaching himself from my grip. "Seriously, what are you doing in town?"

I sink into the threadbare chair next to him. "I didn't get the apprenticeship. You didn't get any of my messages?"

Neil shakes his head as he looks over my shoulder. When I glance behind me, Ollie's hovering by the door, next to the rectangular slit of a window. He's staring down at the barren parking lot below.

"Sorry you didn't get in. That really sucks," Neil says.

I turn back to him and shrug. "I've been trying to reach you all day. What happened? Why did you get so drunk last night?"

"Uh . . ." I've never seen him at a loss for words before. His eyes are spaced out as he rubs a hand through his jet-black crew cut. "I can't remember anything. Did you guys . . . ?" He leaves the unasked question floating in the room.

Ollie answers. "Aisha called your phone after. I told her we were here."

Neil focuses on Ollie again. They say nothing, but unspoken volumes pass between them. My brain works to come up with a translation, but all I'm able to decode is something so excruciating that I'm forced to look away.

"I'm sorry," Neil says, his voice entirely empty. "I didn't mean to . . . I don't know. I just got a little too messed up."

I shake my head. "Why were you drinking by yourself, though?"

Neil lifts and drops his shoulders beneath his hospital gown. "It's not a big deal. For real. I mean, I'm hungover as hell. But other than that, I'm good."

I search his eyes for clues. Why won't he just tell me what's up with him? "You know it's all right if you're not."

He's silent for a moment before letting out a jarring laugh. "Is this the part where I'm supposed to burst into tears or something? Everything's fine."

"I don't believe you," I croak out.

His face drops all at once, and I don't recognize anything in his eyes.

I squeeze my eyes shut for a second, half hoping that this is a nightmare. It's not, though. This is really happening.

When I left school, I knew I needed to get here. Needed to see Neil so I could feel normal again. So I could stop floating away from myself. But here I am next to him, and everything is so incredibly wrong.

His usually warm, golden complexion has a sickly pale, bluish tint. In a flash, I'm imagining what I would have found if Ollie hadn't stopped by Neil's place earlier.

"You good?" Neil asks, right before tears start rolling down my face for the second time in less than ten minutes. "Oh."

Neil and I stare at each other in horror. Crying isn't something we do.

"Ish . . ."

I jump up and turn away from Neil's bed as sobs threaten to overtake me again. The weight of Ollie's eyes settles on me as I rush past him by the door. The hallway is a blur before I burst out of the closest exit and force humid air into my lungs.

God, it was so ridiculously childish to run off like that. I wish this crying thing would stop. It's like a watertight seal has been broken inside me.

After a minute, I collect myself and head back inside. I make my face as composed as I can before I walk back into his room. From how they both stop speaking, I know they must have been talking about me.

"I'm fine," I mutter, crossing my arms and leaning back against the door.

Neil nods before focusing on his phone, which Ollie must have given back to him.

"I e-mailed my dad. He should be back from his business trip soon to sign me out of here. Anyways, I'm probably gonna knock out in a few. Why don't you guys go get some sleep and come back later?"

I nod. "Sounds good. Is your spare key still under the patio chair?"

He doesn't answer me. "Ollie said you can stay at his place while I'm in here."

I shoot Neil a baffled look. "What? Why?"

Risking a glance at Ollie, I find him seated in the chair I vacated. He stares at the floor.

"Could you please stay at his place?" Neil insists. "It's not a good idea for you to stay at mine right now."

I shake my head. "But—"

"Please." There's a desperate edge to his voice that stops me from protesting further.

Ollie gives me an uneasy glance that tells me this probably wasn't his idea.

"Would your parents even be okay with that?" I ask.

Ollie takes in a slow breath before nodding. "No worries, it's cool."

I stumble back as the door I'm leaning on swings open.

The older nurse fixes me with an impatient look. "It's time to go."

Ollie stands then gives Neil a quick one-armed hug and daps him up. I move toward Neil, wanting to hug him goodbye, but I don't trust myself not to start blubbering again.

I squeeze his arm. "I'll be back in a few hours."

*

We take the bus over to Neil and Ollie's sleepy little neighborhood. First light filters through the lush canopy of Neil's willow-tree-lined street. The silence is complete—not even early morning joggers are up yet.

"We can cut through Neil's backyard to get to my place faster," Ollie says when we reach Neil's rustic, burgundy brick bungalow.

I walk around the side of the house and open the latched wooden fence to the backyard.

"It's okay. I can stay here." I turn to face Ollie behind me.

"I promise, I'm not like a weirdo murderer or anything." He attempts a weak laugh.

"I know. I'll be fine by myself, though." I walk over to the small back patio and lift the leg of one of the lounge chairs closest to the door, feeling around for the key.

"I have it," Ollie says. "I know you'll be fine by yourself. But you probably don't want to go in there right now."

I walk over to him and hold out my hand. "Give me the key."

He doesn't move, just stares right through me. The circles under his eyes are stark and hollow.

"What's the problem? Tell me why you guys don't want me going in there."

Ollie blinks slowly and for a long moment I think he didn't hear me.

Eventually, he responds, his voice far off. "He puked everywhere."

"Oh." It finally clicks that they've been trying to spare me from the aftermath. "Well, I guess I'll go with you then."

He doesn't respond, and I can tell he's thinking about finding Neil earlier. I think I might be sick myself, but I swallow down my nausea.

"Hey, come on. Let's go," I murmur, bumping his arm lightly with my elbow.

Ollie's eyes stop fogging over and he examines me closely. I know he's wondering if I'm actually comfortable staying at his place. I keep his gaze for the first time since we hugged earlier. I try to smile in a way that's reassuring.

A shadow of a smile crosses his face before he looks away. "Okay. My house is only a couple minutes from here."

We clear the short chain-link fence, overgrown with vines and weeds, that separates Neil's backyard from a heavily wooded park. Neil and I explored every inch of it when we were kids, racing each other up and down all the winding hiking trails.

We cross the park, climb another low fence, and approach the back of a large but dated two-story house with the same dark red brick exterior as Neil's place.

Ollie pushes the sliding patio door open. "Go ahead. We'll have to be quiet. If my parents wake up, they'll be mad I stayed out all night."

I frown. "You didn't call them? Are you really sure they'll be cool with this?"

"Yeah, it's fine. I just don't want to deal with them so early."

"Okay." I step hesitantly inside the quiet kitchen and inhale the warm scent of saffron and thyme even though there's no food on the stove. The only noise is the hum of the refrigerator, covered in a mess of photos, notes, and drawings. It looks normal enough, cluttered and cozy. A sharp contrast to the sterile, sparse way my mother maintained our house when I was younger.

"Hungry?" Ollie whispers.

I shake my head. I feel starved but can't imagine getting anything down.

He walks past me, leading the way to the front hallway littered with shoes and up the narrow, creaky staircase. The noise is impossibly loud. There's a faint snore emanating from a closed door at the top of the stairs. One of his parents? I think Neil mentioned Ollie has an older sister, but I don't know if she still lives at home. I follow him down the short hallway, holding my breath whenever my footsteps produce more creaks.

He opens the last door, and the first thing I see are records, a wall of them. He closes the door behind him as I step toward the stacked wooden crates. The titles mirror the expansive variety of music on his phone, spanning the gamut of genres, from indie alternative, psychedelic rock, metal, and experimental, to old-school hip hop, Motown, soul, and the Blues. His remaining walls are plastered in band posters.

"Nice vinyl collection," I say under my breath, afraid to speak above a whisper.

"Thanks. You can take the bed. I'll sleep on the couch."

Before I can respond, there's a soft knock at the door. My heart kicks at my ribs, and I shoot Ollie a wide-eyed look.

"It's fine, it's only my sister." He opens the door a smidge. "What?"

"Where were you last night?" a girl's voice whispers. Through the thin split between the wall and the doorframe, all I can see of her is her wavy, deep brown hair, the long version of Ollie's own.

"Out."

"Are you *kidding* me right now? If you're not gonna come home all night, maybe let me know so I can cover for you? You're so lucky Mom and Dad turned in early."

"Can we do this later?"

"Have you been crying?"

I shouldn't be here listening to them. I'm tempted to take a step back, but I'm afraid she'll catch sight of me moving.

"I'm just tired. Can we not—?"

"What's wrong?"

There's a pause before he sighs. "It's Neil. He's in the hospital."

"*What?* What happened?"

"He's gonna be fine."

"But—"

"Sophie." He's trying to keep his voice down. "Not now. I can't . . ." Ollie trails off into silence.

She steps forward to hug him. I don't move a muscle, but her eyes are closed.

"Sorry. You can tell me later. I know it must have been hard, being back there."

I have the feeling I'm intruding again, like I shouldn't have heard that. It's awkward that I know she's probably talking about when Ollie was in the hospital. Neil didn't go into any detail, but he mentioned someone at his school beat Ollie up pretty badly in ninth grade.

"Christ, get off me." He wriggles himself out of her grip, and she spots me, her mouth dropping open.

Sophie's head swivels between me and Ollie.

"I'm Neil's friend," I sputter, my face flaming. "I just needed a place to crash."

"All right . . . Nice to meet you . . . ?" Sophie looks me up and down quizzically.

"Aisha."

She nods before raising an eyebrow at Ollie.

He rubs a hand over his face. "Don't say anything to Mom and Dad."

"Why? I'm sure they'd let her stay for a few days. I mean, probably not in your—"

Ollie cuts her off. "Just don't."

I'm standing in the middle of the room, unsure what to do now. I fold my arms around myself, my face still boiling.

She rolls her eyes at Ollie. "I won't. Come up to the roof later so we can talk. Oh, and stop leaving the bong up there. Mom and Dad might spot it."

Ollie nods briefly before he shuts the door in her face.

"You said your parents wouldn't mind."

"They won't, I swear. But they'll probably start asking you all about your parents and everything." He's quiet for a beat. "Neil said your dad works out of the country like his dad. What about your mom?"

I press my lips together, containing a groan. I have no idea how to explain that my dad has basically forbidden me from seeing her, without sparking way more questions about my messed-up family.

I focus on the complicated pattern of the large rug beneath my feet. "I don't wanna get into it."

"That's fine," he says, his voice betraying his exhaustion. He crosses the room and aims himself at an old blue and gray plaid couch under the window. "Bathroom's by the closet if you need it."

I perch on the edge of his bed, feeling guilty that I didn't insist on taking the couch. But my muscles do ache more than usual from being cramped in the hard plastic hospital chairs for hours, so I'm thankful for the chance to sleep in an actual bed.

I glance at my phone as I get under the covers. I should call my dad, but I don't know what I'd even tell him. He was already worried about me staying with Neil. He'd shit a brick if he knew I was crashing with some random boy he doesn't know.

Okay, Ollie's not exactly a random boy. I honestly have no clue how

I would have survived last night without him there at the hospital. I peek over at him. He's already fast asleep, his breathing slow and even. One of his arms dangles off the couch onto the floor.

I find myself thinking about when he wrapped his arms around me and everything stopped being so horrible for a second. I take a deep breath and try to stop thinking about it, but his bedding smells exactly like he did. The sharp pine scent of guy's soap, citrus laundry detergent, and a hint of something sweet I can't name.

My cheeks start getting all hot again. *Stop being weird.* Why the hell am I thinking about how this kid freaking smells? I need to focus on Neil.

I can't even begin to process all the things that happened in the last twenty-four hours. My insides feel tattered and raw. I'm so confused about why Neil did what he did. I had no idea he was feeling shitty enough to drink that much on his own.

Is this something he's been doing a lot or was it a one-time thing? Even though he tried to brush it off as an accident, I can't stop thinking about how empty his eyes got when I called him out. Shuddering, I wrap the blanket tighter around me. Neil's supposed to be the one person I know better than anyone, yet I don't have the slightest clue what's going on in his head.

I squeeze my eyes shut and try not to hyperventilate. I'm such an awful friend for missing how much he was struggling, for not pushing him to actually talk to me. How am I supposed to fix any of this? How am I supposed to get Neil to admit there's something going on with him?

Darkness seeps into the edges of my vision, and my brain starts flickering off. I'll have to figure things out after I get some sleep.

Unable to keep my eyes open any longer, I let unconsciousness pull me under.

4

Delicate strumming guides me from a deep, dreamless state into the impossibly still realm between slumber and the waking world. My eyes stay closed even as I break free of the last remnants of sleep.

For a long moment, I think it's the murmuring of Ollie's record player. But when I eventually open my eyes, I find him sitting at his desk with an acoustic guitar, his back to me. He's singing but so softly I can't hear the words. His tone nearly lulls me back into the serene, middle space I just stepped out of.

Late afternoon light beams in through the window, streaking his dark curls with honey and molasses. He stops for a moment to reach for a pen and scribbles something into the open notebook in front of him, muttering lyrics to himself.

I sit up, and he spins in his chair.

"Didn't mean to wake you up." He puts his guitar down by his feet.

"That's okay," I say through a yawn. "What're you playing?"

He closes his notebook and starts rubbing at his forehead. "Just trying to get this song done for my audition for school tomorrow."

"Don't stop on my account," I say as I get out of bed, automatically moving into my morning stretches.

Ollie stares down at his closed notebook like he can read right through the cover. "I was done." He gets up and heads for the door. "I'll grab you something to eat, okay?" He's gone before I can respond.

I let out a sigh as I finish up my stretches. He probably hates having me here, taking up his space. For a moment, I consider going over to Neil's, but I don't think I can stomach cleaning up over there.

My phone rings, and I grab it off the nightstand. It's my dad. Shit. If I start avoiding his calls, he'll definitely know something isn't right.

Bracing myself, I sit on the edge of the bed and pick up. "Hey, Dad."

"Hey, honey. Did you get in okay yesterday? Sorry I couldn't call earlier, I've been slammed at work."

"Yeah, I got back fine, everything's cool," I say, forcing my voice to be light and normal. "Anyway, I'll let you get back to—"

"Hope you like Algerian food." I turn quickly to see Ollie has entered the room again, carrying two large plates. "That's pretty much all my mom makes, and there's a lot of lamb involved. Are you vegetarian or anything?"

I frantically put a finger to my lips.

"Who was that?" my dad asks.

Ollie winces and mouths an apology as he sets my plate on the nightstand before sitting back at his desk with his own.

"Uh, that was Neil. We were just about to eat. Call you later."

"Okay." I'm not sure if he buys it or not. "Tell him I said hi."

"I will, bye." I hang up quickly.

"I didn't realize you were on the phone," Ollie says. "Everything good?"

"I think so. This looks great, thanks," I say as normally as I can manage even as my heart starts to pound erratically. I pick up my fork, sticking it into a piece of dolma, a bite-sized bundle of rice wrapped in a grape leaf.

I haven't had rice in years. It always goes straight to my hips and thighs. Mom used to hate whenever Dad would make jollof for dinner. It was so packed with cayenne pepper that it made my eyes water, but I still loved it.

"She can't eat that stuff anymore," Mom grumbles at him across the dinner table. *"I already told you her ballet teacher said no carbs—"*

I shake her voice away, but I'm still acutely aware this is the first time I've eaten in front of someone in a while. At school, I usually grab something small from the cafeteria and eat alone in the studio or my room, avoiding the skin-crawling feeling of anyone watching me. I shoot Ollie a quick glance, and my gut unclenches when I see he's completely focused on his own plate. I take a cautious bite of dolma. There's a little explosion of flavor in my mouth, notes of cumin and a hint of cinnamon mixed in with the rice and ground lamb. I gobble down a few pieces before I force myself to stop. Pushing around the couscous and leg of lamb on my plate, I nibble at some peas. My stomach starts to rumble. Ignoring the guilt, I finish off the dolma.

I make myself put my fork down. "This is super good, but I'm not that hungry."

"Do you want water or anything?"

I shake my head. "We should probably talk."

He finally looks up from his almost empty plate. "About what?"

"Neil." If I'm going to figure out how to deal with whatever it is that's going on with him, I highly doubt I'll be able to do it on my own. "Was this . . . ? Is this the first time that he . . . ?" God, I'm so bad at this.

Ollie nods when I don't finish. "Yeah. This is the first time he ended up in the hospital. He's been blackout drunk a lot, though."

"Have you asked what's up with him?" Like I should have. Neil's *my* best friend after all. I mean, I thought he was.

"I asked," he says.

"How?"

He looks at me sideways. "How what?"

"How did you ask him?"

Whenever Neil seemed in a bad place before, he would always brush me off when I asked about it until I just stopped. It went both ways. I know he could tell how bad things got for me at school sometimes, but I would never get into it, so he left me alone about it.

"I just said he seemed off," he says. "You know how he is. He said he was fine. I told him if he ever wants to talk about anything to let me know. That was about it."

"I don't know how to make him talk about this," I admit.

"We can't make him. But he really needs to cool it on the drinking," Ollie says. "I don't think he's gonna want to hear that, though."

"We still have to talk to him about it. I mean, not like a big intervention thing or anything but like . . ." I trail off not knowing how to finish.

Ollie nods. "We should get back to the hospital. If you wanna avoid my parents, we'll have to climb down the tree by my window."

*

Back at Mercy General, we get visitor passes and head to Neil's room. When I open the door, I freeze, not expecting to see Ollie's sister, Sophie, sitting by his bed. They turn and she jumps up from her chair.

Ollie blinks at her. "What're you doing here?"

"I, uh . . . gotta get going." Sophie moves toward the door, nodding at me briefly. She reaches out and squeezes Ollie's arm, and he pulls away. "Later."

I plop down in the seat Sophie just vacated. Up close, Neil doesn't look as pale anymore. "What was that about?"

He shrugs. "I think my condition may have been slightly exaggerated. Should I be expecting any other surprise visitors?"

"No," Ollie sighs out from his perch at the window. "I hardly even said anything to her."

They exchange a long look, and I clear my throat. "Anything else exciting happen while we were gone?"

"Hmm." Neil thinks for a minute. "A shrink came by a couple hours ago."

"How'd that go?" Ollie asks carefully as he walks over and takes the seat on the other side of Neil's bed.

"Swell."

Ollie and I wait for Neil to expand, but he says nothing else.

"You know, some shrinks can actually be decent," Ollie says after a minute. "Mine's pretty helpful."

My mouth goes dry, and I swallow painfully.

"That's cool for you, man," Neil says easily, but his voice rings false. "I don't need a shrink, though. I just need to get out of here."

Ollie shrugs. "I think everyone could stand to see one now and then."

I start checking out. I'm pulled back exactly two years ago. The summer my life smashed unceremoniously to the ground, the pieces of it never quite fitting together again.

"The sooner you open up, the sooner you'll get out of here." The doctor's trying to come off as genuine, but his voice sounds too practiced.

Discomfort settles on top of me like an itchy wool blanket, shrouding the sunlit clinic office. It weighs down and smothers me, slowly sucking the air out of the room. He taps a pen against my closed file, the only sound in the room. Inside it are all the things this stranger has no right to know about me. Things that have been snatched from me and prodded at without my permission.

He silently appraises me but not in the way I'm used to when Madame examines the lines my body creates. Instead, he's appraising my mind.

I fiddle with the friendship bracelet Neil gave me for my ninth birthday, right before we won our first competition together. The braided rainbow band is frayed, hanging dangerously loose on my wrist. I imagine ripping it off—

"Aisha."

Ollie's voice snaps me back into the present. I find him eyeing me with his brow knit up. He's probably wondering why I'm being a catatonic freak instead of helping him to get Neil to talk.

When I focus on Neil, he's looking at me strangely as well.

Get it together. I take a steadying breath. "Or you could just talk to us."

Neil pulls away from the hand that I don't remember wrapping around his wrist.

"I'm fine. I just feel shitty because I'm here."

I stare at him until he meets my eyes. "And you're here because you felt the need to get completely obliterated by yourself. You'd had to have been feeling pretty shitty to do that."

He shrugs. "Or bored."

I gnaw at the inside of my cheek. It's like he doesn't get how messed up yesterday was. How terrifying it must have been for Ollie, finding him like that. How for hours we weren't sure if he was okay or not.

There's no way I can say any of that, though. I'm sure he must feel guilty about it, even though he's not showing it.

"You—" My voice warbles, and I swallow hard. "You get that you need to take a break from drinking, right?"

"You tryna be an AA sponsor or something?" He snorts. "It's not that serious. It was just a bad night."

"Bullshit," I blurt out, my voice bouncing off the walls of the tiny space. "Don't you remember calling me in the middle of the night almost every night lately? Or were you blacked out then too?"

Oh God. I regret it the moment I say it.

"Nice." Neil's smiling, but his eyes are dark. "My dad should be back to pick me up in a bit. You guys don't have to stick around here all day."

"Neil . . ." I start quietly, but he closes his eyes.

Ollie sighs as he gets up. "All right, man. We'll see you later."

*
*

Back at Ollie's place, I sit up on the roof with him and his sister, watching sunset fall over the park just beyond their backyard. Neon pink and orange clouds float lazily beneath the tall trees. I plant both hands firmly against the sun-heated shingles, pressing down until they almost burn my palms.

Ollie hasn't said anything about how I lost it on Neil earlier. Which somehow makes it more embarrassing. He offered me his earbud again on the bus on the way back, which helped me shut off my brain for a little before we got back here.

Sophie takes a long hit of a bong before holding it out to me. "Do you want—Oh sorry, you said you don't smoke. I'm just an automatic passer. Not trying to, like, peer pressure you."

I lean back on my elbows, shrugging. "No worries; didn't think you were."

"Don't you have to be cool for peer pressure to work?" Ollie asks as he takes the bong from her.

Sophie swiftly hits Ollie's arm. "Shut your trap."

He grins. From what I've observed in the last hour, the only difference in his demeanor when he's high is that he's able to crack more than a half-smile. When his sister's around, he can even muster a laugh. He finds me staring at him, and I quickly turn toward Sophie again.

"I'm so screwed," she groans as she picks up the sketchbook that she's been doodling in sporadically. She holds it close to her chest so I can't see what she's drawing. "I've been putting off finishing my portfolio all summer. I have, like, ten pieces to get done by tomorrow. Ollie, did you finish your audition song?"

He rubs a hand over his face. "Can we not talk about auditions?"

"Fine. How did Neil seem to you guys today? He looked okay when I saw him earlier," she says, her eyes focused on her notebook.

I'm remembering how scared she sounded when Ollie told her he was in the hospital. Neil never really mentioned anything about Sophie to me, but it certainly seems like they're closer than either of them are letting on.

Ollie sighs. "Can we not talk about that either?"

"Okay, jeez," Sophie huffs. She looks over at me as her pencil glides across her sketchbook.

"Uh, are you drawing me?" I ask.

She holds her sketchbook even closer to her as I lean over to try and get a peek.

"Soph, stop," Ollie says. "Maybe she doesn't want you to draw her."

Sophie shoots me a sheepish look. "Sorry, but you're, like, the perfect subject," she says before turning to Ollie. "She's gorgeous, isn't she?"

In an instant, I'm itchy and hot everywhere. My gaze involuntarily goes to Ollie again. He digs his fingers into his eyelids and stutters something under his breath that I don't catch.

Sophie laughs as she closes her sketchbook. "Anyways, I'm gonna be up all night so I'd better get to it. See you guys," she sing-songs as she scoots to the edge of the roof and back through the attic window.

I can't make myself look at Ollie. God, why did she have to say that? I think my face is about to melt off.

The quiet between us is so unnatural, I blurt out the first thing I can think of, still avoiding his gaze. "So you guys have auditions every year at your school?"

"Yeah. To keep our spot in the program."

I keep running my fingers across the warmth of the roof. "If you grab your guitar, I can help you practice if you want."

When I risk a glance at him, he's staring intently at his hands even though he's not holding anything. "I don't know. It kinda sucks."

"What I heard earlier sounded really nice." He finally looks at me and my face somehow gets even hotter.

"It's not really ready."

"Hence the practice. You said your audition is tomorrow, right?" I bite my tongue, wondering if I should drop it.

"Right," he concedes. "Okay, one sec."

He heads back inside, leaving me alone on the roof. The sun's disappeared, and a glittering sliver of moon has taken its place. I try to relax as I watch the appearance of the night's first stars.

"You have to promise not to laugh or anything." Ollie sets his guitar on the roof before he climbs back out through the attic window.

I roll my eyes at him before I collapse onto my back, focusing on the endless indigo above us. "I promise."

He takes a seat beside me and tunes his guitar for a while before starting to play. This is the first time I've heard him use his full voice, and I'm taken aback at how much feeling he puts into it.

Retreat to the underground
Never making a single sound
I'm losing my mind
Trying to drown out the noise
You planned to defeat me
Stuck in your monstrous void
But I wasn't destroyed, wasn't destroyed . . .

My eyes fall closed, the sound of his voice and the chords washing over me. The last of the tension in my body dissolves into languid stillness.

"That was beautiful," I find myself whispering when he's done.

Ollie's quiet for a terribly long second. "Sorry, what?"

I wince, keeping my eyes shut. I'm sure he heard me. He's just giving me a chance to say something not quite as mortifying. "I said that was great."

He snorts quietly. "You're half asleep."

Ollie puts his guitar down and lies back next to me, so close that his shoulder brushes mine. I try to act like this is normal, as if he's done this before.

"Unrelated," I say, finally glancing at him. "And, um, I get how hard it is to deal with people being assholes."

He tilts his face toward me at that, his eyes searching. "You do?"

I nod, looking away for a moment before I refocus on him. "Anyway, you're gonna do great tomorrow."

"Thanks, Aisha." His dark eyes bore deep into mine.

Whoa. My stomach starts doing something indescribable. I'm thinking about what his sister said and his reaction. Was he just embarrassed because it was so awkward, or does he actually . . .

Stop. Just stop. He's so close I feel like my thoughts are out in the open. I tear my eyes away from him, focusing on the smattering of stars bright enough to not be blotted out by the city's perpetual light.

I say the first thing that pops into my head. "Question for you."

"What is it?" He's still looking at me, and my stomach won't settle down.

"Would you rather have to listen to only your favorite song on repeat for the rest of your life or never be able to hear it again, but instead you'd be able to listen to any other song you want anytime?"

He laughs, lifting the weight of the last few minutes.

"Is that even a question? Why would anyone choose to never hear their favorite song again when they could hear it 24/7?"

The corners of my mouth curl up as I shrug. "I think after a while I would lose it, just listening to one song. It'd be like torture eventually."

"I don't think I'd get tired of it." Something about his tone makes my brain go all fuzzy.

"Uh . . ." I try to form words. "Do you wanna practice again?"

"Sure." He sits up and grabs his guitar.

My stomach finally relaxes. I close my eyes as he starts, all my thoughts floating off into the dark.

5

The next morning, when my phone buzzes, it takes me a few moments to untangle myself from the mummified position I rolled myself into last night.

It's Neil calling. "What's up?" I croak out.

"I'm home." His voice is dull. "My dad picked me up if you want to come over now."

"I'll be right there," I say quickly before hanging up.

I grab my bags by Ollie's closet. He's still dead asleep on the couch. I reach out to shake his shoulder, but I can't bring myself to touch him. My hand hovers over him for a moment before I retract it and wrap my arms around myself. *What the hell is wrong with me?*

"I'm leaving now." I try louder when he remains passed out. "Ollie, I'm going."

I stare at him like he'll suddenly just wake up, but I'm not brave enough to say anything else. If he does wake up, I'll have to thank him for being cool about letting me stay here and being so nice to me. I'm sure I'd find a way to mess that up somehow.

I realize how long I've been looking at him, and my face starts to burn, but I don't look away. He's nothing like the kid I first saw over FaceTime in ninth grade. His baby face is gone, and he's grown into his features in a way that I first noticed last summer when Neil and I were planning my visit. He doesn't just look different, though. He's still quiet, but his voice is deeper and more assured—he stutters less than he used to.

When he starts to stir, I turn away and open his window. As I climb down the oak tree in his backyard, I think about how charged everything was last night. When we got down from the roof and went to bed, I couldn't sleep for a long time. Even as he snored softly on the couch across the room, the memory of his closeness was kept alive by the fresh scent of him permeating his sheets.

God, I need to stop deluding myself. Just because he's a decent person doesn't mean he's into me. It was probably all on my end. Plus, I'm only here for a few days, and I have bigger things to worry about.

I'm at Neil's a few minutes later, praying his dad will be in a semi-decent mood. When he swings the door open, I try to smile convincingly.

He returns it for the briefest moment. "Hello, Aisha," he says, leaving the door open for me and heading toward the kitchen. "Neil said you'd be dropping by."

"Hi, Mr. Roi," I call after him as brightly as I can and follow him inside. Neil's at the kitchen island, eating scrambled eggs. "Sorry to intrude."

I take a seat beside Neil and shoot him a small smile. He returns it for a moment before he continues stuffing his face. I don't think he's still upset about yesterday.

"Don't be silly," Mr. Roi says as he pours most of a pot of coffee into a giant travel mug. "I'm glad you're here. Please keep an eye on this idiot for me."

I bristle but manage to keep my pleasant expression mostly in place.

"She always does," Neil says through a mouthful of eggs.

It's totally silent for a moment.

I flinch when Neil's dad snaps, cursing him out loudly. I don't speak Korean, but the words for "stupid," "embarrassment," and "failure" have become familiar to me over the years. This goes on for a while, and I just stare at the floor. When I risk a glance at Neil, he's nodding at his dad as he keeps chewing. I slowly get up and grab myself a glass of orange juice from the fridge.

Neil keeps cramming food into his mouth, looking unbothered. When his dad finally stops shouting, it looks like it's only because he's too winded to continue.

Mr. Roi sighs and catches his breath.

"Why can't you be more like Aisha? She respects and obeys her parents instead of always making trouble."

The orange juice in my mouth sours. Neil starts to smirk but contains himself when he sees my face. He straightens in his seat and looks at his dad solemnly.

"You're right, Dad. Don't worry, Ish can teach me how to stop being such a shameful disgrace."

Mr. Roi looks like he's going to start yelling again but stops short when he glances at his phone.

"I'm late for my flight. Good to see you, Aisha. Tell your parents I said hello."

"Will do. Have a safe trip," I say with fake cheer as he leaves the kitchen.

When the front door slams behind him, I glance at Neil. "You okay?"

He shrugs, not meeting my eyes before he stands up. "Perfect. I'll make some more eggs."

Glancing around, everything looks exactly the same as it did last summer. The kitchen's steel surfaces are all clean. The modest living room beyond it looks tidy as well, the big cozy couches that I've spent endless hours on look as inviting as ever. I have a feeling Neil's dad must have made him clean everything up when they got home.

I swat the thought away. "I can't believe I have to be back at school in less than a week. I know the next few days are gonna fly by, and then it's back to the corps."

Without the apprenticeship, my permanent position as a background dancer is guaranteed again this year.

Neil looks over his shoulder from the stove. "Why don't you stay then?"

I give him a puzzled look. "What do you mean?"

He turns back toward the frying pan. "I mean, don't go back."

I snort. "Funny."

"No, really. I know you hate it over there, Ish," he says as he adds lots of paprika and red pepper to the eggs.

I stare at his back, but he doesn't turn to face me again. "It just really sucks I didn't get the apprenticeship. It's like . . ." I bite my lip. "Like it doesn't really matter how good I am. I just don't have *the look*," I say in a haughty accent before I fake a laugh.

Madame Turner's dismissive frown pops up in my head, and my stomach plummets at the thought of having to face her back at school.

Neil turns back around at that, but he doesn't laugh along. I glance away, unable to take the pity in his eyes.

"It's their loss, Ish. Even though Huntley doesn't have an apprenticeship program, you'd definitely be able to land some leads that would look good for college apps."

I have to admit I'd do almost anything to get a lead, but switching to a public school would be a huge step down for my ballet career.

I wonder if that's Neil's plan—to get into a dance college. It's been a sore subject whenever I've brought it up. Like so much else, he always brushes it off, claiming not to care if he gets into *any* college . . . even though his dad would absolutely lose it if he ever heard Neil say that.

I know he was bummed about his dad not being able to afford a private dance academy after we stopped competing. But he's never wanted to talk about it, and since then he's always acted like he doesn't give a shit what happens with his dance career. But I know he still loves dancing. He was super excited when he told me about scoring a lead in his Modern class piece last year.

I shake my head, coming back to the moment. "You really think so?"

He breaks into an infectious grin as he brings a fresh plate of eggs over to me. "Of course. You're really talented, Ish."

I make a grossed-out face before grinning back. "Thanks. You are too." I consider asking if he'd think about taking ballet at his school. It would be amazing to *pas de deux* with him again after so long. I decide against it, not wanting to risk ruining the moment.

"I know," Neil says as he sits next to me again.

I give him a swift kick in the shin. "My dad won't go for it, though."

As I pick up my fork, I can feel his eyes on me. I take a big bite, pretending like I don't notice, like it doesn't bother me. He spiced the eggs just how I like them—I don't even try to resist scarfing them down.

Neil's shoulders relax. "You never know. He might."

"It's not like he's gonna let me live with you. It took some convincing to even get him to let me stay here this week. And he's *definitely* not gonna let me stay at my mom's." Neil knows how my dad feels about her.

"Right, but if you want to transfer and he won't let you stay at your mom's," Neil says through a mouthful, "he'd have to be cool with you staying here instead. My dad would be fine with it."

I shrug, not saying anything as I dig into my plate. My parents pay a fortune every year for my tuition and ballet equipment. Every time I've even considered quitting in the last couple of years, I've thought about how much money they've spent. The cost of pointe shoes alone is astronomical. They're a hundred dollars a pop and only last a few days. My parents never talked about money in front of me, but I heard them whispering about it behind closed doors before the divorce. They've sacrificed so much for me that the possibility of giving up on ballet school seems unfathomable.

"The dance program auditions are tomorrow," Neil says when I don't respond. "You could always just try out and see what happens."

My head shoots up from my plate. "Tomorrow? There's no way I'd be ready by then."

"You'll be fine winging it."

"Is that what you're doing?"

He grins. "Always."

I roll my eyes. "I guess it couldn't hurt to audition. Maybe a contemporary ballet piece I choreographed last year could work?"

He nods. "That should be good. Don't worry, the teachers are always thrilled when anyone with a lot of classical training shows up."

"Is it closed auditions?"

"They're open. Most of the school comes out for them to do the whole summer catch-up thing."

"Lovely," I intone, putting down my fork.

Just from the sheer volume of names he's mentioned to me over the past few years, I don't know if I have the energy to meet that many new people.

"No big deal, though," he adds quickly. "I won't make you suffer through small talk with every idiot I've ever associated with. Honestly, Ollie is the only person from school I can usually stand being around for more than eight hours at a time."

I nod as I run through all the ways I could humiliate myself in an open audition.

"I promise, it'll be fine." Neil squeezes my arm briefly. "Do you wanna come along to the music auditions today? I'd skip it, but Ollie gets pretty bad stage fright."

"Sure. Yeah, he seemed kinda nervous about it. I don't know why— he has a really good voice. I heard him practicing at his place."

Neil nods. "How was that by the way?"

I blink at him. "How was what?"

"Staying at Ollie's."

I shrug, not really sure how to answer. "Good. I felt kinda bad that he let me take his bed and, like, origami-ed himself to fit onto his tiny couch."

Neil laughs a bit. "Cool, glad it wasn't weird for you."

I pick up my fork again and push around the last of my eggs.

He studies me. "Wait. Was it weird for you?"

"No." My voice comes out too high.

"Are you sure?"

"Yeah, he was really sweet—I mean nice. He was nice." *Jesus Christ. Stop talking.*

"Oh?" Neil lifts an eyebrow and breaks into a slow smirk.

Jumping up, I head to the sink to rinse my plate. "What time do auditions start today?"

"At nine. We should probably head over."

*

Huntley is way bigger than my school, but the building itself is like an architectural Frankenstein. Each department we walk through is a different design style of decades past—so unlike the uniform glass and steel minimalism of the academy. Even though I've never been inside before, it's somehow familiar from the grand sum of all Neil's stories.

As he leads the way through the maze of hallways, I try to imagine what it would be like to go here. The prospect of starting at a new school makes me instantly nauseous. But it couldn't possibly be any worse than the last two years, since Neil would be with me. I almost start to relax for a second when my brain reminds me I still have to talk to my dad and pass the audition.

We find Ollie in the music room and head over to the auditorium.

"You okay?" I ask Ollie as we get backstage. He focuses on me, seeming to just now fully register my presence.

"I uh . . ." he trails off, staring blankly at the scuffed floor.

Neil and I exchange a look.

"Hey. You got this, man." Neil hands him his amp. "We'll be right here."

Ollie takes it and nods stiffly before he walks out onstage to set up. He looks out at the packed audience blankly for a moment before he sets to work connecting his amp.

"Quiet everyone," one of the teachers in the front row, a stout older man with glasses, calls out and the chatter stops. Right behind the row of teachers, I spot Sophie sitting with a group of girls. She gives Ollie a wide grin and a thumbs up, but he stares right through her.

"Do you think he'll be all right?" I ask Neil under my breath.

Neil nods briefly. "He should be okay."

"We're ready, Mr. Cheriet," the same teacher says.

Ollie closes his eyes and takes a few deep breaths before he starts playing. When he starts to sing, a few snickers ring out from the audience. He opens his eyes and stops. I follow his gaze to a row near the back, where a group of jock-ish looking boys sit. For what feels like forever, Ollie is frozen, staring at them.

"Oh shit," Neil mutters.

"Assholes," I grumble under my breath at the same time.

Come on, Ollie. You can do this, keep going. I squeeze my eyes shut and try to will him into motion again.

The audience titters. The same teacher tells everyone to shut up after a second.

Ollie reboots at the sound of the teacher's voice. He stops staring at the guys who laughed, closes his eyes again, and continues. This time, though, it seems like he goes elsewhere. Somewhere that's only for him, like I shouldn't be here watching. But I can't imagine looking away.

All the nervous energy in me starts to melt away, just like last night on his roof.

There's a pause when he's done and then everyone claps as he starts disassembling his equipment. I hear Sophie let out a whoop of support over the applause. Ollie doesn't look over at her as he heads offstage toward me and Neil.

"You killed it, man," Neil says.

"That was horrific," he shoots back in a monotone as they exchange a standard bro hug.

"No, it wasn't," I say, and Ollie stares at me with such complete dejection that without thinking, I reach out and hug him too.

He's still for a second, but then both his arms are around me, not like the one-armed back pat he just gave Neil. The thing happens again where my mind stutters to a stop and my eyes fall closed. When I open them a moment later, there's a kid staring at us impatiently since we're blocking the way to the stage. I quickly pull away from Ollie, and the kid brushes past us. I glance over at Neil, but he's gone to grab the amp Ollie left onstage.

"Your pity and lies are appreciated," Ollie mutters under his breath.

"I mean it. You were really great." I want to say I'm proud of him, but he'll probably think I'm patronizing him.

He's looking at me too closely again, so I take off to help Neil.

I really don't know how he was able to refocus and give such a moving performance, despite having to deal with those idiots. The way he blocked everything out and was so completely himself . . . I don't think I would have been able to do that.

My stomach rolls uneasily as my own audition moves to the forefront of my mind again. Tonight, I'm going to have to get in as much practice as I possibly can. Even though I'm not sure if I'm ready to veer off the course I always imagined for myself, I know something has to change. I can't risk slipping any deeper into the terrifying state I was in when I left school.

6

The auditorium is somehow even more crowded than yesterday and it's not even nine in the morning yet.

I take a slow breath, but my heart keeps pounding at a punishing tempo. I recognize a few of the faces Neil introduced me to briefly yesterday, but I don't spot Ollie among them. I didn't ask Neil if he knew if Ollie was going to show up today, even though I wanted to. When we got back to their neighborhood after his audition yesterday, Neil asked Ollie if he wanted to hang out for a bit, but he just shook his head and took off.

Then Neil and I practiced for auditions in his basement. More accurately, I practiced for a little bit while Neil danced around in an exaggeratedly awful way that always cracks me up before the evening devolved into one of our silly little dance parties. Even though we've done the same thing over FaceTime every weekend for the last few years, it's always so much better in person. We stayed up way too late and by the end of the night we were in hysterics. I couldn't believe how easy and normal everything finally was again.

But now I'm kicking myself for slacking off. I got a bit more rehearsal in before Neil woke up this morning, but I still feel less than prepared.

I debated calling my dad last night, but I'm still not sure what I should do. I haven't been able to stop thinking about what Neil said about me possibly getting some lead roles here. I'd get into some college programs if I go back to ballet school, but so will everyone else there who didn't get into the apprenticeship. Scoring some leading roles would really help me stand out on my applications.

When I didn't get chosen for the apprenticeship, it was like my invisibility to my instructors and peers began to manifest into something terrifyingly real. Even though I felt that same disappearing feeling at the hospital, it was nothing like how awful it was at school. The thought of going back makes all the air leave my body, but so does the thought of asking my dad to quit.

I guess I don't have to decide right this second what I'm going to do. I'll just have to see how things go today.

"Yo, Roi!" I snap back into the loud, muggy room. Some guys in the front row are calling out to Neil, and we head over to them, Neil's arm around my shoulder.

Neil shoots the boys a big grin. "What's up?"

"Where have you been the last few weeks, man?" one of the guys asks him. "Weren't you gonna throw an end-of-the-summer party? Your new girl been keeping you busy?" He laughs and the rest of the boys join him.

I lean away from Neil's arm but stick close to his side as people push around us in the packed space.

"Guys, this is my best friend, Aisha." I'm embarrassingly relieved I still hold the title. "She moved away a couple years ago. Aisha, this is Rashanth, Kevin, Dylan, and Scott."

I greet them absentmindedly as I run through my routine in my head.

"Oh, she's not your girl?" Kevin asks. His eyes leisurely make their way down my body. I zip my hoodie up to my chin, but he doesn't stop.

"Saved you a couple of spots," Rashanth says.

Neil shakes his head as he steps slightly in front of me. "Gotta make the rounds, catch you later."

"Later." Scott fist-bumps Neil. "Let me know if you need a hook up. My bro's all stocked up."

I shoot Neil a sharp look, but he ignores it as we take off. I guess I shouldn't be surprised that he's moved beyond swiping booze from his dad's liquor cabinet, but my gut still twists. Ollie said he'd been drinking more lately, but was that guy talking about hooking him up with drugs too? As far as I know, Neil smokes but doesn't do anything harder. It's starting to feel more and more like I know literally nothing about him.

Neil grimaces when he finds me still staring at him. "Sorry about Kevin. I'm not really even friends with those guys."

"Didn't they say you were gonna have them over for a party?"

"They show up at my parties, but I don't actively invite them," he says as another group of kids wave him over.

This process repeats several times, and each time Neil introduces me to a new subset of his school's social landscape. Names fly out of my head the moment Neil says them, my mind almost entirely taken up by visualizing myself moving through my routine again and again.

I'm about to tell Neil we should head backstage to warm up when a blonde girl in a tiny floral dress jumps into his arms.

"Whoa there. Hey, Gwen." Neil detaches himself from her.

"I missed you *sooo* much," she says, leaning in super close to his face.

I raise my eyebrows. Should I know who this is? I don't think he's ever mentioned a "Gwen" to me. What the hell is going on?

Neil pulls back and laughs but not a real one. "Me too. Hey, Tara," he says, addressing an unsmiling girl with a high ponytail who's next to Gwen. "Guys, this is Aisha—"

"I need to talk to you." Gwen grabs his hand and pulls him a few feet away before Neil can protest.

I glance at Tara. "Are they a thing?"

Tara sighs and shrugs. "Not really. She's just been obsessed since they got together at Brandon's party last month."

"Oh." *What does* that *mean? That they fooled around or fully like . . .* Neil hasn't once mentioned any girls he likes, so it takes me a moment to process. I thought maybe he liked Sophie.

For some reason, I assumed he would tell me if he ever hooked up with someone. It isn't a big deal really, but I thought it'd be something we'd talk about since he still considers me his best friend. I guess he thinks I'm too much of an inexperienced loser to relate. My stomach starts to turn again.

"Has anyone ever told you, you're, like, model pretty?" Tara asks. She's scrolling through her phone, not even looking at me anymore.

"No," I lie.

A few people have told me that before, but I know it's only because I'm tall. More often than not, kids at school and at my old studio would say the exact opposite, commenting on my hips, my thighs, and the one thing my self-control can do nothing to change—my skin.

Tara finally looks up. "Well, you are. And your braids are cool. How do you, like, wash your hair, though?"

I'm not in the mood for dumbass questions about my hair right now, passive-aggressive or not. Not shitting myself about the possibility of bombing my audition is taking up the majority of my brain power.

I unzip my hoodie again, not wanting to get onstage with my leotard already drenched in sweat.

"Usually just pop my head off and stick it in the washing machine," I finally mutter, glancing over at Neil. Gwen's pouting at him while he shakes his head.

"Wow, relax." I turn back to Tara to find her glaring at me. "I was just curious. You don't have to be such a bitch about it."

I bite my tongue and refrain from glaring back at her. I don't have the energy for this right now. Fiddling with the zipper of my hoodie, I realize there isn't feeling in my fingers anymore and that my wrists are numb. Closing my eyes, I try my best to force the numbness away, to keep it together.

Neil is suddenly beside me again, herding me away. "Everything good?"

I shrug. "Pretty par for the course," I say as we head backstage. No one else approaches Neil since everyone's busy practicing. "What's up with you and that girl?"

"Nothing," is all he says as we find a spot to ourselves and start warming up.

"Right." I push down the pang of hurt that he doesn't think I'm even worth telling. *Whatever*. I need to focus anyway. As I stretch, I manage to calm some of my nerves, the feeling returning to my hands and wrists. The pre-performance hush of backstage, everyone quiet as they get into their zones, makes me feel as if I'm in the right place.

I put my headphones on and get into my own zone, going through my choreo in my head for the millionth time. After I'm done stretching, I close my eyes and walk through it at a slower speed. Neil speaks and I snap back into the room.

"Here goes," he whispers.

"Good luck," I say before he heads onto the stage.

I step forward for a better view, stopping at the black curtains at the very edge of the wings.

"Let's go, Roi!" One of Neil's louder friends screams from the audience followed by an amount of cheering that makes me genuinely concerned his ego will explode on the spot.

Before getting here, I had the sense from his stories that he was well-liked at school, but I hadn't imagined anything quite like this. Neil grins and winks at the screaming crowd before he closes his eyes. The deep, starkly sparse first notes of piano on a Billie Eilish song clunk out of the stage's speakers.

He starts on the ground in an impossibly slow but controlled floor roll. His eyes finally open, all of his usual humor drained from him. Leaping to his feet, he moves into a series of dizzying barrel turns and contractions, his movements flowing together in a way I can't imagine thinking up on the spot. He expresses more with his body than he's ever said out loud, radiating something so viscerally hopeless that it overwhelms me. I can't fathom that he's showing how isolated he feels so publicly, but then I realize: These people would never connect what he's expressing to the Neil they know.

He completes one last floor roll as he closes his eyes again. Lying stretched out on his back, he goes eerily still as the music ends. The cheering starts, and he jumps up and jogs toward me, his eyes growing big.

"What's wrong?" I sound like I've been kicked in the chest.

I knew that he'd gotten more passionate about modern since I left, but I've never seen him perform that way before. I still can't believe how much of himself he put into it.

"I think I'm gonna throw up," he says before he grabs his water bottle and starts chugging. He gags but swallows it back down.

"*Jesus.*" I pat his back. "You good?"

He nods before he slides to the floor, still panting. "Yeah, I'm just out of shape. You'd better get out there, you're up next."

I take a painful breath and slowly step out to center stage, sweating under the burning hot lights. The silence that greets me usually wouldn't faze me, but it's particularly awful after Neil's fanfare. The only sound is what I assume is Neil clapping and whistling from the wings. I'm too embarrassed to look at him. Clenching my shaking hands, I focus on the teachers seated at a long table in the front, blocking out the rest of the audience.

I instantly recognize Lucinda Anvyi. She's the second-ever Native American prima ballerina at the New York City Ballet after Maria Tallchief, Balanchine's muse.

What is she doing teaching here? I'm sure lots of elite dance academies would love to have her. I can't even imagine how incredible it would be to work with her. God, I hope I don't mess up.

"Name, grade, and style?"

Tearing my eyes away from Lucinda, I focus on the teacher who just spoke. She's a younger looking Black woman with short natural hair and intense eyes.

I force myself to speak. "Aisha Bimi, eleventh grade. Contemporary ballet."

She nods for me to start.

You can do this. Michaela urges me on as my music begins.

I move into my first position, *en pointe.* I start with a series of fluttering attitude turns, spinning into the chords, letting them carry me wherever they please. My thoughts are gone, and so is everything else as I'm lifted into a constant state of motion. I complete a beautiful arabesque with one leg behind me, arching my back. I keep my spine pin-straight as I extend my arms out with ease. As the classical notes of the song fade into something more experimental, my movements mirror them. I move off pointe, my heightened posture relaxing, becoming more fluid. Morphing into something free and expansive as I move into delicate floor rolls.

Then I stop thinking about my choreo—I don't even know if I'm following it. It's just like last night. I'm moving without worrying about being good, without obsessing about getting every move right. Instead of losing myself in the music like I usually do, I'm finding all the things buried within me. All the frustration and disappointment I jammed down every time I was passed over for a role, all of my yearning to be seen bubbles up and bursts out of me in a torrent of unfettered emotion.

When my body stops in time with the music, I find myself curled on my side on the stage floor, my vision a translucent blur. My heart is going triple time, and I can't catch my breath for a moment. I quickly swipe my hand across my wet eyes as I stand and pray it just looks like I'm sweating. My mind reels, trying to make sense of the last few minutes.

"Thank you, Aisha," the younger teacher calls over the audience, shooting me a smile. It's not the muted applause I'm used to—it's loud and sustained.

I nod stiffly as I glance over at Lucinda writing something on the clipboard in front of her. When I get back to the wings, I'm pulled out of my daze when I find Ollie standing beside Neil. As much as I'd wanted him to show up, I kind of hope he didn't catch all that, everything inside me spilling into the open.

Neil envelops me in a careful hug. "You okay?"

"Just glad that's over," I say, letting out a choked laugh as I pull away from him.

"Aisha . . ." Ollie opens his mouth like he's going to say something else but doesn't. So then we're just staring at each other.

I try not to look panicked as I wait for him to speak, but I know it's not working. I glance at Neil, and he patiently waits for Ollie to finish whatever he was going to say and then shoots him an odd look when he stays quiet.

"I, uh . . . didn't realize you were auditioning," Ollie says eventually.

"I thought I'd give it a shot while I'm here. I haven't asked my dad yet—he'll probably make me go back to my school next week anyway," I say as casually as I can manage. I can't imagine saying out loud how much I really want to get in. I don't want to get my hopes up for nothing.

Ollie focuses on his sneakers. "Oh."

Does he sound disappointed? Like he cares if I stay or not?

I catch Neil smirking at me and shake my head briefly, hoping he keeps his mouth shut. I need to stop thinking about this and figure out what just happened to me onstage, but I can't right now. Not in front of everyone. I take a deep breath and start my winding down stretches, gathering everything I left out there and cramming it back inside me.

*

After auditions are over, Neil checks the school's website for the results. I scan the list over his shoulder and spot my name and "A.S. Ballet Level 3–4" recorded next to it.

Neil grins at me. "Congrats, you scored an assistant gig."

I blink at him, not fully comprehending what he's just said. This can't really be happening; it can't be this easy. I was just hoping to land a lead later in the year if I got accepted. I never imagined getting an assistant position.

He laughs at my blank face. "Why do you look so shocked? I told you that you were a shoo-in."

I manage a smile and take in a slow breath, straightening my spine. At ballet school, there would be no chance of me getting an opportunity like this, I'm certain of it. There's no way I can turn this down.

I'm going for it. I'm going to ask my dad if I can stay.

As if on cue, my phone starts ringing.

My heart immediately bounds into double time. I stare down at my dad's name on my screen, my mind whirring.

"You gonna get that?" Neil asks.

"Yeah, I'll be right back." I shoulder my way through the backstage crowd out into the hallway.

I lean against the faded green cinder-block wall littered with musical tryouts and glee-club posters. I take a steadying breath before I pick up. "Hey, Dad."

7

"Where are you?" Dad asks. "I can hardly hear you."

I walk a little farther down the hallway to find a quieter spot. "I'm at Neil's school's auditions. I, uh . . . I just got accepted here."

He's quiet for a long moment. "Aisha, why would you audition without talking to me first?"

I pinch the bridge of my nose. "Sorry. It was kind of a last-minute thing. But I got an assistant position—"

"Slow down," he cuts me off. "I know you were disappointed about the apprenticeship, but now you want to leave school?"

Kids start heading toward the quiet space I found near a back exit, so I step outside into the stifling heat of the school's back lot. I take shelter under the shade of the wooden bleachers.

"At the intensive, my instructor basically said I was better than anyone in the class and then still didn't pick me," I say quietly. I feel sick; my insides start to squirm. "It's basically the same thing during the school year. None of my teachers ever cast me in leads."

"I'm so sorry, honey. I wish I could smack some sense into them," he grumbles. "Why didn't you tell me about this before?"

"I thought I could handle it. Or, like, make them change their minds or something. But they're just . . . They're just not going to see me. But maybe here things could be different since—since I got an assistant gig and everything. Can I stay?"

I hold my breath, waiting what feels like an eternity for a response.

Finally, he lets out a sigh. "Well, you can't stay at your mother's."

"I know, I meant at Neil's."

"Not happening," he says shortly.

My stomach dives to my feet. "I promise we're not together or anything."

"Aisha, I doubt his father would be okay with hosting you for the school year."

"Neil said he'd be fine with it." Mr. Roi thinks I'm a good influence on him, but I know mentioning that won't help my case.

"I already paid your tuition for the fall semester," he sighs out.

"I'm sorry." My voice warbles pathetically. "I know how much you've spent on my school fees, but I can't do this anymore. I really don't want to go back there. Dad, please. I just can't . . ."

He's silent for awhile, and I hold my breath. "If you were *that* unhappy there . . . I still don't understand why you never told me."

And make him feel even guiltier than he already does for moving away? I know he did it for me, so he could afford everything that I'm giving up right now. I tried to make the best of it these last few years, never really letting on how hopeless things felt sometimes and how much I missed him.

"I don't know. A lot of the time I just didn't really feel anything—" I blurt out before biting my tongue. I try to steady my breath as that chilling moment in the locker room comes back to me. The thought of going back there and the same thing happening again is paralyzing. I can handle going numb for a few seconds like when my hands lost feeling before my audition, but what happened at the academy was on another level that I don't know how to deal with.

He doesn't respond for a minute. *Damn it.* I know I've worried him.

"Aisha, I can't get off work to visit until until Christmas. Before then maybe we should look into finding you a doctor if you're feeling—"

I shake my head violently. "I don't need a doctor. I promise . . . it's not like before, okay? And I get that you can't take work off, it's cool." I fight to keep my voice calm and block out the pang of disappointment that he won't be able to visit any sooner than the holidays. "I just think staying here could be a good thing for me. Like, I think I'll feel, um, better here."

He lets out a sigh. "Neil's school is public, right? No tuition fees?"

"Yeah."

"All right . . . Let me get in touch with your school—hopefully, I can get a refund for this semester. And obviously I'll have to speak with Neil's father."

Is he saying yes?

"I'm sorry that your instructors couldn't see how wonderful you are," he continues in a softer tone.

I nod even though he can't see me but I'm too choked up to speak. Everything I let out during my audition—how awful it had been never being enough at school—is coming back up. My eyes start to sting, but I blink them dry.

He sighs again. "I'll give you a call back. Love you."

"Love you too, bye."

Rubbing at my eyes, I groan after I hang up.

God, I'm praying Neil's dad is okay with this. If I can stay, I know things won't be as bad. I'll be able to stop drifting out of myself and start feeling like an actual human being again. Not to mention, staying here would give me some more time to uncover whatever it is that's going on in Neil's head.

✳

"Are you just gonna sit there?" I yell at Ollie over a pounding, synth-pop beat.

A couple of hours later we've ordered food and are hanging out in Neil's basement, dancing around wildly again. I force down the anxiety about what's going to happen next, doing my best not to think about the fact that this might be one of my last nights here. I got into Huntley, plus the assistant opportunity. No matter what happens, I might as well celebrate that small win.

"I'm DJing." Ollie continues staring at his phone, like he has been ever since Neil and I started dancing a little while ago.

I scoff. "I'm sure you can multitask."

He smirks a bit, finally glancing at me. "I'm sure I can't."

Neil laughs. "Do you guys want ice cream?"

I nod incredulously. "Why didn't you tell us there was ice cream? What kind?"

I haven't had ice cream for ages. Since I'm letting loose tonight, why not? I try my best not to think about all those calories. I can go for a run tomorrow to work it off.

"Half Baked. I'll go grab it," he says before he bounds up the stairs.

"Can you believe he was holding out on us like that?" I joke as

I keep dancing. I stop moving abruptly when I glance at Ollie and find him watching me now. I wait for him to look down at his phone again, but he doesn't. The room feels silent even though music's still blasting.

I'm thinking about that moment after my audition again, but I shake myself out of it and take a slow breath. "Can I ask you something?"

He clears his throat. "Yeah?"

Before I overthink it, I go over and take a seat next him against the mirrored wall, under the barre Neil's dad installed when we were still doing ballet competitively. Back when it seemed like Neil and I were going somewhere.

There's still a possibility Neil's dad won't let me crash here for the school year. Or what if he mentions how little he's here and then my dad changes his mind? Or what if he tells my dad about what Neil did? Trying not to panic, I manage to push the thoughts away.

"Do you know a guy at your school named Scott?" I ask as I pick at the tarnished hardwood floor.

"Uh-huh. What about him?"

"He said something about his brother hooking Neil up?"

"Yeah, Scott and his brother have made a little business out of supplying booze to most of Huntley's parties."

"Do you know how long Neil's been buying off of them?"

"Most of last year, I think, but I, uh . . . don't really go to parties with him. He'd been drinking more lately, though, like I said."

I nod, biting my lip. "At his audition today . . ." I don't know how to put into words how much it freaked me out. "It made me think about how he's here by himself a lot. And, like, maybe it's been harder for him than he's ever told me. Does he ever talk to you about that?"

I can feel him staring at me, but I keep digging my nail into a tiny gap between the floorboards.

"Not when he's sober," he says. "But when he's plastered, sometimes he says stuff, yeah."

I finally focus on him. "Like what?"

"What are you two up to?" I manage not to flinch at Neil's voice. He's coming down the stairs with bowls of ice cream and spoons in hand.

I bite down on my tongue for a second before forcing a laugh. "I'm trying to get Ollie to stop being such a drag. Come on, get up."

Jumping up again, I hold my arms out to him, and he smiles a little but doesn't move. Before I can convince myself not to, I grab his elbows and pull him to his feet. I'm acutely aware of where my hands connect with his warm skin.

"Time to dance." My voice miraculously sounds normal instead of all breathless.

"Yes, here we go." Neil hands each of us a bowl.

Neil and I shimmy around ridiculously as we spoon ice cream into our mouths and Ollie just stands there nodding along to the music.

"Dude, come on," Neil says. He puts his empty bowl down before he starts shaking one of Ollie's arms like a ragdoll. "Ish, help me out here."

My stomach does something incredibly weird as I remove the bowl from Ollie's hand, my fingers brushing his. I force myself to stop overthinking everything as I take hold of his arm and grab Neil's arm too, before we start spinning around. We drag Ollie with us into some type of unhinged version of ring-around-the-rosy that involves flailing all our limbs wildly until we trip over each other and fall to the floor, laughing like idiots.

"I'm gonna go grab more ice cream," Neil says before he disappears upstairs again.

"I really liked your audition," Ollie says so softly I almost don't hear him over the music.

I crane my neck to look over at him. We're still splayed on the floor. "Thanks."

"That Gus Dapperton song you danced to . . . It's actually one of my favorites."

"Yeah, I saw it in your most played," I blurt out.

His mouth falls open.

Oh God. Does he think it's weird that I used it for my audition? "Beyond Amends" is one of my all-time faves too. Since I heard it on his phone at the hospital, I started listening to it a lot again and realized it would fit pretty perfectly with the piece I choreographed last year.

Ollie focuses on the stucco ceiling and I silently let out my breath.

"You really captured the essence of it," he says. "Kind of, um, gut wrenching but somehow still hopeful. If that makes sense."

It's my turn to gape at him. I have no idea what to say.

He winces and closes his eyes. "Sorry. That sounded dumb."

I sit up on my elbows. "It didn't."

Opening his eyes, he sits up next to me. "Do you mind if I ask you something?

My stomach squirms at his solemn expression. "What is it?"

"Is it always like that for you when you dance?"

I glance at the floor, my face warming. "Like what?" I ask even though I know exactly what he means.

Ollie shrugs. "I don't know. When I sing, a lot of stuff comes up, and it's sort of hard to deal with in front of people."

I look up at him again, my eyes softening.

"Yeah, I get that. It doesn't happen to me very often, though." The last time I remember feeling so much when I danced was when Neil and I competed in YAGP for the very last time the summer before eighth grade. There was a special sort of alchemy when we danced together that I've never been able to replicate alone. I don't think Neil has either, at least as far as ballet is concerned. Maybe that's part of the reason he doesn't do it anymore—it's just not the same when we're not together. "But yeah, today was . . . I don't really know where that came from, honestly."

Ollie nods, falling quiet. Weirdly, I'm only half relieved that he doesn't ask me any more about it. I find myself thinking about his audition again and how scary it must be going to such a raw place every time he performs.

After a bit he finally speaks again. "So, you might have to go back to Alberta next week?"

I squeeze my eyes shut. "If Neil's dad says I can't stay."

He sighs and I open my eyes to find him staring right at me now. I have to remind myself to breathe.

"Aisha—"

"Guys, come up here!" Neil shouts out from the top of the stairs. "*Billy Elliot*'s on TV."

Ollie leaps to his feet. "Um, it's getting pretty late. I should probably head home actually."

"Uh, okay," I say as I get up. He's already halfway up the stairs. "Later."

When I get upstairs, Ollie's gone already.

"What happened?" Neil asks when I find him in the kitchen making popcorn.

"I thought you were getting more ice cream."

"Change of plans. Why'd Ollie take off so fast?"

I shrug as I take a seat at the kitchen island. "How would I know?"

"Did he ask you out?"

My entire body stills. "What?"

He opens the microwave and takes the popcorn out. "Ow, shit." He throws the bag on the counter and shakes his burnt fingers. "Did he ask you out or something?"

"Why would he?" I try to keep my voice calm as my mind races. God, I really wish I knew what Ollie was about to say before Neil interrupted us. He definitely wasn't going to ask me out, though— that doesn't even make sense. He knows I might be leaving in a few days.

Neil snorts as he dumps the popcorn into a huge bowl. "You see, Ish, when you're into someone—"

"He said he likes me?" I study him as he starts stuffing his face. I'm feeling particularly thankful for the melanin that keeps my face from getting visibly red because I'd look like a goddamn stop sign right now otherwise.

"No," he says through a mouthful. "My eyes do work pretty well, though." He picks up the bowl and starts heading to the living room.

"If he didn't say, then you don't know." I try to tell myself it doesn't matter, but it's not working. I plop down on the couch next to Neil, grabbing the bowl away from him.

"Oh, I know." He turns the volume up on the TV. "And I know you like him."

It feels like my skin is about to slide off my face. "Did you freaking tell him that?"

"No. Relax. I'm not getting involved. Stop hogging the popcorn." He grabs the bowl back from me.

I let him have it and press my mouth shut, training my eyes on the movie even though I'm not paying any attention. This has to be the fiftieth time Neil and I have seen *Billy Elliot* since we were little.

Obviously, there's *something* going on with me and Ollie, but how can Neil be so sure that he would want to ask me out? The whole concept is embarrassingly foreign to me since I've never had time for dating with all my dance stuff. Not that anyone has ever asked me out—besides old creeps occasionally catcalling me in public. The guys at ballet school acknowledged my existence even less than the girls. I did sometimes find myself noticing girls, too, but the only time they noticed me was definitely not in a good way.

And it's very apparent that Neil has way more experience than I do. Besides Gwen, so many girls were flirty with him today. Earlier I thought he felt like I was too much of a loser to talk to about this stuff, but maybe he just didn't want to make me feel bad. Which somehow makes me feel even more pathetic.

Neil rests his head against my shoulder, and I try to relax. I start to lose myself in Jamie Bell's dizzying steps like I always do. Before I know it, my eyes get heavy. I try to keep them open, but I'm completely spent from today. I'm remembering the way Ollie looked at me after my audition and what happened in the basement, and I can't help thinking maybe Neil's right.

I try to get a handle on the sharp fluttering that starts in my core. Whatever's going on with Ollie is totally besides the point—I don't even know if I'm going to be here after this weekend. And if Neil's dad agrees, I'll have to focus on school. I can't mess up this assistant gig. The thought of working with Lucinda Anvyi makes me giddy and nauseous at the same time. Letting my eyes close for good, my mind slows to a complete stop.

*
*

The next day, Saturday morning, I wake up at dawn to go for a run to distract myself from how out of balance I feel waiting to hear if I can switch to Huntley. Once I'm in the park, I start running and my muscles are immediately relieved to be put to good use again. My mind shuts off as I focus only on my breath and the comforting thwack of my sneakers hitting the pavement.

When I come to a stop, the sun is fully up and it's sweltering. I stop in the middle of a quiet hiking trail. Keeling forward with my hands on my knees, I gasp in the humid air.

My phone rings, and my already elevated pulse speeds up even more. There's no way my dad could have gotten in touch with Mr. Roi so quickly. He must be calling about something else.

I pull my phone out of my pocket.

"Hey, Dad," I puff out as I move into a lunge, stretching out my hamstrings. "What's up?"

"You okay? Why do you sound like that?"

"Out for a run," I tell him as I start heading back to Neil's place at a slower pace.

"Good for you." He sounds tired. "God, I haven't been for a run in ages." Dad used to join me on the occasional morning jog before I moved, but he was never a daily runner like me. "So I spoke with Neil's dad."

"Already?" A wave of irritation washes over me. Mr. Roi can pick up my dad's call but not his own son's? "What did he say?"

"He said he'd be happy to host you for the school year."

I stop running and brace a hand against the nearest tree. It's so warm out the bark radiates heat. "Wait, really? I can stay?" Relief floods through me, a grin taking over my face.

"Yes."

I jump up and down for a moment before I manage to contain myself. "That's great!"

"Just a few conditions."

"Okay," I say as I start running again.

"Make sure you mind your manners and do your part helping out around the house."

"Of course."

"And you'll have to keep your grades up. He said Neil's grades have been slipping. That doesn't mean yours can too."

"Not a problem." Since I had no social life at the academy, I'm already way ahead of my grade's curriculum, so I'm going to have a few free periods this year. Lots of time to get my homework done.

My mind races as I wonder what else they talked about. He couldn't have told my dad about Neil being in the hospital or we wouldn't be having this conversation. I have an icky feeling Mr. Roi didn't tell him about that because he's embarrassed or ashamed or whatever. All of the terrible things he yelled at Neil about that morning before he left.

What a jerk. At least Neil will have me now. I'll just have to figure out a way to handle what's been going on with him on my own. If I said anything about it to my dad, he'd flip. There's no way I can ask him to help.

"You'll let me know if your mom contacts you?"

I swallow down a heaving sigh. "Will do."

I don't plan on even telling her I'm here. I can practically see the disappointment on her face if she knew I was giving up on ballet school.

I zone back in as he continues. He says he e-mailed my old school to see if they'll give him at least part of his deposit back. Then he asks me to e-mail him a copy of the registration forms when school starts and everything's pretty much settled. No friends to say goodbye to. I didn't leave anything back in Alberta besides my posters.

Regret tugs at me, but I try to tell myself I don't need them anymore. I can keep doing my ritual with Michaela in my head instead.

"One last thing," he says.

"What is it?"

"I know talking to your old man isn't thrilling, but please call to check in at least once a week, okay?"

I laugh, slowing my pace a little. "You make it sound like a punishment. Obviously, I'll still check in, Dad."

I try never to let on how much it sucks that he's not here, but it's really hard sometimes. It's not like I can be mad at him about it, though—since I'm going to try for a college program now, that's another expense for him to worry about.

"You'd better. Talk to you later, hon."

After we hang up, I pick up speed as I approach Neil's back patio. I'm practically vibrating with excitement to wake him up and tell him the good news. I know he's going to be super hyped too.

Starting at a new school is never easy. But whatever gets thrown my way, at least I know Neil will have my back, no matter what.

8

Auditions were a lot to take in, but the first day of school is downright dizzying. Huntley School for the Arts is massive—there must be over a thousand students. My old school had less than a hundred. When the first bell rings, the stampede at the front doors pushes me away from Neil's side to the opposite end of the front hall. He yells to text him at lunchtime before he's carried away by the crowd.

After I pick up my registration forms from the office, I try to find my first-period English class. It takes me forever—the room is tucked away in the back corner of a large, older wing on the second floor. It's horribly institutional, metal doors and cement walls blending together, all painted a uniform bluish gray.

Somehow my English teacher, a pudgy balding man, takes the entire period to review a mind-numbing syllabus. He seems a little too fond of Shakespeare. We'll be reading ten of his plays this year.

When the bell for second period rings, I climb the overcrowded stairs, gripping the railing so I don't get knocked over. The third floor is slightly less dated and easier to navigate. I check my class schedule again and stop in front of a door I think might be my Ancient History class.

When I step inside, the first person I spot is Neil's buddy, Kevin, in the back row. He looks me up and down, grinning. Pretending not to see him, I scan the room some more.

Ollie's at the far end of the middle row, next to the windows. My pulse trips over itself for a moment. I haven't seen him since he left Neil's so abruptly on Friday night. He didn't stop by again all weekend. I didn't want to seem obsessive or nosy, so I hadn't asked Neil where he'd been.

I'm blocking the doorway, so I make myself head in Ollie's direction. He doesn't see me. His forehead is planted on the top of the tiny desk-chair combo he's crammed himself into.

Act normal. I clear my throat after I take the empty seat next to him. "Hey."

He jerks upright, blinking away unconsciousness for a moment. Then he breaks into a grin. "Oh. You're here."

I just nod like an idiot for a long moment, his smile rendering me mute.

"You look tired," I blurt out and wince internally. "I mean, are you okay?"

Our teacher walks in before he can answer. "Morning everyone. Open your books to page ten."

She goes up to the blackboard and writes "Ms. Lin" followed by the course code. Everybody shuts up and she doesn't do much introductory stuff, just starts the first lesson on Mesopotamia. I'm sure everyone else must be bored out of their minds, but honestly this has all been a novel experience for me.

Because I'd been so focused on dance since I was a toddler, I completed all my elementary school requirements from home. Back at my ballet school, the classrooms were more like boardrooms, with long tables, rolling office chairs and smartboards. Huntley's a genuine school, complete with wooden desks, the scent of chalk and pencil shavings pervading the room.

The tap of chalk against the blackboard pauses near the end of class, Ms. Lin letting us catch up on our notes. I've already neatly written everything down and am just doodling at this point.

I peek over at Ollie. He's hardly written anything. His long, dark eyelashes almost brush his face as he looks out the window, his eyes half-closed.

I kick him lightly and he looks over.

"If you think I'll be sharing my notes with you before midterms, you're mistaken," I whisper.

His lips quirk upward. "Thanks for the heads up," he says under his breath.

Ms. Lin sighs loudly. "Miss . . ." Then she pauses and looks at me questioningly.

I shift uncomfortably in my seat. "Bimi."

She nods. "Miss Bimi. Is there something you'd like to share?"

No one makes a noise, but the second-grade "Ooh, she's in trouble" energy in the room is palpable. I cringe, staring down at my notes.

"No, sorry."

"All right." She stops eyeing me and addresses the rest of the class. "This year's first assignment is a research project on a historical figure of your choosing who lived before the tenth century. You can pair up or work on your own," she says as the lunch bell rings.

I hurriedly stuff my crap in my backpack while almost everyone else has somehow already made their way out of the room in what seems like seconds. When I stand up, I find Ollie sitting on his desk now.

He jumps up and swings his backpack on. "Partners?" he asks.

"Uh . . ." Normally I would say no, given the opportunity to work by myself. Group projects are always annoying. Somehow the work never seems to be equally divided, and I usually end up taking the brunt of it.

"Wow. You're taking a while to think on this," Ollie says as we walk out into the hall. "I promise I won't stick you with all the work."

"You promise?"

He sticks his pinky finger out, and I loop my own around it before I remember what coming in contact with him does to me.

I give him a serious look, ignoring the phantom heat still pressing against my skin as we start down the stairs. "I'm gonna hold you to that."

"Got it." He laughs. The lilting sound of it makes something in my brain short out. I can't help dropping my stern expression and smile like a moron.

He's smiling right back. Does this qualify as flirting? I think it might.

"Come on," he says. "I'll show you where the caf is."

I follow, praying that lunch period isn't going to be a whole complicated thing with unspoken seating arrangements that are tightly adhered to. Back at my old school, I'd usually eat in the studio or my room before getting some extra practice in.

Ollie contains a yawn as we head to the lunch line.

"Didn't get enough sleep?"

"I got home from work pretty late," he says as he puts a blueberry muffin on his tray.

So that's what he was up to on the weekend. "Where do you work?"

"At a record store."

Of course he does. That explains his massive vinyl collection.

I grab a bottle of orange juice. "You guys were open on Labor Day?"

"I do tech for the venue above the shop sometimes. There was a holiday show last night, and the band started almost three hours late."

"Which band was it?"

He smirks a bit. "Not one good enough to get away with starting three hours late."

I snort out a laugh as I reach for an apple. "Sounds brutal."

We continue through the line, and I panic a little when I realize there are no salad options, just sandwiches. I slowly pick out a ham and cheese.

At least it's whole wheat bread. That doesn't make me feel better, but I ignore my unease. I can't just have an apple—that would look weird. Plus, I need to eat something substantial so I have enough energy for my dance classes after lunch. I guess I'll have to start making and bringing my own lunch from now on.

"There you guys are." Neil is suddenly behind us, reaching over me to grab a bag of chips. "Let's go meet some people."

I contain a groan. I was convinced he must have introduced me to every kid in our entire grade by this point.

We walk a short way down the main hall to a group of juniors seated on the floor near the auditorium.

"Hey, Ebi. How was your summer, man?" Neil asks as he takes a seat beside a boy with a hi-top fade. I grab the spot next to Neil, and

Ollie sits right beside me, his shoulder brushing mine for the briefest second.

"It was horrible," Ebi says with a laugh, his perfect teeth a gleaming contrast to his deep brown skin. "My grandparents visited for, like, a month and a half. My parents forced me to hang out with them 24/7."

"Yikes," Neil says.

"Every day it was, like, Ebi!" He switches to a heavy African accent. "Eh! Do you have a girlfriend yet? You have to find a nice Nigerian girl who can cook. She must cook proper jollof rice."

"I guess you didn't tell them about George then," Neil says. "How's he doing, by the way?"

"I enjoy being alive, so no, I didn't tell them," Ebi says with a snort. "But George and I actually broke up this summer before he left for college."

Neil winces. "Sorry. That sucks."

"It's fine." Ebi shrugs before focusing on me. "I think I spot a fellow West African here. Can you make jollof? My parents would love that."

"I only make Ghanaian jollof," I say before raising an eyebrow. "Which is obviously superior."

Ebi kisses his teeth. "You know what, never mind. My parents would rather have me bring home a boy."

I laugh. Neil introduces me to Ebi, his friend Khadija, and some other people in their group. I surmise they're the resident theater kids as soon as they start talking about musical auditions.

"You guys are doing *Chicago*?" I ask. "That's a little spicy."

"Oh, they keep it spicy," Neil says with a grin. "They did *Spring Awakening* last year."

"If I had my way, we would have done this show called *Me and My Dick*," Ebi says.

"Ish, you love *Me and My Dick*, don't you?" Neil asks with a completely straight face.

I shoot him a disgusted look as Ebi snickers.

"What's *wrong* with you?" I shake my head before I focus on Ebi. "But, yeah, that's a great show. All the numbers in it are amazing."

"True. 'Gotta Find His Dick' slaps so hard," Ebi says before he and Neil crack up.

"I'm done. You're such children." When I roll my eyes, I catch Ollie smiling at me briefly before looking at his phone again. He has his earphones in and hasn't said a word since we sat down.

Ebi breaks into a booming rendition of "Gotta Find His Dick," and I can't stop myself from laughing. He somehow convinces me to sing along, which turns into a full routine with some seated choreo.

Before I know it, the bell rings. Looking down at my sandwich bag full of crumbs, I realize I finished my whole lunch without even thinking once about anyone watching me eat.

Ollie finally looks up from his phone again. "Gotta get to Band. Later."

He takes off so quickly that I don't have a chance to respond. Did I do something to annoy him? Everything seemed great after class when he asked me to be partners. I wonder why he clammed up like that.

*

Neil, Ebi, and I head upstairs to the dance studios on the fourth floor, which is by far the most recently renovated. The high ceilings are windowed and vaulted, letting in daylight that illuminates the wide hallway.

"See ya in Modern," Neil says as he and Ebi head off to their Jazz class.

Taking a deep breath, I step into the ballet studio, wishing that Neil was walking in with me. The studio is wall-to-wall mirrors. The sprung hardwood floors bounce back against my sneakers a little as I head toward an empty space.

I lock eyes with a slender, auburn haired girl a few feet away from me, and we recognize each other. Her name is Caroline—she used to train at Madame D.'s old dance studio.

She scoots away, putting some distance between us. I twist to face the other direction as I start to stretch.

To be honest, I doubt she even remembers my name. She and the other girls used to refer to me as "Charity" because they all assumed I was there on a scholarship.

"Hey."

I look up from tying my pointe shoes to find a South Asian girl taking the space Caroline just vacated. She starts to pull on her leg warmers. They're a light brown, matching her skin tone.

"I'm Prasheetha," she says, smiling a little. "You're new here, right? What's your name?"

The corners of my mouth hesitantly turn upward. "I'm Aisha."

"Cool. Nice to meet you," she says before turning to greet Caroline on her other side.

After a moment, Caroline leans in to whisper something in her ear, giggling. Prasheetha doesn't laugh; she just turns to look me up and down impassively.

Great. Same shit, different place. I can already tell this is gonna be a blast. My sandwich turns over in my stomach as I glue my eyes to my feet again.

"Hello, everyone!"

My head snaps to the front of the room as Lucinda Anvyi glides into the studio. I start tying up my shoes at double speed.

"I'm Madame Anvyi. Your usual ballet master is away on maternity leave. I'll be your guest instructor for the year."

As soon as I'm finished with my shoes, I'm on my feet with my hand poised above the barre behind me.

"We'll have two main performance opportunities this year," Madame Anvyi continues. "A solo for the winter showcase and a full class performance in the spring. Can I get this year's assistant up here, please?"

I totally blank until she looks right at me.

Oh crap, that's me. I walk to the front of the room.

When I reach her, she puts a hand lightly on my shoulder. "How long have you been training in the Balanchine method?"

"Almost ten years."

Even though Madame D. was from Russia, where classical is the norm, she'd been fond of neoclassical. I've always loved the sharp, exacting moves of Balanchine's method.

Madame Anvyi nods. "Perfect. We'll be training in Balanchine style this year, which the artistic director has told me will be a change of pace for most of you. Aisha will be assisting me with corrections."

When I glance at the class, no one looks particularly amused. The speed and precision of Balanchine style is famously difficult.

I spend the rest of class helping out with corrections, which is super unnatural for me. I'm used to instructors physically moving me into the correct position, but I've never had to do it to other people.

Tara, the girl from auditions who made the annoying comment about my hair, is struggling quite a bit.

"You have to extend a little more," I say as I pause in front of her and bend low at my knees, demonstrating a deep *plié*. I don't really want to touch her—or anyone, for that matter.

She ignores me. I sigh internally but keep my face unaffected as I move on to the next row.

When the bell rings, everyone collapses to the floor to wind down.

I grab my bag and rush up to the front to talk to Madame Anvyi.

"I just wanted to say I'm really excited to work with you. I loved your *Firebird* at NYCB." I wince at myself, hoping I'm not coming off like a rabid fan.

She laughs warmly. "Thank you. I thought your audition was wonderful. You obviously have a strong background in contemporary ballet."

My eyebrows shoot up. It's wild she thinks that when I haphazardly pulled my audition together from the one contemporary Ballet class I took last year.

"Not really—I have a lot more classical training."

"Well, keep up the good work and you may have a shot at the winter showcase solo," she says with a wink before taking off.

Holy crap. I stand there with my mouth open for a moment before I snap out of it and head out the door toward last period. I grab onto the straps of my backpack to keep from shaking.

"How'd it go?" Neil asks when I get to Modern. I run toward him and start shrieking and shaking him. He and Ebi burst out laughing at my antics. "Pretty well, I guess?"

I tell them what happened while we wait for the instructor to arrive.

Neil grins. "That's awesome, Ish!"

Ebi high-fives me. "Way to go, future prima."

I start to deflate. Things are getting more diverse in ballet, but I know it still isn't likely that I'll ever be a prima at a major company. Not with my complexion.

The teacher with the short natural hair from auditions walks into class. "Okay, guys, let's get started."

She sits down cross-legged at the front of the room, and the rest of the class forms a circle around her. I scooch in between Neil and Ebi.

"I'm Hannah." She doesn't say her last name. "For those of you who are new, this will be a bit of a different experience." She looks at me, and I try not to fidget under her gaze. "We'll be using therapeutic dance exercises to inform our choreography. I want you to think of this class as an exploration of self."

I shoot Neil a wary look, but he's completely focused on Hannah.

"All of the work we'll be creating together this year will be informed by our collective emotions."

Collective emotions? I nod along, like I know what on earth she's talking about.

"As the year progresses, we'll be moving deeper into feelings that aren't always easy to look at. We'll be examining the parts of ourselves that aren't usually exposed to the light."

Okay . . . ? It sounds like she's reciting corny poetry.

"Let's start with a meditation."

Everyone closes their eyes. When I don't, Hannah raises her eyebrows expectantly. I resist the urge to roll my eyes and finally shut them.

"I want you to think back to a moment you were truly at peace. No stress or worries weighing you down. A time when you felt completely safe. What did you feel in your body at that moment? Was there a lightness in your chest? Did a wave of ease wash over you?"

I can't take this seriously. It's like I'm in a hippie yoga class or something. All that's missing is the sage and incense.

"Focus on that feeling. Go fully into it, like you're back there again, completely safe and whole."

Breathing deeply, I pretend I'm visualizing like everyone else. I wonder how long we're going to do this before class actually starts. I start mentally going through the steps of today's ballet routine, wishing I was pirouetting instead. It seems like a century before Hannah speaks again.

"All right, you can open your eyes. Would anyone like to share?"

Neil stands and my eyes widen as he moves to the middle of the circle. He's into this? I guess I shouldn't be surprised given how good his audition was.

Hannah puts on some music, and he enters the same space he did during his audition, exploding into a barrel roll, his limbs contorting in a language that's completely foreign to me. It looks like it comes so easily to him, translating Hannah's words into the physical. His hand movements are quick and effortless as he jumps into a complicated set of contractions, rounding his spine forward and then straightening again. It looks like he's worked on this for weeks, instead of making this all up right now.

The class whoops when he finishes.

"Thank you, Neil," Hannah says brightly as he sits back down beside me. "As this year's assistant, you'll be leading our fall showcase group performance."

I clamp onto his shoulder and grin at him as the next person moves to the middle of the circle. "Why didn't you tell me that you got the assistant gig for this class?" I ask under my breath.

He shrugs me off. "No big deal."

"Have you been an assistant before?" I whisper.

He shakes his head, and I elbow him. "It's a big deal, then."

Neil rolls his eyes as Ebi gives him a firm pat on the back.

This is exactly how he acted when he mentioned he got a lead in Modern last year. But underneath his front, I can tell he's pumped. I know he doesn't want to seem too excited because it makes the pressure more real.

We're the same, in that way at least. I still have no idea how he's able to access a depth of emotion that I feel so far removed from. After what happened at my audition, I can't imagine willingly moving into that place in front of people again.

It looks like Hannah is going to ask everyone to improv today, and I'm really not looking forward to it. Unlike Neil, moving without a plan and not looking like an idiot isn't my forte.

It's almost the end of class, and everyone else has already danced solo. With a deep sigh, I get to my feet and move to the middle.

Hannah starts the music, but I don't move.

"Take your time," she says after a moment.

I nod, but I'm coming up completely blank.

"Don't think about it so much," Hannah says. "Remember that feeling we meditated on earlier. Bring yourself back to that."

I close my eyes and start moving, doing my best to keep my arms in a more rounded position than I'm used to in ballet. My contractions are stiff, and I don't even attempt the hand movements. I feel so stupid. I'm hoping I don't look as awkward as I feel. I end with a basic deep back bend that I remember from my Modern class last year.

When I stop, Hannah doesn't look pleased. The bell rings before she can say anything. I head back to my spot as quickly as possible, grabbing my backpack.

"That was awful," I groan in the hallway.

Neil shakes his head. "Chill. It's your first day."

If I want to stay at Huntley—and have a shot at a spot in a college dance program—I can't afford to do badly in this class. I'm going to have to figure out some way to tap into what Neil did, whatever the hell Hannah was talking about earlier. I've hardly ever seen him open up like that, but I really hope that getting the hang of this can help me start piecing together what's happening inside him.

9

When I get to second period on Thursday, I'm kind of disappointed Ollie's seat is vacant. I start taking out my notes, and when I look up, I find Kevin sitting in the seat directly in front of me. He straddles the back of the desk-chair combo in a completely unnatural way that he seems proud of.

"Hey, Aisha." He takes his time looking me up and down again.

I groan internally. "Hi."

"Guess you didn't see me wave you over to sit with me on Tuesday."

I nod vaguely. This is the first time I've seen him since then because I had two spare periods in the morning yesterday. It was a welcome break from his leering.

He continues, despite my lacklustre response. "Now you're stuck here since Ms. Lin said the seating's permanent."

I try not to grimace. "Uh-huh."

"How're you liking it here so far?"

I fiddle with my pencil case. "Fine, I guess."

"What other classes you got?"

I briefly mention English and my dance classes.

"Oh yeah?" I can tell he wasn't really listening. He's using all his concentration to look at my body.

My hoodie's slightly cropped, and I glance down to check it hasn't ridden up to expose any of my midsection. It hasn't.

"Listen," he says after I don't respond. "Henry's having a party tomorrow night. Do you wanna go with me?"

I squint at him. "Who's Henry?"

"He's a senior. His parties are always hype. You should come."

"I'm not free tomorrow. But thanks," I say as I pick up my pen and focus on my notebook.

I expect him to get up, but he stays put. "No worries. You free Saturday? We could watch a movie or something. I mean, if you want to hang at my place. My parents won't be home."

My stomach sloshes around the leftover chow mein I shouldn't have eaten for breakfast. My hands start to sweat as his eyes keep burrowing into me.

"Not free then either," I say, not even looking up.

He finally gets the hint, and there's that familiar shift in energy from lust to annoyance to anger. I can sense it a mile away at this point, since I've witnessed it in so many strangers. Men who've yelled "bitch" at me while passing me on the street, when seconds earlier they'd been whistling lewdly. Becoming instantly livid when I don't acknowledge them.

He starts to get up. "Okay. You don't have to be like that." I catch him sneering at me from the edge of my vision. "I don't usually even go for darkskins, you know."

My windpipe vacuums shut. My palms are so clammy I'm worried my pen is going to slip right out of my hand and go flying. I grasp it tighter and keep focused on doodling nonsense in my notebook.

When he realizes he's not going to get any reaction, he stalks away. I force out a breath and put my pen down.

I look up just as Ollie appears, scrunching himself into the seat beside me.

"What was that?" he asks. He keeps his face blank.

I turn away from him, focusing on the front of the room. "What was what?"

"Are you okay?" From his gentle tone, I know he heard what Kevin said, and I want to die on the spot.

I shrug, unable to face him. People are still strolling in, but Ms. Lin isn't here yet.

"I'm fine," I mumble, picking up my pen and doodling mindlessly again. "I guess he couldn't handle that I'm not interested."

Ollie's silent. I consider glancing at him to gauge his reaction—to see if there's some clue on his face that *he's* interested in me or if Neil was talking out of his ass.

I still can't make myself look at him.

After a moment he responds. "You're not interested in Kevin? But he's such a catch."

I bite my lip, but a loud snort escapes my mouth. When I focus on him, he keeps a straight face for a second before we both start snickering.

"Okay, everyone," Ms. Lin says as she enters just as the bell rings. "Flip to chapter two."

Ms. Lin has us take turns reading sections of the chapter out loud.

When she gets to the middle row it's Ollie's turn to read, but he doesn't say anything. I look over, expecting to find him half asleep, but he's looking right at Ms. Lin who's staring back at him impatiently.

"Pass," he mutters.

Ms. Lin shakes her head. "Do you want a zero for class participation today?"

I contain a sigh. Why can't she just let him pass if he doesn't want to read?

Ollie shakes his head, and starts reading. He stumbles over his words, and I hear Kevin let out a smothered laugh from the back. I turn and shoot him an unamused look.

"Enough, Mr. Galang," Ms. Lin warns Kevin. "Go ahead, Mr. Cheriet."

"I can go," I chime in. Before Ms. Lin can protest, I start reading where Ollie left off.

I glance at Ollie again when I'm done, but he doesn't look at me for the rest of class.

When the bell rings, he doesn't wait for me, but I catch up with him by the door.

"Ollie—"

"It's cool if you don't want to be partners anymore," he says, still not looking at me.

I blink at him as we head toward the stairs. "What?"

He finally glances over and smiles a smidge. "Totally get it if you'd rather work with someone who can read."

"Okay, cool. I guess I'll see if Kevin wants to pair up then." I roll my eyes. "It's fine. Reading in class is the worst. Ms. Lin was being so annoying about it."

He smiles a little more. "Well, we should probably start working on the project then. Are you free to come over after school tomorrow?"

"Yeah, I should be." I try my best to sound normal even as my heart does a weird little jig. God, I need to chill out. This doesn't mean anything special—it's just an assignment.

I'd started packing a salad after the first day, but I still pick up some extra fruit in the caf. The carrot muffins smell so good, though, I can't resist grabbing one.

We find Neil and the theater kids by the auditorium again. As soon as I sit down, Ebi and Khadija start telling me about their theater director who was apparently on a maniacal power trip at their *Chicago* auditions. I'm absorbed in the drama for a while before I realize Ollie's gone quiet again. He's scrolling through his phone with his earbuds blasting something with screaming guitars.

I stuff the uneaten half of my muffin in my lunch bag before I peek over his shoulder to glance at his phone. "What're you listening to?"

He starts a little and takes an earbud out. "What?"

I ask again, but he glances over my shoulder.

Neil, Ebi, Khadija, and some other kids have all stopped their conversation and are staring at me and Ollie. I give them an odd look before I turn back to Ollie and find him with his eyes glued to his phone again.

"It's, uh . . ." He trails off but holds one earbud out to me.

I put it in my ear and scooch a little closer so it doesn't fall out, careful not to actually come in contact with him.

"Wait, this is Midnight Cavalcade? They finally put out a new album? I've been dying to see them live."

"Yeah. I guess it didn't get a ton of press after Serafina left to go solo." Ollie tells me all about the time they played at the venue where he works. Before I know it, the bell rings.

"See ya." He smiles before he takes off.

I wipe the grin off my face when I turn to find Neil, Ebi, and Khadija all staring at me again.

"What are you looking at?"

Khadija shrugs as she sweeps her thick, waist-length twists behind her shoulder. "Nothing. Just never really seen Ollie talk before. Later," she says before she heads out.

I squint after her before Neil, Ebi, and I make our way upstairs. "What does that mean? He talks."

Ebi smirks. "To *you*."

I sigh. "Whatever."

I had wondered when school first started why Ollie was so silent at lunch compared to at Neil's place and at his place. I sensed after a bit that he just wasn't into inserting himself into larger group settings, but after today, I'm pretty sure it just makes him anxious. Which makes sense considering how freaked out he was at his audition. Our lunch crew isn't as intimidating as the entire school, but I get that it isn't easy being comfortable in every social situation like Neil is.

*
*

In Ballet, I've been trying to get used to correcting the other girls' form. I avoided Tara yesterday, but her posture is so bad today, I have to correct her since Madame is busy correcting someone else on the other side of the room.

I straighten her drooping arms, and she flinches away like I had her in a death grip. I barely touched her.

"Ouch," she whines, clutching her arm. "Relax. You don't have to be so aggressive."

I act like I didn't hear her as I move to the next girl in line.

"Freak," she mutters behind me.

Caroline and the other girls in earshot giggle quietly.

This shouldn't get to me. I should be used to this kind of thing by now—I'm always the sore thumb in Ballet, sticking out front and center to be picked at. I'm the tallest girl in the class and the only person of color here other than Madame A. and Prasheetha.

Madame's still fully absorbed in assisting the girls at the end of the room. My gaze lands on Prasheetha as I move to help the girls in her row. When I find her already staring at me, I give her a short nod. She studies me stonily for another moment before turning away.

I can't tell if she's annoyed on my behalf about Tara's comment or if her irritation is aimed at me for some unknown reason. Maybe Caroline made up some particularly foul rumor about me.

God, none of this pettiness even matters anymore. Here at Huntley, I actually have a shot at getting a solo, and that's all I need to worry about.

*

"You good?" Neil asks me when I get to Modern after Ballet's finally over.

I try to relax my face as I sit next to him on the studio floor. "I'm fine. How about you?"

"Great," he says automatically.

I feel like an idiot even asking at this point. At home, things have been normal enough, but he still hasn't really opened up about how he's been doing since the hospital. I know my best chance at an actual answer is trying to interpret whatever escapes him when he's dancing.

Hannah starts with the meditating thing again. "Think back to the last time you felt truly carefree. Completely filled with joy even at the smallest things. Feel the pureness of that joy radiate from within you, lighting up everything around you. Move fully into that unself-conscious space."

I lose focus almost immediately like I have the last few days. Tara and Caroline are snickering at me in my head, and then Kevin's sneering face joins them. My lunch starts to inch its way up my throat. I squeeze my eyes shut even harder, but I can't force myself to focus.

Hannah asks us to share, and Neil goes first again. His jumps are bursting with momentum as he flies around the circle, as free and uncontrolled as he was when we were small. When he used to come over and we'd play in our own little realm, away from the pressure of practice and rehearsals.

As I watch him, I find myself back there with him, *jeté*-ing around with my glittering wand. It feels full of power, like I can summon anything I want into being. A tea party of woodland fairies appearing from beyond the yard. A parade of songbirds flying down from the trees to twirl around me. A pile of my stuffed animals joining me for an impromptu formal ball in the garden. That one magical hour between getting home from the studio and dinner time was all mine. Anything I could imagine existed within it.

When he's done, I slowly make my way to the middle of the circle. Taking a deep breath, I focus on channeling Neil's energy. I spin in a series of dizzying *fouettés*, moving like I did before I knew the limits of what used to seem like a world of endless possibilities. Before it mattered if I was in my yard or in front of hundreds of people. All that mattered was that I was dancing. I finish off with an ecstatically high flying *tour jeté*.

Hannah's smiling at me for the first time since my audition. "Thank you, Aisha."

Neil grins and nudges my side as I sit back down next to him. Containing a laugh, I poke him back.

Well, that wasn't so awful today.

Actually, that was kind of great. I feel way better than I did earlier. Hannah might be onto something with this stuff. At the very least, I'm not quite as worried about failing this class. Besides that, maybe I'll be able to rediscover the connection Neil and I had when we danced together when we were kids—despite everything that's happened.

10

"Good job today."

I blink slowly into the present as I head out of the ballet studio. My mind was entirely focused on my breakthrough in Modern yesterday, wondering if I'll be able to do as well today. Turning around, I find Prasheetha behind me, her face deadpan as usual.

After a moment, I realize she's talking about the routine demo Madame had me show the class earlier. None of the girls had seemed thrilled to be an audience to it—I'd avoided their gazes after I finished and we got into corrections.

"Oh," I say slowly. "Thanks?"

She hasn't really spoken to me since the first day last week—why is she talking to me now?

"How long have you been doing ballet?" she asks as we head for the door. "Do you compete?"

"Not anymore. When I was younger I—"

"Hey, hon," Caroline cuts me off. She brushes past me at the door, taking my place beside Prasheetha and linking arms with her. "Did your parents say you can come to my sleepover tonight?"

"Yep, I finally convinced them," she says, not even glancing at me again as Caroline leads her away down the hall.

Right. So much for that then. I don't know why I even briefly entertained the idea that Prasheetha might be different. I suck in a sigh and head toward Modern.

*

"Ish. Aisha!" Neil says loudly, and I finally snap out of my daze, turning my attention toward him. We're sitting on the floor, waiting for class to start.

"What?"

"What's up with you?" Neil asks as he starts stretching.

I grab my water bottle out of my bag. "Just tired."

He shakes his head. "How could you be tired? You fell asleep super early last night and you didn't even get here until lunch."

Instead of spending my spare periods in the library this morning, I opted to stay home. Neil's assuming that I woke up late because I was still on the couch when he left. I was too tired from rehearsals to go out for a super early run like usual. He didn't cook breakfast and was really quiet leaving—I think he was trying to give me a chance to sleep in, which was sweet of him. I suck at sleeping late, though, so I got up pretty soon after he headed out and started researching for my History project that I'm doing with Ollie.

"Okay, guys," Hannah says as she walks in. "We're going to do something a little different today. Pair up."

I shift closer to Neil as I wait for her to say what we're doing.

"For the next two minutes, I want you to look into your partner's eyes. Connect with what they're feeling without exchanging any words."

I fake a soundless gag as I turn to face Neil. God, this would be so incredibly awkward with anyone besides him. The thought of looking into someone's eyes without saying anything for that long makes me want to crawl out of my skin.

Neil and I used to have staring contests all the time at our old studio before class started or when we were waiting to get picked up. He starts in with his usual ridiculous faces, and I bite my tongue not to laugh since the room is totally silent. I cross my eyes at him but stop when Hannah shakes her head at us. Neil contains a snort, his expression serious now.

Time stretches out in the quiet of the room. I keep my gaze in the general vicinity of his face, but honestly, it's just too weird staring straight on for this long. I can feel him doing it, though, so finally I meet his eyes. There's something behind them that I instantly recognize as concern. Probably about me zoning out on him earlier. The leaving-my-body thing hasn't been as bad as that last day at ballet school, but Neil's definitely noticed it happening.

I match his expression. I get that he's worried about me spacing so much, but I wonder if he gets how little that matters compared to whatever I've been glimpsing inside him since I got back here. I've given him this look before, and at this point he'd usually look away and change the subject. Now there's nowhere for him to go.

I expect his eyes to harden, but they don't. I can tell he knows how much it scared me when he shut me out like that at the hospital. He's not hiding anything from me now—I can feel exactly how miserable he is.

"That's time," Hannah says, and I blink, turning away from Neil. "We're going to take whatever you just found in each other and translate those feelings into an improv pairs piece. Who's ready?"

Ready as I'll ever be, I guess. I look over at Neil, and he nods before we get up and move to the middle of the circle.

I expect Hannah to start the music, but she studies us for a moment. "Can you share any emotions that came up for you during the exercise?"

I'm silent, staring at the hardwood floor.

"Isolation," Neil says, and my head shoots up, my mouth falling open.

I never expected him to say any of the things that had just passed between us. I try to search his eyes, but he's looking at Hannah. She nods at Neil before focusing on me.

My heart thunders at a concerning speed, and I swallow painfully.

"Hopelessness," I force out.

"We're getting somewhere." Hannah finally starts the music and gestures for us to start.

Facing Neil, I don't let myself think as I begin moving. He follows my lead, and I feel myself shifting into a new plane where the language of his movements starts to become familiar. A form of communication that I'm not only beginning to understand but learning to speak.

My right hand juts across my body and into the air, and Neil mirrors me the opposite way. We simultaneously bring our arms down and around before bending back into a floor roll.

Our eyes connect and I communicate to him that I get how alone he's felt and that I've felt it too. That I'm so glad we're finally together again. When we come to a stop, we're eye to eye, and for a horrible second, I think we both might cry. He pulls me into a hug as the class claps. I let him for a second before pulling away. I cross my arms, trying to keep myself in one piece.

"Thank you for sharing that," Hannah says, smiling gently. "You two have danced together before?"

"Yep." Neil's immediately closed off again. He somehow looks completely unfazed by what just happened. "We used to do competitive ballet together when we were kids."

My chest constricts sharply, my lungs deflating. He said it so casually. Like it meant nothing to him, like it was so easy to throw it all away.

Hannah nods. "You have a really unique chemistry that I think you should keep exploring. Aisha, I'd like you to join Neil in choreographing the group performance for the fall showcase."

Me? I nod, unable to speak. I'm having trouble processing what's happening, a high-pitched ringing echoing in my head. I can't do this.

Calm down. It's a huge opportunity. I have to try.

"Thanks, Hannah," I get out before I quickly head back to my seat, Neil right behind me.

He grins. "This is gonna be sweet."

I nod, trying to let his excitement seep into me.

This is a good thing. It'll be something else besides my ballet assistant position to put on my college apps. That doesn't change the fact that it's still way outside of my comfort zone.

Over the years, lots of instructors have told me that I would be "better suited" for modern. I knew what they really meant, though. They thought modern was where Black dancers belong, not ballet. But the unfailingly defined structure of ballet has always come easier for me than this unsettlingly amorphous form.

I'll just have to figure it out. Besides this being good for college, this is the closest I've gotten to understanding how Neil's actually feeling. I wish I was glad that I've made some progress with him. But the gravity of how awful he really feels, and feeling all of that within myself . . . it was a lot. And some instinctual part of me knows I barely even scratched the surface.

After the bell rings, Ebi comes over to us. "Congrats! I'm having some people over tomorrow night if you're in the mood to celebrate."

"I'm down," I say, trying not to sound too excited. Even though I'm sure this is a daily occurrence for Neil, I think this is the first time I've ever been genuinely invited to a real, party-shaped event. After what happened with Caroline and Prasheetha, it's nice to feel like my presence is wanted.

Crap, maybe I shouldn't have agreed so fast. If people will be drinking, that won't be a good scene for Neil.

"Sounds like a blast, but I already told Rashanth I'd stop by his place tomorrow to check out this game he just got," Neil says as we head out of class. "I have to warn you, though, Ish. The drama kids like to get pretty rowdy on the weekends."

Ebi snorts. "Don't scare her. I promise it won't be the drunken den of debauchery Neil's making it out to be."

"I'm not scared," I say, and they both start laughing. "Wow, I love that I'm giving off desperately sheltered vibes."

"Not desperately," Ebi says, and I swat his arm. "I'm kidding. See you then, all right?"

*
*

"Where're you going?" Neil asks when we get home and I immediately start toward the back door.

"Ollie's. We have a project. I'll be back later."

"Ah, okay. Have fun," he says with a grin as he jumps onto the couch and reaches for the remote.

"We're writing a paper—how much fun could we possibly have?" He grins wider and I sigh. "I'm leaving."

Heading out the back door, I clear the fence and walk through the park over to Ollie's place. The summer's been lingering heavily, and I'm sweating in the scorching heat.

Maybe I should have taken a shower before I headed over—I probably reek. When I lift the neck of my T-shirt over my nose, I don't smell anything, so I think I'm okay.

I spot Ollie and hurriedly stop sniffing my shirt like a weirdo. I wasn't expecting to find him sitting outside on his back patio.

"Oh, hey," I squeak out.

"Hi." He gets up as I walk over. Hopefully he didn't catch what I was doing. "What's up?"

"Uh, did you still wanna work on the project?" I ask.

"Yeah, did you?"

I nod. "Yeah." *For the love of God, how is it humanly possible to sound this stupid?*

He opens the sliding door, letting me inside the steaming kitchen. It smells even more strongly of fragrant spices than usual.

His mom looks over from the stove, and I give her a small wave. "Hi, Mrs. Cheriet." She smiles warmly. "Hi, Aisha."

I wonder how she knows my name since we've never met.

"I like to make it my business who's in and out of my house." She shoots me a quick, knowing look but doesn't seem annoyed.

"Christ, Mom," Ollie mutters. "Can you not?"

I'm just about ready to melt into a pool of humiliated goo. I don't even want to imagine what she must think I was doing sneaking into her son's room. "It's nice to meet you," I manage.

"You too, dear. You can call me Anissa if you like. Are you hungry? Dinner will be ready in a bit, but I have some dolma ready now—"

"We're good," Ollie says quickly before he leads me out of the kitchen.

"Sorry about that," he says when we get to his room.

"No prob." I shrug my backpack off and take a seat on the couch. "So, I had some time to get started this morning. I was thinking we could do Cleopatra for our historical figure. It might be kinda fun. Or at least not unbearably boring."

"Sounds good," he says as he flips through a pile of albums by his record player. "Any requests?"

"Whatever's fine," I say as I take my notes out of my backpack.

Why is he putting music on? I thought he wanted to work on this.

Relax. Why wouldn't he put music on? He's always listening to something. Even in class sometimes, he'll put an earbud in and cover it with his hand, so Ms. Lin doesn't catch him. He picks out a sleepy alt rock album that isn't too distracting.

"That's what I've done so far." I hand him my research notes as he sits next to me.

His fingers feather over mine as he takes the notes and my breath catches. I yank my hand away a little too fast and he looks at me sideways. I busy myself retrieving my textbook and pencil case from my backpack.

"You did this all today?" he asks as he scans the pages. "I thought you said you didn't want to get stuck doing all the work."

"Oh, don't worry. There's still lots for you to do," I assure him.

"That sounds ominous." He laughs, and my stomach does a jittery little loop-de-loop.

*

An hour later, he's typed up the first draft of our paper.

I peer over his shoulder at his laptop screen. "Looks good. I'll work on the second draft this weekend." I should have some time before Ebi's thing tomorrow.

Wait, should I invite Ollie? Maybe Ebi already told him about it, so it might be weird if I ask him to come too. Besides, he already told me he doesn't go to parties, so it's probably not something he's even into.

"Cool." He closes his laptop before he stands up and stretches. "Do you mind if I put something else on?"

"Uh, no. I mean, I don't mind. Why would I mind?" I wince at myself as I stuff my notes back in my bag.

"How's everything going with your dance stuff?" His back is to me as he leafs through his records again.

"Today was weird," I mutter.

He glances over. "What happened?"

"We did this exercise in Modern and Neil and I, like . . ."

"Neil and you what?"

I shake my head, not knowing how to start. "Remember what you said in the basement? About Neil saying something about not feeling great?"

Ollie nods as he puts a new record on, another older indie album, something a bit more bass heavy and upbeat. "When he's been drunk a few times, yeah."

"What exactly did he say?"

He rubs his eyes for a moment before he takes a seat on the rug by the record wall.

"Why? What happened in your class?"

"We did this improv thing, and it felt like I got through to him a little bit, but I have this feeling that something's really wrong. I thought things would be better now that I get to stay and everything. But he's still not okay."

Ollie sighs and looks at the rug. "Yeah."

"So what did he say when he was drunk?"

He keeps staring at the rug for a while. "I wish he'd consider going to therapy."

My stomach clenches as soon as he says it. Neil won't even talk to me. He won't open up to some random stranger who doesn't know anything about him. I wish Ollie would just tell me what Neil said.

I chew at my lip. "The improv was actually part of this dance therapy thing. Neil's super good at it."

"Do you think that's been helping him at all?" Ollie asks.

"Maybe? I don't really know. Our teacher asked me to help Neil with leading our class performance. I could try to figure out what's going on in his head while we're working on that together."

He meets my gaze again. "That sounds like a good plan. You'll let me know how it goes?"

I nod. "For sure."

"Okay, cool. And congrats on the lead. That's awesome, Aisha."

"Thanks." I focus on fiddling with the zipper of my pencil case. "Anyway, uh . . . Are you going to Ebi's party tomorrow?" I blurt out.

Ollie shakes his head. "No, not really my thing."

"Oh, okay," I say, jumping up and grabbing my backpack. "See you later then."

I make my way downstairs, cringing at myself. I *knew* I shouldn't have asked him about the party.

"Bye, Anissa," I murmur as I book it toward the back door.

"Are you sure you can't stay for dinner?" she calls after me.

"Smells amazing. But that's okay, thank you," I say quickly before heading out.

At least I got a chance to talk with Ollie about what's up with Neil. He pretty much confirmed that Neil's still been off. I'll have to figure out whatever Ollie wasn't telling me on my own.

11

On Saturday evening, I take the bus to Ebi's place, which is close to Mercy General. His apartment building towers over the strip mall beside it. Tiny balconies with peeling paint run the length of the building. I step into the lobby and enter his buzz code.

When he picks up, I can hardly hear him over singing in the background. "Come on up!" he yells over the noise.

Once I'm on his floor, I don't have to search for his door number; I just follow the muffled echoes of "All That Jazz" blasting from a unit near the stairs. When I try the door, it swings wide open.

"Aisha!" Khadija greets me. She gives me a big hug, the Heineken bottle in her hand cold against my back. "Glad you made it."

"Thanks," I say awkwardly when she lets go. She's never greeted me this warmly at school. "Where's everyone?"

"In the living room." She takes my arm, leading the way through the narrow, carpeted hall. Traditional West African paintings and sculptures punctuate the cozy space, reminding me of my grandparents' old place. The faint smell of fried plantain permeates the air.

A gaggle of theater kids are spread out in the small living room in front of a flat screen TV that takes up most of the wall.

I take a seat on the carpet in front of the couch next to Ebi. "Oh, I love this part!"

Lucy Liu's onscreen, being led through a jailhouse in handcuffs. She kicks one of the swarming paparazzi to the ground and grins wickedly.

"I know," Ebi says as he passes me a beer. "Kitty Baxter always has me out here questioning my sexuality."

"Honestly, same," I say as I take it from him, and he cracks up.

"Love that."

The night is more laid-back than I thought it'd be. We all sing, dance, and recite iconic lines together for the last half of *Chicago*. Then Ebi leads a Fosse-themed game of trivia that devolves into a heated debate over the artistic merit versus historical accuracy of some Fosse biopic show. After that, things wind down and people slowly start heading out until soon it's only me, Ebi, and Khadija left.

"When are your parents supposed to be back?" I ask Ebi as I sprawl out on the newly vacated tan leather couch.

"They're in Nigeria until next week for my cousin's wedding," Ebi says. "I told everyone else they'd be back tonight so they'd leave at a decent hour."

"Genius," Khadija says as she flips through a magazine next to me.

"Let's get a pic," Ebi says, pulling out his phone. "I meant to get some earlier when everyone was still here. Come on."

Khadija and I lean into the frame and he snaps a few shots.

"I need final approval if you're posting any of those," Khadija warns.

"Pick one then, I'm gonna post in a sec. George has been checking my stories lately. He needs to know I'm not just sitting around pining after him. He's been posting at frosh parties non-stop all week."

"Your ex, right?" I ask.

Ebi nods as he hands Khadija his phone.

"George is such a wasteman," Khadija says, examining the photos Ebi just took. "Stop engaging."

"What can I say? I love trash," Ebi says with a sigh, leaning back against the couch. "Particularly hot trash."

I guffaw. "So you wanna get back together with him?"

"Nope. Just make him jealous. Well, mostly. I mean, I'd for sure take him back if he asked." Ebi groans. "I need a backbone. Anyway, where's your dude tonight?"

"Neil's at Rashanth's."

"No, I mean Ollie," Ebi says, wiggling his eyebrows at me.

"Yeah. What's up with you two?" Khadija asks.

"Nothing." I shrug, looking away from them.

Khadija snorts. "Liar."

"I'm not. Nothing's happened with us."

"But you like him, right?" Ebi asks.

I press my beer against my cheek to cool down my face. "He's okay."

"Aww, you're *so* into him," Khadija squeals. "How did you even get him to talk to you?"

"We have History together."

"I had like three classes with him last year, and he never talked to me for, like, more than ten seconds."

"And she really tried it." Ebi laughs. "Multiple times."

She shrugs. "He got unnecessarily hot last year. What was I supposed to do?"

My eyes dart over to her. "You like him?"

"Don't worry, he's all yours," she says. "Honestly, until you got here, I figured we might not play for the same team."

Ebi gives her a dull look. "You're kidding, right? Just because he wasn't into you, you thought he was gay?"

She laughs. "Of course not. But people used to say that he was, a lot. I think because he used to paint his nails and wears his jeans so tight—"

Ebi raises an eyebrow. "So? Who cares? Huntley's an art school for God's sake."

"Who started the rumor that he's gay?" I ask.

"Thomas, this obnoxious asshole who graduated last year," Khadija says. "When we were in ninth grade, he and all his buddies used to make fun of Ollie and picked fights with him constantly. It got really bad. But anyway, I guess he's straight." She shrugs. "Or bi. Have you told him you're into him?"

The lyrics of Ollie's audition song whir on a loop in my head. I have a feeling it must have been Thomas who landed Ollie in the hospital in ninth grade. I absolutely hate that he had to go through that.

This is so uncomfortable, talking about him like this. Especially about his sexuality. I'm not totally sure yet what *I* even identify as. I can't imagine how weird I'd feel if I knew people were speculating about who I'm into.

My lungs start to burn, and I let out a half-choked breath.

"I think he's probably figured out that I like him at this point." There's no way he doesn't know after how bizarrely I acted at his house yesterday.

"I don't know," Ebi says. "He seemed pretty clueless the entire time Khadija was throwing herself at him last year."

"I didn't throw myself at him. I mean, I didn't *physically* throw myself at him." She fixes me with a serious look. "You should ask him out. He probably won't ask you since he's shy."

"Not a huge fan of humiliating myself," I mutter. Even though it seems to be quickly becoming a hobby of mine.

Khadija looks baffled. "But he likes you back."

"Yeah, you should definitely go for it," Ebi says.

My stomach does a quick round of somersaults. *Should I?*

I can't. As much as I think he does, maybe, like me that way, what if I'm wrong? At the hospital, everything was so terrifying and heightened that it's possible I read too much into him being so *there* for me. He could feel obligated to be nice because of the situation with Neil. Or maybe he just thinks of me as a friend, but I'm so clueless and starved for romantic attention, I've been misreading things.

I pry myself off the couch. "I gotta get home, guys."

"Think about it!" Ebi calls after me as I take off.

*

When I get home, Neil's still out. I settle in front of the TV and end up falling asleep. I'm jolted awake at the sound of jangling keys in the front door.

I sit up and let out a yawn. "Hey, what's up?"

"Not much." I can tell Neil's been drinking as soon as he enters the living room. His cheeks are flushed and he's smiling a little too big. "How was the party?"

"Good," I mutter as he plops down next to me, laying his head in my lap.

Goddamn it. How do I handle this? It's not like it's my job to reprimand him. Not that he'd listen to me if I did.

He rolls his eyes at my grim face. "Chill. I just had a few beers."

"Right." He's obviously had more than a few.

"Why do you have to be such a buzzkill?" He rubs his eyes.

I bite hard at the inside of my cheek, but the words still slip from my mouth in a whisper. "Did you do it on purpose?"

I'd been pushing it as far away from my conscious mind as possible, but it's all rushing to the surface. What Ollie wouldn't tell me yesterday.

He blinks up at me, remaining silent.

"You said it was an accident at the hospital . . ." My voice cuts out as tears start to well up behind my eyes.

He closes his eyes. "What does it matter?"

An intolerable pain pierces my chest. "Why would you say that?"

"People die every day. It doesn't make much of a difference in the grand scheme of things." He lets out a snort. "Not to get all philosophical or anything."

I shove him off me, jumping up to fix him with a glare.

"Sure, that makes sense. What difference does it make that Ollie found you here, probably half suffocated in your own puke? Who cares that if he hadn't found you, I would have? That wouldn't be your problem if you were fucking dead."

He's staring at me upside down with his head lolling off the edge of the couch. There's nothing in his eyes.

I make a quick break for the bathroom.

Christ, why did I say that? I splash water on my face and try to take in a full breath. The room slowly starts to spin.

Bracing my hands against the sink, I look into the medicine cabinet mirror.

For a split second, my perspective is reversed. Instead of looking into the mirror, I'm suddenly viewing my real self through it. I try to open my mouth to yell out, but my empty body doesn't move. My face is completely blank.

Neil's bedroom door slams across the house, and I'm jolted back into myself. Tearing my eyes from the mirror, I stare down at my hands gripping the white porcelain. I lock my knees to keep from crumbling to the tile floor.

After a moment, I get a hold of myself again, straightening up. Burying my face in a towel, I let out a muted groan.

I'm literally losing my mind. I shake away the thought that whatever's happening to me is getting worse. That it's not something that I could just leave behind me at the academy after all.

I hate that I just went off on Neil like that. But how could he say that it wouldn't matter if he died? Does he not get how that would have destroyed me? Does he really hate being alive that much?

Losing his mom so young must have been harder than I can imagine. And his dad being so awful to him. But I thought he knew that I got it. That I'm always here for him. I guess I'm not enough anymore.

Ollie's right about Neil needing to see someone. I have no idea why I thought I could handle this when I'm so beyond screwed up myself.

My phone buzzes in my pocket. I'm surprised my dad's calling so late. When I look at the screen, my mom's name flashes across it.

The room starts to spin again as my heart shoots up into my throat. She must have found out I left ballet school. I can't handle the thought of her chewing me out about quitting.

When my phone stops ringing, I thud the back of my head against the bathroom door. I squeeze my eyes shut and bury my face in the towel again.

12

By Thursday the next week, I'm exhausted. Since Saturday night, I've made myself get up even earlier than usual to go for a run before working on my routine for my solo tryouts. Working with Neil in Modern has been strained, so I've been putting my attention into scoring the ballet lead to take my mind off it.

Now I'm trying to focus on the computer in front of me. Ollie and I are sitting in the frigid library, finishing up the slides for our project. Ms. Lin is letting us work on them all period. In our History classroom upstairs, it's boiling since the AC doesn't work as well, but down here it's so cold I have to zip my sweater up to my chin.

Kevin and his partner, Scott, start snickering at something across the room. I hardly spare them a glance as the librarian shushes them.

"I think we're done." Ollie's voice is so close to my ear that my stomach goes into a violent spin cycle. It gets worse when he turns to me and his knee bumps mine.

I stare down at our knees, and he quickly leans away. "Sorry."

"It's fine," I breathe out.

His eyes scan my face. "What's up?"

Through the windows of the computer room, I spot Ms. Lin in the main area of the library. She's busy at the prehistoric photocopier, trying to get it to release tonight's homework.

"Is something up with you and Neil?" he asks when I don't respond.

I guess he noticed at lunch that Neil and I weren't really talking as much. Neither of us has mentioned Saturday night.

After a moment, I reluctantly meet his gaze again. "After Ebi's party on the weekend . . ." I trail off as the librarian shoots us a look. "I'll tell you later," I murmur.

When the librarian turns away, Ollie leans in so I can hear him. "Can you come over after school? We still have to write the presentation script."

I nod, managing not to visibly shiver when his breath brushes my ear. "I'll drop by after rehearsal." I try to quell the excitement bubbling up in me by reminding myself that we have to focus on our project and figuring out what we can do to actually help Neil.

*

Madame Anvyi's voice calling out the eight-count becomes a sleepy hypnotic rhythm. I try to stay focused as I zero in on the positions of my classmates' limbs instead of their faces. The girls who've never done the Balanchine style before are finally getting used to the speed. They're dragging behind the count less this week. I stop in front of Nina, a petite blonde who's struggling with her arabesque position.

"Open up your left hip a little more," I say before doing a quick demonstration. "That'll help your arabesque line look better."

Nina rolls her eyes and looks toward the front of the room. When I glance at Madame Anvyi walking the studio's perimeter, she's looking right at us. I quickly return my attention to the task at hand, examining the form of the girl in front of Nina.

I take a step forward, and the next thing I know I'm on the ground, staring up at the rafters. Panic rushes through me as a dull throbbing starts in my left ankle.

Madame's A's face is suddenly above me. "Are you all right?"

Sitting up slowly, I let out a breath. It stings, but the pain isn't blinding. "I think so."

Madame turns to Nina and stares at her unblinkingly for a moment. "Did you trip her?"

My jaw clenches as I focus on Nina. I'm pretty sure I felt her foot against mine before I fell, but I'm not sure if she did it on purpose. She's far from the most coordinated girl in class, so it could have been an accident.

The color drains from Nina's face as her green eyes widen. "No, of course not."

Madame offers a hand to help me up. When I put my weight on my ankle it aches, but I don't think it's broken.

Thank God. I'm praying it's not sprained.

Nina's face has gone from paper white to deep pink. I study her hard, but I can't decipher if she's lying or if she's ticked off about being accused in front of everyone.

"Let's call it a day," Madame says as the bell rings. She turns to me. "Let me check out your ankle."

Everyone else heads for the door as I take a seat on the studio floor again. Madame presses her fingers lightly into my skin. It's uncomfortable, but not unbearable.

"I don't think you sprained it—there's no swelling. How's your pain?"

"It's a little sore." I keep my voice light even though I'm freaking out. What if she doesn't let me audition for the solo?

I become aware of her trying to read me, so I force a smile.

She doesn't return it. "I've been there, Aisha. I know how difficult it can be when there aren't many girls in your classes who look like you."

My stomach knots up again. I retract my ankle from her hand and start untying my other pointe shoe.

"It's not that bad. I mean, compared to my ballet school in Alberta," I say, pushing out a tight laugh.

I look up from my shoes to find her smiling at me sadly. "If you ever want to talk, let me know."

Usually, my instructors act like they don't notice when girls start in with their bullshit. It was cool of her to even acknowledge what happened.

Standing up, I grab my bag, fiddling with the strap for a moment. "Thanks, Madame. Do you mind if I ask you something?"

"Not at all, go ahead."

"Why did you decide to teach here?"

"You mean at a public school instead of private academy?" She gives me a knowing look, and I feel silly for asking after what she just said. It's not like it would be any easier being a person of color in ballet because she's a teacher instead of a student.

"Sorry to pry." I stare at the floor, and she places a light hand on my shoulder.

"Don't worry about it. No dancing for the rest of the day and then see how you feel in the morning, all right?"

"Okay." I keep avoiding her gaze. I know she's trying to be supportive, but I'm not feeling particularly resilient right now. "Thanks again, Madame."

Gingerly, I make my way over to Modern. Neil notices me not putting weight on my ankle right away. When I tell him and Ebi what happened, I'm relieved when Neil automatically drapes an arm around me, which he hasn't done all week.

He sighs. "Those girls are something else. I guess they must be scared about you nailing your solo audition."

"For real." Ebi shakes his head. "You almost got Tanya Hardinged."

"If she'd broken my ankle, I swear to God. She'd be the one getting a crowbar to the knee," I mutter.

I'd seen girls occasionally pull stuff like this at my old school, but I'd rarely been the target. There wasn't much of a point since I was never up for leads.

When Hannah starts class, she has us focus on the feeling of anger, which I'm able to summon immediately, thinking about Nina. My chest burns and my breath starts to quicken. Instead of pushing it down I let it run through me, heating up the blood in my veins.

I'm itching to dance after, but I sit out the rest of class and our fall showcase rehearsal like Madame suggested. As much as I hate not being able to release everything boiling inside me, it's pretty satisfying to see how well the class is doing with the choreography Neil and I have been working on. The showcase is coming up next week, and I'm glad it looks like it's coming together.

"Don't forget to ice it," Hannah says when we call it a day. "We need you all better tomorrow."

I nod at Hannah. "Will do. Thanks."

Neil sticks around after rehearsal to hang out with some of his buddies. When I say I'm taking off, he doesn't offer to come with me.

I'm not sure if he's still mad about what I said on Saturday. Neil doesn't usually hold onto stuff like that, but things haven't felt right since. Which isn't going to make it any easier to talk to him about getting help. I'm praying Ollie can help me figure out how to finally get through to him.

※

When I get to Ollie's, I knock on the front door for once.

A tall, dark-haired older man who I'm assuming is Ollie's dad answers. "Yes?"

"Hi, I'm looking for Ollie."

"*You're* looking for Olia?"

Apparently, Ollie's mom left him out of the loop about me. He seems overly surprised, and I try not to wonder what exactly about me has shocked him.

"Yeah . . . We go to school together."

"Oh, it's Aisha! Isaac, let the girl in," Anissa says from behind him.

He opens the door and I step inside. "Aisha? That's an Arabic name. A beautiful name for a beautiful girl," he says.

"Uh . . . That's nice of you to say, Mr. Cheriet."

"Aisha means—"

"Alive," I say, shoving a smile onto my face.

He grins. "Ah, smart girl."

"Are you hungry?" Anissa asks. "You look hungry. I'll get you a plate."

My shoulders instantly tighten, but I manage to keep my expression friendly. She leads me toward the kitchen and I follow, not want-ing to seem rude. I can sense she's trying to be welcoming and didn't mean to insult me.

She hands me a large plate and starts filling it with dolma and an array of stuffed vegetables. My stomach rumbles at the scent of roasted peppers and potatoes filled with rice and lamb.

"This looks amazing," I say as she continues to pile food onto my plate. I resist the urge to tell her to stop. "Thanks."

"Of course." She winks at me. "Make sure Ollie eats some too."

I nod as I start to head out of the kitchen, but she puts a hand on my shoulder. "You're limping."

"Oh." I shrug as Anissa makes a beeline for the fridge. "I just tripped and hurt my ankle a little."

"Put this on it." She places a bag of frozen peas in my hand.

"Okay, thanks again," I say before I head upstairs and knock on Ollie's door.

"Get lost, Soph," he yells out.

"It's me," I say.

He swings the door open, and I shoot him a grin. "Hey, *Olia*. I thought your full name was Oliver."

"Oh, great. You've been talking to my mom. Awesome. Sorry if she accosted you." He eyes the towering plate of food before glancing in confusion at the frozen peas.

"I fell in ballet. It's not serious or anything." I put the plate on the coffee table before I ease myself onto the couch, resting the peas on my elevated foot.

He studies me closely. "Are you sure? We can do this later—"

"Just rolled my ankle. I'm fine. We should finish up the script."

After we're done writing, we start practicing our presentation. I have my parts down pretty quickly, but Ollie keeps blanking on his lines.

He stops short and swears under his breath. "Can we start over?"

"Yeah, no prob."

We go from the top, but he trails off again and rubs a hand over his face.

"You're good. Keep going," I say. He looks over at me and I smile, hoping he'll do it back, but he doesn't.

He shakes his head and gets up from the couch. "Sorry."

I shrug and pop a piece of dolma in my mouth. "You've got it. Relax."

"I can barely get through a sentence," he mutters as he flips through his records for something new to put on.

"You're overthinking it. You memorize lyrics all the time, right?"

"That's different." He replaces the hum of a Blues album on the record player with some big band fifties rock. "Lyrics are like stories that aren't hard to remember. This stuff is just useless facts."

I stare down at the script as he collapses back on the couch beside me. "Isn't this sort of like a story too, though? There are all the boring dates and everything, but it's still about people who cared about the same stuff everyone cares about even if they lived centuries ago."

His mouth curves upward for a fleeting moment. "Okay, I guess I can see that."

"You wanna try again?"

He doesn't say anything, just closes his eyes. I study him as his chest slowly rises and falls under his shirt. His brow gradually unfurrows.

"Uh, you ready?" I ask after I let him have a moment.

When he opens his eyes, his face is relaxed. "Yep."

We get through the entire script this time without too many hiccups.

I grin over at him. "That wasn't so bad, was it?"

He lets out another slow breath. "It's different at school in front of everyone."

"Don't think about everyone. Just keep focused on anything that keeps you from getting distracted."

He nods and I think he's about to say something, but he stays quiet and that thing happens where we stare at each other a little too long. I look down at the melting peas on my sock. I can't put off this conversation anymore.

"About Neil," I say. "I think you're right."

"Right about what?"

"He needs to see someone. On Saturday, he came home drunk and basically said . . ." I trail off, the endless void of Neil's eyes after I freaked out on him filling my brain. "That it wasn't an accident."

Ollie sinks back against the couch. "Yeah."

"Is that what he told you when he was blacked out? That he wants to . . ." I can't finish.

"Not in so many words," he says.

I peel down my damp sock and check for swelling again. My ankle looks okay, and icing it helped with the soreness. "You, um, said you have a therapist, right? How did you get one?"

He doesn't reply, and I bite my lip. "Sorry if you don't want to—"

"It's fine. I asked my parents."

I'm sitting in the kitchen after dinner. I'm facing the backyard, but it's so dark out all I can see is my own wet face reflected back at me in the kitchen window. Dad's watching me across the table like I might explode into a thousand pieces at any moment. Mom is staring down at the already cleared table. Dad's mouth is moving, but I can't hear him over the sound of my own voice. "I'm not going!" I screech. "You can't make me—"

"Aisha?" Blinking back to the present, I find Ollie frowning at me.

I shake my head. "Neil's dad isn't really into that stuff."

"There's a counsellor at school. That might be a good start."

"Okay, but . . . What if he gets pissed at us for bringing it up again?"

He shrugs. "I don't see any other options at this point."

I inhale and nod after a moment. "You're right. Things are pretty hectic with rehearsals. Let's talk to him after the fall showcase."

Neil and I are both going full tilt right now, so I'm hoping it can wait until the pressure's off. Maybe once the showcase is over, dealing with this won't be quite so overwhelming.

I try to imagine Neil taking us seriously, but I can't. No matter how he reacts, I'm going to have to find a way to keep it together. I can't lose it on him again or he might shut me out for good.

13

I shut my eyes against the other girls zeroing in on the bag of ice on my ankle as they walk in the backstage door. Slapping my headphones on, I visualize every step of my routine as I stretch. My ankle was still kind of sore yesterday, so I didn't fully prep for this morning's solo auditions. Earlier I ran through the choreo, but not on pointe. As annoying as it was not being able to practice, I knew better than to potentially injure myself worse by dancing on my ankle before it was ready. Michaela wouldn't risk hurting herself like that. I move to the rosin box, the bittersweet smell stinging my nostrils as I give my pointe shoes an extra coat. There's no way I'm slipping onstage today.

You can do this in your sleep. I can almost hear Michaela's assured voice in my ear. I've watched this version of *Coppélia*, where she plays the title character, a mechanical doll, about a hundred times. It's burned into my brain.

"Aisha, are you ready?" Madame Anvyi's voice breaks through my daze.

I put my ice pack down and don't look at the other girls as I head out onstage.

"Break a leg," Nina mutters, and I resist the urge to shoot her a scalding look. What a horrid bitch. She for sure tripped me on purpose.

I miraculously manage to slow my breath when I get to center stage. When I get on pointe, my ankle is a little creaky, but I work through it without wobbling, keeping my face entirely empty. I pirouette around the stage in stiff staccato rhythm, my muscles as tightly wound as a mechanical toy. Perfectly replicating Michaela's routine, each endlessly practiced step falls into place.

When it's time for my final *jeté*, I think of my ankle and my pulse flutters wildly. I know what I need to do, as much as I hate it. I can't risk landing wrong. I slow down a bit as I leap into the jump, getting only a fraction of my usual height.

When the music stops, I stare at my feet. No one in my class claps. I can practically feel the smirks from the wings.

I can't even look at Madame as I walk offstage. After I put my headphones back on, I roughly untie my shoes before turning every bit of my attention to stretching.

"Thank you, girls," Madame calls out when the bell for first period rings. "The soloist and understudy will be announced in class this afternoon."

Tuning out in English class, I replay that pathetic jump in my head on a loop. I press my pencil to my notes so hard that I break the lead.

Finally, the bell for second period rings, and I head over to History. I find Ollie at his desk with his face buried in his script.

He glances at me briefly when I sit down before focusing on his notebook again. "How was your audition?"

"Not great—"

"Okay, everyone," Ms. Lin starts at the blackboard. "Do we have any volunteers or am I going to have to pick names?" When no one responds, she continues. "Pick names it is. Miss Bimi and Mr. Cheriet, you're up."

Ollie and I head to the front and set up our PowerPoint presentation. It goes smoothly until we're almost finished. For a second, I think I missed my line, but Ollie's stopped short, staring into the middle distance.

I whisper his name, and he focuses on me but still doesn't say anything.

Angling myself away from the class so Ms. Lin doesn't see, I mouth his next lines to him. He lets out a breath and continues for a moment before he starts to stutter.

Kevin and Scott start snickering.

"Boys," Ms. Lin warns.

Moving from the computer, I nudge Ollie's arm with mine. "Do you wanna take over the slides?" I ask under my breath.

He nods woodenly before we switch spots. I finish up the rest of his part and our closing statements.

Ms. Lin doesn't look amused as we take our seats. I glance at Ollie, but he stares unseeingly out the window. A few other people present and then the lunch bell rings.

"Sorry about that," he mutters as we head out the door.

"No worries, it's no big deal. I completely bombed my audition earlier if that's any consolation."

He shakes his head. His thumb brushes mine for half a second as we turn toward the stairwell, and I stop breathing for a long moment.

Did he do that on purpose? I'm vividly picturing his fingers wrapped tightly around mine, his warmth lighting up all my nerves, but his voice snaps me out of it.

"What happened?"

After a moment, I register his question. "I choked on my final jump because I was worried about my ankle."

"Is it still sore?"

I shake my head. "I didn't want to reinjure it."

"Your teacher probably gets that."

"Maybe she'll make me the understudy," I mutter as we head into the cafeteria.

Madame A. told us on the first day of school that this would be the only solo opportunity of the year. It's the only one I've been remotely close to getting in years. I know playing it safe was probably for the best, but part of me wishes I just went for it, gave it everything I had.

*

After lunch, when I get to ballet, I find everyone huddled around the solo casting list by the door. I step closer for a look and Tara pushes roughly past me, practically stomping in indignation like a six-year-old.

Prasheetha's right behind Tara and rolls her eyes at her antics before nodding at me.

"Congrats." Her tone is begrudging, but I don't think she's mocking me.

Okay? Guess I scored understudy. I know Caroline must have gotten the solo since she had the strongest ending jump during auditions.

I return her nod before continuing toward the list to see for myself.

Squinting, I think my eyes are playing tricks on me when I read my name above Caroline's.

Winter Showcase First Soloist — Aisha Bimi.

Hands clap down on my shoulders, and I look up to find Madame Anvyi beaming at me.

"Keep taking it easy on that ankle, and you'll be great," she says before heading to the front of the class.

Putting a hand to my mouth, I mask the manic grin that takes over my face. My entire body is buzzing, and I have to press my feet together to keep them on the ground. I can't believe she thinks I can do this.

You can *do this*, Michaela's voice echoes in the back of my head. *You're gonna kill it.*

I float through the rest of class before heading to Modern.

"I got it!" I scream at Neil and Ebi before they can ask.

Neil grins and gathers me in a tight hug. I don't push him away, thankful things are finally starting to feel normal again. I try not to think about how Ollie and I are going to confront him next week, but my mood starts to droop.

With our class performance coming up, we rehearse even longer than usual. Hannah takes off after a while, leaving me and Neil to finish leading rehearsals.

"Guys," I say to the group. We're taking a short break, but now that Hannah's gone it's turned into everyone lounging around talking. No one's paying attention to me except Neil and Ebi.

"*Hey,*" I try louder this time. "Let's run through it one last time and then call it a day, okay?"

People groan but start moving to take their places again.

After we finish, I chug the last of my water and plop down on the floor next to Neil.

"That was pretty good. But we're still not as tight as we could be," I say.

He wipes a towel over his face. "I know. As much as I hate Saturday rehearsals, I think we'll need them."

Hannah booked the auditorium for our class tomorrow, so I'm hoping we'll look better by next Wednesday. If we nail this, maybe Neil will be in a more receptive mood when Ollie and I talk to him afterward.

*

The next few days are a blur of non-stop modern and ballet rehearsals. I spend my spare periods on Tuesday morning running through my parts alone and end up working through the entire lunch period a couple of times. My muscles are constantly on fire, but whenever I feel like I can't take another second, I tell myself that it's a good thing that I'm present in my body. I'm lucky that I don't have to rehearse on pointe until a few weeks from now, closer to my solo. As busy as I am, I remind myself that this is everything I'd wanted when I switched to Huntley. There's less of a chance of my nerves getting the better of me in the moment if I get in as much practice as possible.

The next thing I know it's Wednesday, the night of the fall showcase. I peek out at the audience from the wings. The room is jam-packed, even more than it was for auditions—parents there alongside the students and teachers.

I try to breathe through the building pressure in my chest. I wish with everything in me that my dad was here right now. He called me earlier to wish me luck, but it's not the same as seeing his face in the crowd. *Even having Mom here would be* . . . I shake my head. She doesn't care about modern dance as much as ballet.

Turning away from the audience, I find Hannah behind me.

She shoots me a concerned look. "Nervous?" she asks.

I shrug vaguely, my mind mostly on the choreo.

Hannah tucks away a braid that's fallen out of my top knot, and I blink back into the present.

"I know it's uncomfortable and even painful sometimes to put all of yourself in the open," she says. "But when you let yourself go like that, I promise you'll find something that survives beyond tonight."

I nod, annoyed that I'm so transparent about how awkward this is for me. "Thanks, Hannah."

"*Merde.*" She grins before she makes her way to her seat.

I find Neil backstage doing some final stretches, and I join him.

"You ready?" he asks.

"Yeah. I just hope no one screws up the choreo," I mutter.

"I mean, Tara will for sure screw up," he says under his breath. "But hopefully not badly enough that anyone besides Hannah notices."

"Come on." I sigh as I adjust the shorts of my plain black costume so they don't ride up my butt. I wish I was back in my sweats. "Let's do this."

Neil and I take our places onstage along with the rest of our class.

I look out at the audience again. Khadija and the other theater kids are in the third row by the doors. Ollie is sitting next to them with his sister and a few of her friends. He catches me staring and smiles at me, the widest I've ever seen him smile, his dark eyes lighting up in the dim auditorium.

Wait. Did he just . . . *check me out?* His eyes don't linger long; I almost don't catch him. He's still smiling at me, but I forget how to operate my face. The music starts and I close my eyes, taking a steadying breath.

Neil and I turn to each other at the same time, and he swings me up into a fish dive lift. Around us, everyone else is moving, their bodies sharp and concise.

I stop thinking after that—I can only feel the weight of my movements. The emotions behind them tear through my body before shooting out of me in unrelenting waves. It's so intense I almost shout out, but I swallow it down, letting my being speak for me.

In rehearsals, I did my best to put myself in the mindset that I was playing a character, like in ballet. But now all of that is gone. All of this is me, and it's way too real.

Everything I don't have words for explodes from me with stunning force. Unchecked fear and frustration escape me in thundering waves. Our bodies turn, barrel-rolling in opposite directions like rapidly unspooling thread. We face each other again, dropping to our knees as the song tempers out.

The audience erupts in deafening noise. I'm so drenched I don't worry about anyone spotting my wet eyes this time.

I think I kind of know what Hannah meant about taking something away from this. I feel somehow lighter and heavier all at the same time. The pain I released refuses to dissipate, staying put right on top of my chest.

"Hey, you good?" It's Neil's voice. I become aware of him hugging me once we're in the wings. He pulls away and looks at me carefully when my arms stay limp at my sides.

I'm above my body all at once. The corners of my vision start to darken. *Please, not now.*

Then I can't see anything. I'd scream, but I don't have access to my vocal chords anymore.

"Ish? *Aisha.*" Suddenly, there's a firm pressure against my hand and I can see again. Neil's staring at me, along with almost everyone else backstage. I want to vomit.

"Do you wanna sit down?" Neil asks.

Looking down, I realize he has a grip on my shaking hand. I'm flashing back to our last rehearsal together before I moved away. When he squeezed my hand and looked at me this exact same way.

"I'm fine," I mutter, ripping myself from his grasp.

He's silent. I know he felt exactly what I did onstage. We were so in sync I could sense it.

"I'm gonna grab water." I'm halfway to the door before he can protest, blocking out all the curious eyes on me.

When I get out into the hallway, I spot Ollie by the backstage door.

"Hey." His brow knits up when he sees my expression. "What is it?"

Shaking my head, I walk away from him.

"Uh, where're you going?" he calls out right behind me.

I keep shaking my head. The invisible weight crushing my chest grows even heavier, rendering me unable to speak. Pushing through the back doors, I pick up my pace. The sun's almost set, the backfield cloaked in semi-darkness as I head toward the empty bleachers.

"Go back inside," I choke out, still not turning to face him.

"Why?"

My body collapses in on itself, my knees hitting the gravel under the bleachers before I'm gone again.

I'm in the kitchen after dinner. My hands are shaking so badly I hide them under the table while I glare at my parents. "Neil and I have YAGP in New York in two weeks."

Mom says nothing, her eyes glued to the delicately embroidered place mat in front of her.

Dad's voice is low and weighted with exhaustion. "Honey, you heard what the doctor said—"

"This isn't fair!" My voice echoes through the entire first floor. "I'm not going!"

I jump up from the table and run up to my room, slamming the door behind me. I flop on my bed and stare at my bulletin board full of ribbons and medals. Right in the middle is a picture of Neil and me with Madame D. at YAGP from the year before. My vision becomes a moist blur as fury overtakes me. Neil destroyed it all—everything we've worked for. I bury my face in my pillow until the burning in my lungs spreads to every inch of my body—

"Whoops, my bad." A loud laugh startles me, and I fold back inside myself. I still can't see anything, but I hear footsteps receding. "Dude, let's go smoke in the alley."

I blink, trying to get my bearings. My face is smushed against something warm and woodsy like cedar or pine . . .

When I realize I'm pressed up against Ollie's shoulder, I pull away. It's too dark to see, but I think I've snotted on his shirt like I did at the hospital.

"Sorry," I croak out as I rub my eyes.

His hoodie is draped over my bare shoulders now. I can't believe I ran outside in just my leotard.

Ollie says nothing, holding his water bottle out to me. I take it, remembering I told Neil I was going to grab water. He must be wondering where the hell I went. I didn't even take my phone with me.

"How long have we been out here?" I ask when I hand his bottle back.

"About a half hour?"

"*What?*" I didn't think it could have been more than ten minutes. "Really?"

He nods, biting at his lip for a moment before he speaks. "Your performance . . . I just wanted to tell you . . . It was really powerful."

"Thanks, Ollie," I murmur.

"It looked super intense for you and Neil."

"Yeah." I stare at the rocky ground between us. "I really did my best to connect with whatever's going on with him, but he can shut down everything he's feeling so fast. I can't instantly turn off like that."

"That sounds really overwhelming," he says quietly before pausing for a second. "Do you wanna tell me what happened just now? I mean, we don't have to talk about it if you don't want to . . ."

I look up at him again, and my breath hitches at his expression, worry etched across his face.

He didn't have to do this. He didn't have to stay out here with me, but I'm suddenly overcome by how glad I am that he did.

I blink hard and find myself nodding. The words tumble from my mouth before I can overthink them.

"This thing's been happening where I blank out so badly it's like I'm not even in my body anymore. But just now was way worse than usual. I couldn't see anything and then I was . . ." I clamp my mouth shut for a long moment. "I don't know. I'm just going crazy, I guess."

"Welcome to the club." He gives me the slightest trace of a smile, his voice dry.

I stare down at my raw, scraped up knees. "Sorry I freaked out."

Ollie shrugs. "I dissociate all the time."

He must mean when he spaced during his audition and our presentation. That night in Neil's basement he told me that difficult stuff comes up for him, too, when he performs. But freezing up for a few seconds is nothing compared to how bizarre I just acted.

"But you never zone out for as long as I did." I cringe, imagining him trying to get me to respond for all that time while I was catatonic.

"Well yeah, it's just part of my anxiety. But maybe you have an actual dissociation disorder?"

I bite my lip, still staring down at my knees. I don't want to think about what specific type of messed up I am.

"You're okay now?" he asks.

"Yeah." I slowly get to my feet, bracing myself against the cold metal frame of the bleachers. "Thanks."

"It's cool." He jumps up to steady me. We both take half a step toward each other in the tight space and suddenly we're hugging again.

Let go of him. My arms refuse to obey, staying wrapped around his neck. I expect a wave of humiliation to hit me any second. Instead, my brain slows to a standstill, my eyes closing.

"*There* you are." Neil's voice cuts through the silence, and I break away from Ollie. Even in the near darkness I can see the glint of his grin.

"Hey," I squeak out, climbing out from beneath the bleachers. "Sorry I took off—"

"Don't mention it. I grabbed your stuff—you guys ready to go?"

"I'm just gonna change first." I take my bag from Neil and pull out my phone as we head toward the back doors. My breath shortens when I see a voicemail from my mom. Without a second look, I shove it back into my bag.

All Hannah's advice about uncovering our true emotions sounded nice . . . up until my mental breakdown. Whatever dark places she wants us to keep exploring, I'll have to do it from a distance. At least while I figure out how to get a handle on whatever's happening to me, away from prying eyes.

It was different talking with Ollie, though. It's hard to believe that I let him see me like that and nothing bad happened. I actually feel a little better. As much as I detest talking about this stuff, I think talking to someone might be the only way to stop whatever the hell that was from being on full public display ever again.

14

The next day, I get to school halfway through lunch. For once I slept in since I hardly got any sleep last night. I dreamt about my performance, falling onstage in a horrible drop. The crack in my big toe felt way too real, viscerally similar to my tendonitis when I first started on pointe. The screaming pain shot me awake, my heart nearly going nuclear in my chest. For once I stayed in bed late, since I hardly got any sleep last night.

"Hey," Ollie says when I walk up to him in our lunch hallway. He smiles the same utterly overwhelming way he did when I was onstage yesterday.

I let out a weird, wheezing laugh instead of responding, and he grins even wider. Christ, I really can't function when he looks at me like that.

Neil fake coughs and then bursts out laughing. Ebi and Khadija join him.

Damn it, why does he have to make this so awkward?

Giving Neil a deathly look, I sit down between him and Ollie. I change the subject immediately, pretending not to notice Ollie's whole arm is flush against mine. "What are you guys up to?"

Khadija tells me about some guy from her drama class that she asked out last week. He's taking her to see a Tarantino marathon tomorrow at The Forum, an old theater that plays classics downtown.

"If he wasn't so cute, I think I'd bail," Khadija says. "*Tarantino?* So basic, it's embarrassing. That pasty old man was really in *Pulp Fiction* saying the hard 'R' with his whole chest."

I scrunch up my nose. "Gross."

Khadija goes on about other reasons she thinks Tarantino should be cancelled, and I tune her out, wondering if she mentioned asking that guy out to nudge me about the Ollie thing.

What would I even say? I feel like such a goddamn idiot. Why is this so difficult? He likes me, and I know he knows I like him. But he's still so quiet sometimes. He hasn't even looked over at me since I sat down.

Shifting a little closer to him, I lean over his shoulder to see what he's writing in his open notebook. He snaps it closed and focuses on me. "What're you doing?"

"What're you working on?"

"I have to finish this song for next week."

"Can I see?" I reach toward the pen he's used to bookmark his page.

His hand flies out to grab mine when I touch the notebook, keeping it firmly closed. "No."

Our eyes meet for a beat too long. My stomach lurches downward before catapulting into my mouth. Finally, he lets go of my hand.

I look at him sideways. "Why not?"

He scrubs a hand through his hair. "It's not done."

"So? You don't wanna show me what you have so far?"

He shrugs and opens his notebook again, flipping to a blank page. He jots something down in tiny letters, and I lean in to read it.

When do you think we should talk to Neil?

I let out a sigh. We'd agreed to talk to him after the showcase, but we hadn't decided on an exact time. When we took the bus back after I freaked out last night, Ollie stuck around for a couple of hours. We got pizza and just lazed in front of the TV before he headed home. I know he got that I wasn't up to confront Neil last night, but I guess he still wants to do it soon.

I take his pen, leaning in even closer to write something next to his words. I'm amazed my hand doesn't shake. He's so close I can smell the Sprite he just downed on his breath.

I'll talk to him.

He turns to me, his nose nearly brushing the side of my face. "Are you sure?"

"Yeah." I don't lean away now that I'm finished writing. I force myself to stay put, not moving a muscle as I stare back at him. "I have to talk to him about yesterday anyway—"

"What are you two whispering about?" Neil's stopped talking to Ebi and is raising an eyebrow at us.

I turn to Neil and force out a thin laugh. "Just me losing my shit last night."

Neil's expression turns grim. "Oh."

"So I, uh . . ." I stare down at my feet as I start to get up. "I guess it's pretty clear that I need professional help. I'm gonna go make an appointment to see the counsellor."

"Do you want me to walk over with you?" Ollie offers as I grab my bag.

I shake my head quickly. "Thanks, but . . . Neil, can you come with me? I have to talk to you."

"Yeah . . ." Neil says slowly as he gets up.

I shoot Ollie a reassuring look over my shoulder. I hope it's convincing.

He nods at me before he opens his notebook again.

Neil catches me looking back at Ollie and chuckles. "Why do you want me to come with you? Aren't you and Ollie a thing now?"

"What do you mean?"

"You're dating now, right?"

Heat slowly rises up my chest toward my face. "Uh, no."

Neil shakes his head. "God, you guys are hopeless. What about last night?"

"What about it?"

"I found you because some stoners told me you two were making out under the bleachers."

I just about choked on my own spit. "I would have told you if we kissed."

His shoulders shake with barely contained laughter as we enter the office.

"Glad I'll get the play-by-play. What were you doing for so long then?" he asks in a quieter voice as we take a seat in the reception area.

We sit in silence for an excruciating minute as I fall right back into how awful yesterday was. I shake myself out of it and inhale as deeply as I can before I speak.

"I was spacing out. Like, um, after our performance, but it got way worse." I avoid his gaze. I know he's noticed me spacing out before last night. "Ollie said it's probably this thing called dissociation. He thinks I have it."

Have it. Like it's a thing that belongs to me now that I can't throw away.

He nods and stares down at his sneakers. "That really sucks. I'm glad you feel okay to talk to someone about it."

"Thanks." I squeeze his wrist, and he looks up at me. "Do you wanna make a deal?"

"About what?" he asks.

"I'll make an appointment if you make one too."

He pulls his arm away. "Why would I make one?"

I close my eyes and contain a sigh. "Just one appointment, okay? If it sucks, then we'll forget about it."

My stomach feels full of lead. Those stupid doctors I had to see at the clinic my dad sent me to were terrible. I hated every humiliating question they asked. But I have to believe this might be different.

"Yes?" We look over at the receptionist, who's focused on us now.

I get to my feet and glance back at Neil. He lets out a sigh and follows me up to the front desk. After we sign a sheet, she gives us both cards with our appointment times on them. One of the counsellors is on leave, so they're backlogged. Our sessions are a few weeks away.

"At least it's during class," Neil says as we head out of the office, sticking the card in his pocket. I took note of his time as well so I can check in with him if he actually ends up going.

"Anyway, I know I said I wouldn't get involved with your stuff with Ollie, but . . ."

I give him a quizzical look. "But what?"

"It's his birthday tomorrow. Why don't you get him something to, like, you know . . ." He wriggles his eyebrows. "Shoot your shot."

"*Tomorrow?* Why are you just telling me now?" It's weird Ollie didn't mention it either. "What should I get him?"

He shrugs. "No idea."

"Helpful," I say as the bell rings.

✳

Ballet goes by uneventfully. I stay ultra-focused on giving corrections, pushing out the inkling of hurt when literally everyone in class gives me the cold shoulder. I feel Madame A's eyes on me and smile when she gives me an encouraging nod before I get back to the task at hand.

Afterward in Modern, I sit on the floor next to Neil with my eyes closed as Hannah goes through today's meditation.

"We've explored all the facets of anger quite a bit these last few weeks with your group performance. I really appreciate you all pouring everything you had into that last night. But now we're moving on to explore some even more difficult emotions."

Awesome. I gnaw at the inside of my cheek.

"I want you to think of a time when you felt like you'd done something wrong. Something that you regret saying or doing, that you'd give anything to take back. Or think of something that someone did that made you feel small. Like your opinions or what you wanted didn't matter. For as long as you feel comfortable, sit in the discomfort of that moment. Stay with it without judging whatever comes up for you."

Neil and I are twelve. We're in Madame D.'s studio scooting across the slippery floor in our socks. Madame yells at us to stop messing around, but

her voice doesn't have any real heat behind it. Practice is over—we're wait-
ing for our parents to pick us up. We slide to the floor, giggling like little
idiots.

"Aisha." My mom's sharp voice makes me shoot to my feet. I quickly get
into my sneakers and pick up my bag.

I grin at Neil. "Later, loser."

He sticks his tongue out at me, and I laugh as I reach Madame D. near
the door beside my mom.

"Bye, Madame," I call out.

"See you tomorrow, my dear." She pats my butt with her cane and looks
at my mom. "No second helpings at dinner, all right?"

I deflate, ducking my head from my mom's disapproving gaze. She nods
at Madame before she takes a firm hold of my shoulder and crouches down
to my level—

Stop. I open my eyes even though the meditation isn't over yet. I'm
not doing this right now. I close my eyes again and try to focus on
literally anything else.

I'm remembering the feeling of Ollie's hand closing around mine
when I tried to open his notebook. His sugary sweet breath brushing
over my face when he turned to me—

Neil pokes my arm and my eyes snap open. Hannah's finished the
meditation and improv is starting. When it's my turn to go, I contort
my face into appropriately somber expressions as I move. I mimic my
emotions instead of letting myself really feel anything that deep.

After class, Hannah asks me and Neil to stay behind as everyone
else files out.

I worry my lip between my teeth as we approach her at the front.
She shoots us a wide grin and I exhale.

"You two were wonderful last night. Neil, your emotionality was stellar, and Aisha, your technique was a great balance to that. I want to invite you two to choreograph a pairs piece on your own for the winter showcase."

Neil squeezes my arm and grins. He's not muting his excitement about this, and I'm glad he's allowing himself to be more invested. I hope it makes him think more about the possibility of college.

Things in Modern have been feeling more and more like when we were kids, lately, our synchronization becoming something that doesn't really feel like work. This seems like a natural progression for Neil, but I still feel a little unsteady and new to this. I'm not totally sure I'm as ready for this as Neil is.

"Thanks, Hannah," I manage.

She considers me for a long moment. "Aisha, can we talk for a few minutes?"

"Uh, sure." I shoot Neil a wide-eyed look as he heads toward the door.

He nods at me. "I'll wait for you by the front doors."

"Are you feeling okay?" Hannah asks once Neil is gone. "You seemed upset last night."

She must have caught on when I zoned out backstage and ran off.

I press my lips together and shrug. "I'm fine."

"Are you sure?" She's using this soft voice, like I'm a hapless child. "Is everything okay at home? I noticed your parents didn't attend."

I cringe internally but manage not to make a face. "Everything's fine. I've just been a little stressed lately."

"If you're not sure about the showcase that's totally—"

"No," I say a little too loudly. I make myself lower my voice. "I'll be fine doing the showcase."

She considers me carefully. "All right, if you're sure. If you need to take a break to take care of yourself, let me know anytime. And you can always see the school counsellor—"

"I made an appointment," I mutter.

"That's great." She's visibly relieved. "Just let me know if you change your mind."

"I will," I assure her before I head for the door.

Rubbing my eyes, I try to block out the last few minutes. That was so goddamn embarrassing. I try to focus on the fact that Neil and I get to choreograph our own piece and perform as a pair again. I can't believe I'm going to have two performances at the winter showcase now.

You deserve this. Michaela sounds convinced as always, but I'm not quite so sure.

What if Hannah's right and I can't handle this? I'll just have to pray that counselling actually helps this time so I can stop freaking out after I perform. As much as I tried to put on a brave face for Neil, the thought of talking to someone is still kind of petrifying considering how bad the clinic was.

My phone beeps with a notification that my last voicemail is about to expire. Bracing myself at my open locker, I put my phone to my ear and listen to my mom's message.

"Hi, Aisha." My name sounds foreign coming from her mouth. "I know you're back in town. Hope you're doing well. If you wanted to meet up for coffee to catch up—"

I feel like my windpipe is swelling closed, and I fumble with my phone, quickly pressing the delete button.

Shit. I should have listened to the rest of the message. Now I don't know why she wants to meet up. She didn't sound angry or annoyed.

Maybe she really just wants to catch up? It's possible she won't be so disappointed that I quit ballet school since I'm getting lots of leads here.

You're not supposed to meet up with her. I slam my locker shut. Dad would be pissed if he knew I entertained the thought for a second. My head starts to pound as I head for the front doors. I haven't even told him she contacted me, like I promised him I would.

"Everything go okay?" Neil asks when I find him on the front steps.

I force a smile. "All good."

15

"Happy birthday," I say to Ollie as he takes the seat beside me in History the next morning.

"Thanks for the playlist." Sunlight streaks through the windows of the muggy room and he squints against it, avoiding my gaze.

I lift and drop my shoulders. "No prob."

Did he hate it? I spent hours agonizing over what songs to include and the right order, making sure it all flowed naturally the way his playlists always do. Worried my tastes were too pedestrian, I'd psyched myself out of sending it. But then he texted me after he finished work, just before midnight, to ask how it went with Neil at the office earlier. After I filled him in, I sent the playlist along, my heart racing the moment I hit *send*.

He hearted it but didn't say anything after that. Around one in the morning, I stopped checking my phone and went to bed. Maybe he hadn't had a chance to listen yet.

The sun's still in his face as he looks over at me, transforming his dark eyes into a liquid amber. "It was perfect."

A warm glow starts in my core and travels all the way to my fingertips.

"Oh. Good." After a second, I'm able to form full sentences again. "What are you doing to celebrate? Got plans with your family?"

"Nope. Not really a big birthday person."

"Me neither." I concentrate on flipping open my notebook. "Do you have work later?"

From the edge of my vision, I see him shake his head.

"So, you're free to chill at Neil's after school?" My heart gallops as wildly as a spooked horse. I want to wipe my sweaty hands on my pants, but I don't want to be gross.

"Definitely." I'm still not looking at him, but I can hear the smile in his voice.

*

In Ballet and Modern, I can't stop thinking about Ollie coming over later. Neil said I should shoot my shot or whatever, but I don't really know what that entails. Wasn't the playlist enough? Some of the songs I included were so transparent there's no way in hell he didn't get the hint.

But after school, it's pretty anticlimactic. Neil and Ollie smoke for a bit in the backyard and then we just sit around in front of the TV like usual.

The doorbell rings around six.

"Who's that?" Ollie asks, but Neil's already headed for the door.

Ollie looks over at me, and I shrug helplessly. Neil didn't mention he was having anyone over. We hear a commotion, and he returns with Ebi, Khadija, and about ten other theater kids in tow.

"Surprise!" Neil says.

Ollie stares dully.

"Did you really think we were gonna do nothing for your birthday?" Neil asks as everyone starts making themselves comfortable around the room.

Ebi grins as he plops down on the carpet and grabs the TV remote from my hand.

Khadija pulls a couple of beers out of her bag. "BYOB, right? These are warm. Can I put them in your fridge?"

I jump up and grab them from her before Neil can offer. "Yeah, I got it."

In the kitchen, I swear under my breath as I stick the beer in the fridge.

"Are you good with pizza again?" Neil asks as he enters the kitchen, focused on his phone.

I grab it away from him, slapping it on the kitchen island.

He blinks at me. "What're you doing?"

I fix him with a hard look. "Why didn't you say you were gonna have people over? Ollie seems less than psyched about this."

I want to say more, that this isn't a good idea for him, but I know he'll say I'm overreacting and shut down.

He grins. "I can get everyone to leave right now if you want him all to yourself."

"Shut the hell up," I whisper as I peek into the living room.

"Chill. Don't be a party pooper. Loosen up a bit tonight, okay? Trust me. You'll like it." He winks before he grabs his phone and heads back to the living room. "Who wants to go in on a couple pizzas?"

I groan and head back out after him. Okay, I can handle this. Ollie and I can keep an eye on him and everything should be fine.

But Ollie's disappeared from his seat on the end of the couch.

"Where'd he go?" I ask Ebi.

"A little busy here," he mutters, biting his lip as he focuses on his phone.

Khadija looks up from peering over Ebi's shoulder at his screen and juts her head toward the back door. "I think he went for a smoke."

I find Ollie sitting on the back patio with his earphones in. He takes them out in a rush when he sees me.

"Sorry about this." I perch on the patio chair across from him. "I would have given you a heads up if I knew."

He smiles, but it doesn't quite reach his eyes. "I know. It's okay."

"If you wanna take off, I can keep an eye on Neil—"

"I can stick around."

"You're sure?"

"Yeah, I can stay." He gets up, taking hold of my hand and slipping his fingers through mine. "Come on."

As he pulls me up, every molecule of the cool evening air is sucked out of the yard at once. He doesn't let go until we reach the patio door. Before he pulls away completely, his thumb gently traces the edge of my palm. I gawk at him as he pushes the door open and steps inside like he did nothing.

This is happening. I try to remember how to think as we reenter the living room.

"Just in time," Ebi says. "We're doing trivia."

"Fosse again?" I say as I take a seat next to Khadija on the crowded couch. She scooches over to make room for Ollie and me on the end.

"I told you theater parties get real wild," Neil says with a snort.

Ebi elbows Neil on the carpet beside him and laughs. "You're just salty because you lost last time."

"I don't recall," Neil says, the corners of his mouth quirking upward.

"Of course you don't, you drunk," Khadija's friend Beth says. My eyes shoot over to her before going to Neil. He just laughs.

"Okay, here we go," Ebi says, focusing on his phone as he starts with the questions. He's branched out from Fosse to more general musical trivia. I do love quite a few musicals, but I'm out of my depth in current company. Pretty soon, I'm scraping the bottom of the barrel of my Broadway knowledge. Ollie and I have paired up and, to be honest, I've been carrying us so far. Then we get to the rock-opera category, and he starts pulling out some answers that get us back in the game again.

Beth snorts after Ollie names some obscure lyric from *The Wall* and we pull ahead. "*Please* don't tell me Pink Floyd is your favorite band."

When Ollie says nothing, I glance over at him and realize his arm is stretched across the couch behind me, super close to my shoulders. I'm not sure if he noticed Beth was talking to him or not—his face is neutral. We're practically squashed together, but I press my leg even closer to his and give him an expectant look.

When he still doesn't respond, I turn back to Beth and fill the silence. "Has anyone in Pink Floyd done something unsavory?"

"Not that I know of. It's just the most music-snob crap, ever," she says, looking over at Ollie again. "I've seen you rock that *Dark Side of the Moon* shirt."

He finally laughs quietly. "You're gonna rag on me about my Zeppelin one next, aren't you?"

"He isn't a music snob." I can't help sounding a little teed off. "Do you hear *him* trying to gatekeep what people like to listen to?" I raise my eyebrows pointedly.

"Everyone ignore Beth," Ebi drones as he flips through more questions. "She's projecting about her douche of an ex."

"He was in a . . ." Khadija pauses and squints at Beth. "What did he call it? A *post-screamo* band?"

"I've blocked it out," Beth says, shuddering.

Everyone laughs and Ebi shouts over us. "Enough stalling. Back to the final round. We're doing lyrics to an entire number, and everyone has to *actually* sing." He looks right at me as he says the last part. I'm notorious for my lip syncing at lunch because my voice is crap.

Khadija and Beth nail "Out Tonight" from *Rent* and then it's Ollie's and my turn.

"Okay, we've got a duet for you—'Come What May' from *Moulin Rouge*," Ebi reads out. "Y'all ready?"

Ollie nods and looks at me. "You know it?"

"I think so?" I've seen *Moulin Rouge* a ton, but I haven't listened to the soundtrack on its own or anything.

Ollie starts singing, and I join him a half-second later. He's got it down, so I let his voice drown out mine for the most part. He doesn't hesitate at all. I can't deny it's a beautiful song, but it's so ridiculously over-the-top romantic that Ebi must have chosen it on purpose to be annoying. I try not to look at Ollie directly as we sing since it's already strange enough being practically in his lap. Then he raises his voice to a register I didn't know he had for the final chorus. His tone is so lovely I can't help but just stare at him.

Ollie's eyes are closed, but he opens them to find me staring. Everything tightly wound inside me starts to unravel, like he's pulled on a loose sweater string. My stomach becomes a tangled mess.

He stops short and scratches the back of his head. "You're not singing."

It takes me a moment to form words. "Oh. I forgot."

Everyone cracks up except Ollie, who searches my eyes so deeply I get the uncanny feeling he can see into my brain. I suddenly become aware that his arm is draped over my shoulders, his skin warming the back of my neck.

Laughter sounds from the kitchen. I look away from Ollie and realize Neil's disappeared.

Jumping up, I head into the kitchen to find Neil with about ten other kids from school, talking to Rashanth, Dylan, and Scott. I'm not particularly compelled to interrupt them since Scott seems to be such good friends with that dumbass Kevin. I don't spot Kevin anywhere, though, thank God. I groan when I notice a kid pulling out a brown bag and red plastic cups. Just what we need, more alcohol in the house.

I can't just hover in the doorway forever worrying if Neil's going to drink, so I head back to the living room. We do more trivia for a while until the crashers in the kitchen start to increase in volume. When I peek in a couple more times, Neil isn't holding a drink, thankfully. The theater group starts to dissipate until it's only Ollie, Khadija, and me left in the living room.

When she says she has to get home, we go to the kitchen to grab her beers. I look through the fridge, but I can't find them.

"Anyone see a couple Heinekens?" I call out over the noise. I frown when I look around but don't spot Neil in the kitchen anymore. He walks back in a second later, holding a deck of playing cards. I let out my breath.

"Oh, sorry." A short guy with sleepy eyes turns to us. "Thought those were for everyone. There's some Bud Lite left."

I tear my gaze away from Neil to find Khadija rolling her eyes. "I'll pass. See ya at school, guys. Happy birthday, Ollie."

*

After a bit, the handful of kids left migrate down to the basement. It's getting late, so I'm praying people will start heading out soon. Neil still seems okay. I haven't spotted him with a drink yet—he's been focused on showing his handsy friend Gwen his card shuffling tricks as they play a game of Kings. Ollie and I are sitting away from everyone, DJing in the corner by the stairs.

"I'm sick of your wallflower bullshit," Neil's slurred voice calls out.

My head snaps up from Ollie's phone to find Neil standing right in front of us.

Shit. I was supposed to be keeping an eye on him, but I got distracted by Ollie's closeness, his arm finding its way around my shoulders again as we pored over his party playlist.

"Come on, we're starting a new game." Neil heads back over to everyone in the middle of the room, expecting us to follow.

Ollie and I exchange a grim look.

"What the hell happened?" I whisper. "I didn't see him drinking at all, did you?"

He shakes his head. "I saw him head to the bathroom a little while ago. Maybe he slammed some beers then?"

"Damn it." I let out a heavy exhale as I pull away from him and get to my feet. "How about we just get through one game and then we tell him it's time to call it a night, okay?"

Ollie drags himself up. "All right, fine."

They've switched from cards to truth or dare when Ollie and I join the circle.

"Truth," Gwen says, giggling.

"Who's your crush?" Dylan asks her.

Gwen giggles harder. "Oh my God, Dylan! You know."

He shrugs. "Just say it then."

"Neil, obviously. He's, like, the hottest Asian."

I wince, rubbing my throbbing temples.

There's an awkward pause before Neil laughs and says, "Taking that as a compliment, Gwen. You're not too bad yourself."

Gwen's face flushes. "Okay, Rashanth, it's your turn. Truth or dare?"

I check out for a little bit before I realize that the song Ollie's just put on is from my playlist. Glancing over at him, I find he's bailed from the circle to play DJ again. He smiles at me, that slow one that I can't deal with. Even though no one else knows about the playlist, it feels more intimate than it should.

"Okay, Roi, you're up," one of the guys says. "What'll it be?"

"Dare," Neil says instantly.

"I dare you to kiss Gwen."

Neil shrugs. "Okay."

He scooches closer to Gwen and beckons her to sit in his lap. She turns red again but climbs onto him. And then he kisses her, like for real, not a stupid little game kiss. I get skeeved out and have to look away as his buddies start howling.

I can't believe he's doing this. How drunk could he possibly be already? I wrack my brain, trying to find some non-confrontational way to end this ordeal but come up blank.

"Yo, Aisha," Scott says.

"What?" I glance over at him and find that Neil and Gwen have mostly detached themselves from each other, but she's still in his lap.

"Truth or dare?"

"Truth, I guess." As much as I want to bail right now, I can't just leave Neil here like this. If I play along for one round, I'm praying Neil will be less inclined to argue when I tell him it's time to call it in a few minutes.

"What's your body count?" Scott asks, and then he starts to laugh along with some of the other guys.

I stare blankly at him.

"He means what's your number," Gwen explains. "Like how many people have you had sex with?"

My face boils over. "Oh. Zero."

Scott snorts. "You're staying here with Neil, right? Like you guys have never hooked up."

I grimace. "It's not like that." *Asshole.*

Neil's voice comes out lazy and staggered. "She hasn't even kissed anyone yet."

I stare daggers at him. I can't believe he just told everyone that. He must be even more wasted than I thought.

Scott laughs. "Sure. Kevin told us that you gave him his black belt," he says, snickering along with Rashanth and Dylan.

Nausea and humiliation slosh together in my stomach.

"Kevin *wishes*," Neil mutters darkly. "What a goddamn liar."

"Hmm, I don't know. He was pretty descriptive," Scott says.

I sneer at Scott, trying to think of a good comeback, but I'm too pissed off to think straight.

"Kevin's full of it and you know it, Scott," Ollie says. "I know why you're really saying this."

"Ollie," I say, finally managing to look at him. "Stop."

He does and stares at me while everyone else stares at us.

Scott snickers again. "Wow, Cheriet. You really do like Black girls, don't you?"

I shut my eyes like if I do it hard enough I can make this stop happening. My stomach turns even more, all the pizza I just downed attempting to make a break for it. I've been so stressed tonight that I didn't even keep track of how many slices I ate. I need to get out of here, but I've already lost feeling in my feet.

"Your question doesn't make sense," I hear Ollie say tonelessly.

"Sounds pretty simple to me," Dylan chimes in.

Ollie speaks slowly, like he's talking to five-year-olds. "How can I say I like an entire group of people based on the fucking color of their skin?"

Scott snorts. "Jesus. Relax."

"Ask a question that makes sense then. Did you mean do I like girls, generally? Then yes, I like girls."

"Definitely wasn't sure about that, Cheriet," Scott says, and Dylan and Rashanth start snickering again.

I finally open my eyes and catch Ollie's dark glare go utterly blank for a long moment before he turns to Neil.

"Awesome party, man."

"Uh-huh," Neil says distractedly, his voice muffled. I glance at him and realize he and Gwen have migrated to a dim corner of the basement and their shirts are off. Gwen's not paying attention to what's being said—her hands are all over him.

"You blacked out yet?" Ollie asks Neil.

I shoot Ollie a sharp look, but he doesn't glance at me.

"Getting there," Neil mumbles out.

"Fantastic," Ollie says bitterly. "You selfish dick."

I force myself up and grab Ollie's hand, dragging him to the opposite corner of the room by the stairs.

I let go of him, overly aware of everyone staring. "If we're going to get him to listen about calling it a night, you've gotta cool it a bit, okay?"

Ollie blinks before shaking his head. "Do you seriously still think he's going to listen to us at this point?"

"Cheriet wants his birthday cake!" Dylan shouts before making obscene clapping sounds, and the rest of the boys lose it.

Ollie turns to them. "You guys can get out now."

"Dude, this isn't even your house," Scott says.

"Okay, party's over," Neil mumbles, and I heave a sigh of relief. "You guys gotta go. Except for you, Gwen. You don't move. Ish and Ollie, you can stay, but take it upstairs."

All of Neil's buddies groan in annoyance.

I race up the stairs as quickly as possible, not stopping when I hear Ollie's voice behind me.

He catches up to me on the back patio. "You okay?"

"I'm fine." I sink into a lawn chair. "But what's up with you? I mean, I get that this was not an ideal birthday. But you know it's pointless getting in arguments with people that dumb." I've never seen him that outspoken around so many people.

"I know," he mutters as he sits in the chair across from mine. "Scott's such a piece of shit, though."

"Look . . ." I struggle to find words for a moment. "It's hard to call people out on their bull every single time, okay? But you get that I don't need you or Neil to do it for me, right?"

I absolutely hate having to talk about this with him. I wish the last ten minutes never happened.

He nods. "I get that it's tiring for you. I'm sorry, but you don't always have to do it by yourself."

I'm silent. I don't want to think about this anymore.

We can still hear my playlist blasting out from the open basement window. "Say It" by Maggie Rogers comes on next. It's the one song I almost didn't include, worried he'd read way too much into it; worried it might give away all the things I can't fathom confessing, even to myself.

"This one's my favorite," he says suddenly.

I stare at the dead grass in front of me. "Hmm?"

"This is my favorite song on your playlist." His eyes burn into me.

"Oh," I say dumbly.

"Wanna dance?" He stands and holds his hands out.

I stare at them, but I can't move.

"Come on." He pulls me up, and I don't push him away. His touch is the only thing I can focus on.

His hands slide from my elbows to my waist, and I can't even describe what this does to my insides.

He searches my face intently. "This okay?"

I nod, trying not to be aware of how clean he smells. My arms wrap themselves around his shoulders as I breathe him in. My body relaxes against him of its own volition, and my thoughts stop pounding against my skull.

There's the distant thud of the front door slamming. My eyes snap open, and I pull away from Ollie, heading back inside.

We find Neil alone in the kitchen.

"I told Gwen to leave too. She's an idiot," Neil says, his filter completely gone as he grabs another beer.

"Why don't you cool it?" I mutter, grabbing the bottle.

"It's getting late," Ollie adds. His bitterness from before has dissolved into exhaustion.

"Okay, Mom and Dad." He teeters out of the kitchen into the bathroom.

He's in there for so long that we start to get worried. I knock on the door, but he doesn't answer.

"Goddamnit," I mutter at Ollie.

"Open the door, man," Ollie calls out before rubbing a hand over his face.

We wait, but there's nothing but silence. I'm trying to stay calm for Ollie's sake, but I can't handle this, not again. I squeeze my eyes shut and try to quell the nausea rising in me.

"Okay, we're coming in." I try the doorknob, my hand shaking.

We find him sprawled on the tiled floor, and my knees give as I rush toward him.

"*Neil?*" My voice is shrill as I shake him. "Neil, wake up."

He winces and pushes me away, and I let out a breath, nearly overcome with relief that he's responsive.

I do my best to keep my voice firm. "We're just gonna get you to your room. Stand up. Come on."

"Nah, I'm good," he says, dozing off a bit.

"Nope. Up." I look over at Ollie and realize he's frozen in the doorway. As terrified as I was a second ago, I can't imagine how he feels being in this position again.

"It's okay, I've got him." I try to drag Neil to his feet, but he's dead weight.

Ollie forces himself from the door and grabs Neil's other arm.

We manage to walk Neil down the hall to his room. Letting him drop onto his bed, I roll him over so he's on his side.

I push his trash can next to his bed. "If you have to puke, the can's here."

"Rad," he mutters before closing his eyes again.

Ollie mumbles something I don't catch, still looking shaken as he bolts from the room.

Focusing on Neil again, I crouch by his bedside and stick my hand in his hair, rubbing at his scalp like I used to do when we would take naps together when we were really small.

Letting out a trembling exhale, I close my eyes. "God, you're a mess."

"When my dad picked me up from the hospital, you know what he said?"

My eyes open again to find him staring up at the ceiling. "What?"

"That I'm weak." He lets out a dark chuckle. "Just like her."

He never talks about her, but I know he must mean his mom. Is he saying that she . . . ? I shake my head, blinking back stinging tears.

"I can't believe he would say something like that." His dad's an asshole most of the time, but that's the cruelest thing I've ever heard.

His face contorts for a moment before it goes completely blank again. "He's right."

"Neil." I breathe out, resting my head next to his. "No. You just need help. I'm glad you made a counselling appointment because I can't . . ." My voice cracks. "I really can't do this with you anymore."

"Fine." He turns away from me, facing the wall. "You don't have to, then."

"Fine," I spit back.

My eyes threaten to well over as I stand, balling up my shaking hands. Spinning on my heel, I head out of his room.

I find Ollie in the living room, perched on the couch with his head in his hands.

"Oll, you okay?" I sit down next to him. "I know this must have sucked after . . . after last time."

"Yeah." He takes a few deep breaths.

Before I can think about it, I reach for his hands. Ollie immediately wraps his fingers around mine and leans forward until our foreheads are pressed together. Neither of us moves for the longest time.

"Aisha?" he murmurs as he pulls back a little.

"Yeah?"

"I've, um—I've never kissed anyone either," he mumbles, staring at his feet.

"Oh." My breath stops completely for a moment before picking up at twice its normal speed. My pulse becomes a loud hum, filling my ears. "Did you . . . Do you want . . . ?"

"Yeah," he says, but he doesn't move a muscle.

"Like right now, or—"

Ollie leans in and the moment his mouth brushes mine something in the base of my stomach jolts wide awake. My brain starts to overheat and everything goes out of focus. It's just like when he sang earlier but so much more overwhelming. Wrapping my arms around his neck, I pull him even closer.

Without warning, he jerks away from me.

My eyes fly open, and I search his face, but he avoids my gaze like the plague.

"What's wrong?" I manage to get out, still breathless.

He shakes his head. "I, uh . . . I gotta go."

"Wait, *what?*" My voice is a strangled squeak.

Before I can process, he's off the couch, pulling the back door open.

"Later." He's gone before I can say anything else.

I sit there frozen for a moment before folding my legs up toward my chest. Curling into a ball, I squeeze my eyes shut as sobs shudder out of me.

16

Incessant ringing drags me slowly out of a dead sleep. My eyes open in slits, the morning sun a laser that pierces the front of my skull.

Reaching around, I find my phone stuck between the couch cushions.

"Hey, Dad," I groan out as I pull my aching body into a sitting position. I rub at my sore, puffy eyes. "It's early."

"Aisha, it's me." Mom's voice comes out unnaturally high pitched, nothing like her usual deep velvety tone. But I still recognize it. "Sorry, did I wake you up?"

Damnit, I should have checked my caller ID.

"That's okay," I say slowly, tightening my grip on my phone. "Uh, how are you?"

"I'm doing all right. And you?"

"Good." I open my mouth, but I can't for the life of me think of anything else to say. An absolutely cavernous silence falls. I rub at the crick in my neck, bracing myself against her next words, whatever they might be.

It's quiet for so long I think she may have hung up, but then her crisp voice fills my ear again. "Are you free to meet up for coffee today?"

"Um . . ." My dad's disapproving face flashes into my mind. "I don't know if that's a good idea." There's no way she checked in with Dad about this—he would have told me.

"Oh." Her voice falls flat for a moment before perking back up. "I just thought . . . I thought it might be nice to catch up since we haven't seen each other in so long." It's almost a year since I saw her last Christmas. "I've really missed you, Aisha."

"Me too." I'm not sure how much I mean it.

She lets out a breath. "So could today around noon work for you?"

If I agree and Dad finds out, he'll freak. On the other hand, meeting up with her is better than sticking around here all day. I swallow hard as all the memories of last night come flooding back. "Okay."

"Great, I'll text you the details."

"Bye," I say quickly before hanging up. "Crap."

I shoot up from the couch and start pacing the living room. Maybe I should text her to cancel.

Rubbing at my throbbing forehead, I walk into a disaster of a kitchen. Plastic cups and pizza boxes are scattered across the island. Neil can deal with it. I grab a tall glass of water before nibbling at some cold pizza.

I'm startled when Neil comes stumbling into the kitchen. He always sleeps late on the weekend, and with the hangover I'm sure he's nursing, I didn't expect him to be up for hours.

"Morning," he says through a yawn as he grabs the water pitcher next to me.

I keep my eyes on my plate as I mechanically chew the congealed cheese and dough.

"You okay?" he asks as he heads for the fridge.

Getting up from the island, I drop my plate in the sink, the porcelain banging loudly against the stainless steel.

"What's up with you?"

I stare at my hands as I wash them before yanking the tap closed, hard.

"Look, I'm sorry about last night," Neil says, following me back into the living room.

"Sure," I mutter as I sit on the couch and flip mindlessly through my phone.

He flops down beside me and covers his eyes against the sunlit window with his forearm. "I mean it, Ish. I'm really sorry."

I finally look up at him, my eyes sharp. "Sorry for what? Do you even remember anything from last night?"

He removes his arm from his face, grimacing. "Enough."

"Whatever." I get up and go to the bathroom, slamming the door behind me.

*

On the bus ride over to my old neighborhood by the lake, modest two-story houses grow into roomy three-floor homes before becoming sprawling mini mansions mostly hidden behind towering, perfectly landscaped hedges. The bus exits the long, winding residential streets after a while and comes to a stop at the local high-end mall.

Mom's standing in front of the artisanal coffee shop close to the crowded entrance. Put together as ever, she's in a silk blouse and pencil skirt.

She looks up from her phone, spotting me when I'm a few feet away. I'm an inch taller than her now, even in her heels. It feels wrong, looking down at her as she gives me a bright smile.

I try to return it, but my mouth barely moves.

"How are you?" she asks.

"Fine." I know I should say more, but my brain's stalling. I look into the coffee shop, but there are no empty seats. "Did you want to get in line?"

"How about we do a little shopping first and come back?" she suggests, her eyes scanning my plain T-shirt and joggers. "Might be nice to grab a pair of jeans or something? Nothing too fancy."

I hate shopping, but I shrug, not wanting to start an argument within the first two minutes. At least she's not gunning for me to try anything frilly or floral. Mom leads the way through the sea of people to some snooty department store.

She starts flipping through blouses, and I head over to the jeans section and look at the endless piles of incredibly similar looking denim. Picking out a pair in my size at random, I head toward the dressing rooms.

"I'll meet you there in a few," Mom says as I pass her.

In the dressing room, I struggle to pull the jeans over my thighs. Holding my breath, I finally jump into them. They barely zip.

The mirror reflects my bulging hips, which seem to have appeared on my body out of nowhere. Aren't store mirrors supposed to make people look slimmer? I look like a disgusting fun-house version of myself.

I can't believe I've been letting myself eat so much crap lately. Neil and I have been ordering pizza way too often. I thought I could get away with it since I've been running and dancing a lot, but obviously it's caught up to me.

"Can I see?" I hear my mom ask outside the stall.

"They don't fit," I call out.

"Too big or too small? What size do you need?" she asks, like she works there or something.

I'm silent as my heart starts to race. The thought of telling her how many sizes I've gone up makes me feel like I'll be sick all over the floor. I hurriedly rip the jeans off and get back into my forgiving joggers.

"Can we just go?" I say as I open the door.

She opens her mouth, but thankfully, when she sees my face, she just nods instead of pushing it like she would have in the past. Since she's been so persistent about meeting up, I guess she realizes if she wants me to agree to see her again, this isn't the way to go about it.

Back at the coffee shop, we snag a small table. I told her I only wanted coffee, but she grabbed us both salad wraps anyway.

I pick at the wrap as we sit in silence. There's a young family seated at the table behind us. The two toddlers giggle over their cake pops as their parents grin at each other.

"So, are you staying at Neil's house?" she asks.

Here we go. I brace myself for her to start in about how stupid it was for me to leave ballet school. "Yeah."

"I'm surprised your father is all right with you living with your boyfriend." Her voice is mild, but I study her closely as she takes a small sip of her coffee.

"I don't have a boyfriend." I swallow and blink hard for a moment, focusing on the family behind us again. "I mean, you know Neil and I are just friends."

"Do you want to be more than that?" she asks quietly.

Sighing, I set my wrap down. "No."

"Are you sure?"

"There's this other guy," I find myself muttering, and she raises an eyebrow. God, why am I even mentioning this to her? I guess because I have literally no one else to talk to. Ebi and Khadija are cool, but they do love to talk whenever there's juicy drama.

"He's . . . He's Neil's friend from my new school."

Her eyes darken for a moment at the mention of school, but she composes herself, taking a longer sip of her coffee. "Oh yeah?"

This is so weird. We've never talked about stuff like this. All our conversations used to revolve around my dancing. I wonder what's up with her. I was sure she would have brought up ballet school by now.

"It was his birthday yesterday. We hung out with Neil and some kids from school, and he was really . . . I just thought he felt like I did. But he didn't." Or he did up until he kissed me and realized he wasn't interested after all.

"How do you know he doesn't feel the same?"

I'm back in the living room now, Ollie's eyes refusing to meet mine after he pulled away from me and bailed last night.

When I don't respond, she continues, "Don't worry. Boys your age have no idea what they want."

I manage a shrug.

"How's everything going at school?" Her voice is level, but I still tense up at the question.

"Good."

"How are your classes going?" she asks.

"I don't have that many classes this year since I finished most of the courses required for my diploma at my old school. Next year, I'll just have electives. I'm keeping my grades up, though."

She nods. "Glad to hear you've stayed focused. What're your favorite classes?"

I examine her closely as she takes a dainty bite of her wrap. *Here we go.* "My dance classes."

Her face clouds again before going placid.

"And how's that going?"

"I have a ballet solo, and I'm choreographing a modern pairs' piece with Neil for the winter showcase."

Her eyes brighten. "You have *two* performances in a showcase?"

"Yeah, and I'm assisting my instructor in Ballet. It's Lucinda Anvyi from your old company."

My mom was a soloist at NYCB before I was born. It was only for a few months. When she had a career-ending knee injury, she stopped dancing and started studying law.

"That's impressive. Congratulations." She doesn't really sound that excited, but my heart still leaps at the rare praise. "Oh, and I have something for you."

She grabs one of her shopping bags off the floor and places it on the table between us. While she was checking out at the store, I didn't pay any attention to what she was buying, counting the seconds until we left.

I gingerly reach inside the bag and pull out a navy-blue satin dress. It's really pretty, but I know I won't ever wear it. I'm not into dresses, other than wearing dance costumes. "Thanks."

"I *think* it should fit," she says. My face flames, and I fight the urge to shrink in my seat as she assesses my figure. I let out a silent breath when she stops studying me. "I have tickets to the ballet next week. I thought you might want something to wear. If you're interested in coming with me."

I still remember the very first time my parents took me to the ballet, when I was seven. The production of *A Midsummer Night's Dream* inspired so many of my fairy-princess-themed backyard performances.

"Okay," I find myself saying, unable to resist. Despite ballet being my life, I haven't had a chance to see a company production in quite a while. My dad's frowning face pops up in my head, and I quickly shove the image away. I can tell my mom is trying to connect, even though today's been a little awkward. It's just one night—he doesn't need to know. It doesn't have to be a big deal.

17

I'm able to avoid Ollie and Neil for the most part on Monday. I spend my free periods and all of lunch in the ballet studio, practicing for my *Coppélia* solo. Because I missed a few weeks practicing on pointe while my ankle fully healed, I need to make up for that time.

In Modern, I don't sit next to Neil, and he doesn't try to talk to me any more than necessary while we rehearse for our pairs performance after school. Our rehearsal is pretty much a disaster, both of us completely off with our timing.

On Tuesday morning, when I take my seat next to Ollie, I feel his eyes on me, but I don't turn in his direction.

"Hey, Aisha." His voice is raspy and raw.

I pretend not to hear him as I pull my books out of my bag. He lets out a quiet groan and puts his head on his desk, turning away from me.

Halfway through class, he flicks a note onto my desk.

I don't pick it up and focus up front again. He nudges my foot and I turn to glare at him.

"Open it," he mouths.

I pick up the note just to avoid looking at him any longer. We pass it back and forth for a few minutes.

Do you hate me now?
Yes ☐ No ☑
I'm sorry about Friday night.
Okay then.
I'm an idiot.
That doesn't explain anything.
Are you free later?
For what?

The lunch bell rings and I shoot out of my seat as quickly as possible. Before I can take off, Ollie catches me by the arm. I almost stop breathing as I stare up at him.

"I have to do this original song in my music class tomorrow, and I'm—I'm probably going to bomb again," he stutters out. "Would you, uh . . . Would you mind helping me practice?"

I focus on his face for the first time today. The hollows under his eyes are unusually dark.

Letting out a sigh, I pull away from him and head for the door. "Fine."

"Yeah?" He keeps pace with me, and I avoid his gaze again. "For real?"

I manage a tight smile as we get to the stairwell. "I can stop by after rehearsal."

"You're a lifesaver," he calls out from behind me as I start up the stairs to the dance studios. "Are you coming to lunch today?"

"No, I gotta practice. Later."

*

I have the entire studio to myself, so I prop my phone up on my bag and watch Michaela's performance as The Doll in *Coppélia* yet again. In the mirror, I make sure every single one of my *piqué* turns are as smooth and steady as hers. Whenever I falter, I start over from the beginning, challenging myself to do it all the way through without any issues five times in a row.

When girls start entering the studio at the end of lunch, I stop dancing. Putting my headphones on, I watch the video a few more times as I stretch.

Someone says my name, and I look up, pulling off my headphones. Caroline and Nina glance over at me before turning away.

"I think she heard us," Nina attempts to whisper.

Caroline snorts. "So?"

I press my lips together, my jaw tight as I put my headphones back on. *Don't they have literally anything better to do? This is getting pretty damn old.*

Madame A. enters and we get to work. I move through corrections as swiftly and efficiently as possible, adjusting the girls' posture and repositioning limbs before moving along without giving them a second look.

"Good job, girls!" Madame calls out. "Everything all right?" she asks as she passes me.

"Fantastic," I mutter, instantly regretting my tone. I know she's just trying to look out for me.

Madame shoots me a sideways look, but I move along to the next row before she can say anything else.

*

"Hey!"

In Modern, Ebi plops down in front of me. We're at the windows, a little away from the rest of the class.

I pull my headphones off. "Hmm?"

"What's up, you little hermit? Where've you been at lunch this week?" Ebi asks as he sprawls out on his side.

"Just getting in some extra studio time," I say, leaning back on my elbows.

"Okay, sure. You have to spill, though. What happened with you and Ollie at his party after we left?" He winces when he sees my expression. "Oh no. Did it not go well?"

I just shake my head.

"You can't keep me hanging like this," Ebi groans out. "Do you even get what it was like to watch you two, like, *genuinely* fall in love, right then? I couldn't take it, y'all were too cute."

I squint at him for a long moment. "In *love*? Are you *on* something? And you totally set me up with that sappy ass *Moulin Rouge* song."

He shrugs. "Well, it worked. Or so I thought. What happened later?"

"Neil got wasted with his asshole buddies, and then Ollie and I had to take care of him. Super romantic," I drone out as I focus on my phone. There's no way in hell I'm telling him about the complete and utter humiliation of what happened with Ollie after.

Ebi winces. "That sucks."

Hannah claps to get our attention. "I've got some fun news. Pointe Noire, my former company, had some last-minute tickets open up for a dress rehearsal of their latest show, *Subverting the Margins*."

Ebi grins, and some other kids in class perk up as she passes out permission slips. I've never heard of Pointe Noire, but a field trip does sound like a nice break from the unrelenting intensity of Modern.

During meditation, I completely block out Hannah's voice, not wanting to risk feeling anything that could set me off.

After class, Hannah sticks around to see what Neil and I have so far for the winter showcase.

She stops the music partway through our routine and turns to us.

"I feel like you've taken some steps back here." It's a bit of an understatement since we're somehow more of a mess than yesterday, our movements even less in tandem. "How about we work through it together?"

"How do you mean?" I gasp out, my chest on fire from exertion.

"I think sorting out the core of this piece could really help you two get back on track."

I contain a frustrated groan. God, why does she always want to talk about everything?

Neil shrugs. "That's okay. We're just a little off today, but we'll keep working on it."

"I really think it would be useful to explore the journey you two are taking."

"We're just running through it." My irritation bleeds into my voice, and Hannah raises an eyebrow at me. "I mean, for the performance we'll be in character."

"That's the thing. I don't want to see a character," Hannah says. "I need you guys to bring out something real inside you. To truly connect with each other and the audience. Every single time you run through this, I want you to put everything into it. You can't just pull it out of nowhere the night of—you need to home in on your connection."

I nod, even though the thought of going back into that unfiltered, exposed place again sounds like a nightmare. Especially considering how uncomfortable things have been between us since the weekend.

"Can you tell me a little about the themes of this piece? What are some of the main emotions you're aiming to evoke?"

Neil and I fall into a choking silence. I pick up my water bottle and chug, refusing to be the one to fill it. This is essentially his piece that I'm trying to unravel, the strands of it knotting uselessly in my mind.

Finally, Neil clears his throat. "Letting go, I guess."

"Of what?" Hannah pushes.

"Resentment," he mutters before focusing on me. "The past."

I hold my breath while I stare at the floor. I don't understand why he wants to dredge up our past when all I want is to forget it.

She nods at him. "Okay, that's a start. What do you think it's about, Aisha?"

When she turns to study me, I release my arms from their tightly crossed position over my chest.

I blink hard as I stare at my bruised, bare toes.

"I don't know. Forgiveness?" Everything in me wants to be in motion, moving as far away from this conversation as possible.

I can feel both of them watching me, but I refuse to look up. Pressure builds in my lungs, making it difficult to catch my breath again.

Hannah sighs. "I know you both come from a type of classical training that doesn't encourage vulnerability. But if you want to excel at modern choreography you're going to have to work against that training. I know it's asking a lot. But this could be healing for you if you let it."

I flinch, knowing she means I'm a head case who obviously needs some outlet for all my massive issues. Going to a counsellor is one thing, but I'm not putting everything out in the open for everyone to see ever again.

I still have no idea how to shut myself on and off like Neil does, and there's no way I'm asking him. I wish all my horrible feelings would go away right after I dance. But once those dark bits escape, they have free rein to try and suffocate me. Which isn't exactly what I would call "healing."

When I finally look up, Neil's smiling thinly at Hannah. "We'll keep at it. Right, Ish?"

I swallow hard. "Right."

Hannah gives us a last doubtful look as she heads for the door. "See you tomorrow."

Neil focuses on me when the door closes. "Ready?"

I only nod as we begin our next run-through. We're supposed to finish the piece facing each other, but I keep misjudging my last turn and end up facing away from him.

"Okay." Neil sighs. "Let's go again."

I shake my head as I grab my bag. I really don't want to deal with this anymore. "I'm done."

"Look, I know you don't want to talk to me. But we still have to get this."

"It's fine, we've got it. Let's just do the ending facing apart."

"I don't think we should end it that way," Neil says slowly, his voice low.

"What's the difference?" I snap.

He sets his jaw and his eyes darken, but he doesn't say anything.

"I gotta get going," I say, quieter now. "Later."

Neil stares after me as I head for the doors. I can't for the life of me read his expression.

Hannah's words echo in my brain no matter how hard I try to block them out. I get that I need to suck it up and figure this out—I can't embarrass myself in front of the whole school and mess up my grade in Modern. And despite what happened at Ollie's party, I still want to help Neil somehow. But I'm just so tired of all this, of trying to fix everything. How am I'm supposed to do any of this without falling apart?

⁑

When I get to Ollie's place, his mom insists I bring food upstairs again.

He sighs when he sees the heaping plate.

"We literally just ate dinner. I don't know why she always does this."

I set the plate down and sit on the couch. I'm really tempted to pop just one piece of dolma in my mouth, but I tear my eyes away from it.

It's way too quiet for a moment.

"So, uh . . . How're things with Neil?" he asks.

"Pretty bad," I admit. "Our rehearsals haven't been going well. And Hannah wants us to be more emotive. It's kind of a lot."

"That sounds really tough. Have you been feeling okay?"

I nod quickly as my breath starts to shorten. "Anyway, are you ready to practice?"

God, why did I agree to this? I have to make sure I don't go all googly eyed when he starts singing. Remembering him leaving that night should be enough to keep me from getting caught up again.

He grabs his guitar, and I wait for him to start, but he just sits there, staring out the window behind me.

"You okay?"

"Um. You know what, never mind," he says, putting his guitar down.

"Never mind what?"

"I'm good. I should be okay for my class." He wipes his hands on his jeans and stares vacantly at the floor.

"What's up with you?"

Ollie looks up at that, and something in his eyes makes my heart bang against my ribcage like it's trying to escape. The point where one of us should look away comes and goes. I'm screaming at myself to stop, but it's like I'm stuck in a trap.

After an eternity, he looks away, rubbing at his eyes. "I was exhausted when I wrote this. It's just a brain dump, not an actual song. I might do something else instead."

I nod. "Do you have something else ready?"

"No," he sighs out.

I feel bad this is making him so stressed. "Well . . . You might have to stick with what you have then."

"It's just kind of—it's kind of personal."

We're staring at each other again, and my stomach is twisting and leaping into my throat.

"That's okay, you can trust me." I wince at how out of breath I sound.

"All right." I almost think he's going to back out again, but then he picks up his guitar and starts.

When you danced
I tripped and fell

Fell into a waking dream
You're inked inside my memory
It never stops
You're on repeat
At night I can't
I never sleep . . .

Ollie searches my eyes to gauge my reaction, but I can't move a muscle. The molten heat that's rushed to my face spreads across every inch of my skin.

Finally, he closes his eyes, releasing me from his gaze. He keeps singing, but now he's talking about something else. From how choked up his voice gets, I can tell he's talking about something horrible that happened to him.

If you knew I lost it all
Everything I thought I was
All my pride ripped away
Would you still look at me
Think of me the same way?

When Ollie finishes, he doesn't open his eyes.

I wipe my soaked face on the sleeve of my sweater before I get up and sit next to him. Taking his guitar from his hands, I set it down next to me.

"Oll?" I take his hand and he opens his eyes, staring down at our fingers as they wrap around each other's. The lyrics repeat in my head, a terrible truth clicking into place. "Is it okay if I ask you something?"

He nods, not looking up from our hands.

"When you got beat up in ninth grade, did, um . . ." A sickening dread fills me, smashing down on my chest. "Did something else really bad happen too?"

After a while, Ollie meets my gaze, and I'm stunned by his expression. I don't think I've ever seen someone look so afraid. He takes a few deep breaths before he calms down and nods again.

I tighten my grip on his fingers.

"I'm so sorry. It was really brave of you to write this. Thanks for sharing it with me."

His eyes brighten for the briefest moment. "Thanks for listening."

"And Ollie . . ." I stop and try to steady my voice.

"What is it?" His dark eyes sear right into me, turning my insides to jelly.

"What happened to you doesn't change anything about, like, my feelings for you." My words are so clumsy and inadequate after how beautifully he expressed how he felt about me. Ignoring my paralyzing panic, I try to find even a fraction of his courage within myself. "I really like you."

His eyes soften. "I like you too. I'm so sorry about that night."

"I know. It's okay."

"Aisha, is it—" He stops short and takes a deep breath. "Is it okay if we try again?"

"Yeah," I murmur. "We can try again."

We lean into each other, my eyes falling closed. His fingers brush the back of my neck before he takes my face in his hands and presses his lips gently to mine.

When I can breathe again, I lean away and search his eyes. "Are you still okay?"

He nods before pulling me back toward him, and my mind dissolves into nothing. I'm fully present and tuned in to my body as everything inside me completely takes over.

18

After school the next day, I skip out of rehearsal early, still unable to take how awkward things are with Neil after Hannah confronted us. We're still not getting anywhere with our choreo since I don't even really want to look at him for too long.

On the train ride downtown to meet my mom at the National Ballet of Canada, I distract myself from my aching muscles and my nerves about messing up at the showcase by thinking about what happened last night with Ollie. The grimace on my face finally eases, a goofy grin taking over.

When I arrive at the ballet theater, I take in the looming three-story structure made entirely of glass, patrons of the arts in expensive fare clearly visible from all angles as I approach.

I almost miss her since I'm so preoccupied thinking about Ollie, but eventually I spot my mom waving and smiling widely at me in the bustling auditorium lobby.

"Glad the dress fits," she says, and a warm rush of relief shoots through me. The last few days, I've been way stricter with my food choices and went out for some longer runs than usual. I only just managed to zip myself into it. "You look great."

"Thanks. You too." She's in a long, black dress form-fitted to her slim figure.

We head to the concession stand and, to my surprise, she orders me a white wine along with hers, handing me the glass with a wink.

After finishing our drinks in the lobby, we go find our seats. We make it to the front of the orchestra section as the lights go down and the first act starts.

It's a production of *The Red Shoes*. The way the prima ballerina, Victoria Reyes, *bourrées* across the stage is otherworldly—she's practically floating. Even though I don't want to, I find myself comparing my body to her impossibly tiny one. And her light brown complexion to my deeper tone.

I'm painfully aware there isn't a fully Black female dancer in the entire show. Victoria Reyes has an Afro-Latin and Asian background. Siphesihle November is the only fully Black principal dancer in the company, and he doesn't happen to be performing tonight. My mom and I are some of the very few Black people in the audience.

Despite my initial unease, toward the end of the show, I'm completely enthralled in the prima's movements, her *fouettés* faster than I can see. By the time the curtain falls, I'm drawn back to when I was here as a kid—the dancing, sets, and costumes all making me feel like I've been transported somewhere magical.

I turn to Mom and grin widely as the lights come back up. "That was amazing!"

She stands and motions me forward with her program. "Come on. I have a surprise for you."

I rise slowly, giving her a curious look as she leads the way out of the auditorium. Instead of turning toward the exit, she heads down a narrow, dimly lit hall, and then we're backstage.

My jaw drops as the night's dancers move around us in a flurry, making their way to the dressing rooms in their intricate costumes embroidered with sequins, crystals, and shimmery thread. After a moment, I realize I've stopped to gawk while Mom has walked ahead. I quicken my pace as she moves toward the main stage wings.

Mom places a hand on my shoulder when I catch up to her talking to the prima.

"Victoria, this is my daughter, Aisha."

"Lovely to meet you," Victoria says as she pops some bobby pins out of her bun. Up close she's so delicately beautiful, I feel like a gangly giant next to her.

"You too," I manage as my heart thumps out an erratic rhythm. "You were incredible tonight."

Victoria tilts her head as she gives me a gentle smile. "That's so sweet of you."

Mom's hand reaches across my shoulders, her grip tight. "Aisha is a dancer herself. She's only in her junior year and she's a student assistant with two leads in her school's next showcase."

"That's wonderful!" Victoria sings out. "Congrats!"

"Thanks." I bow my head a bit as Mom pats my shoulder firmly.

"Victoria did a short stint at NYCB while I was there," Mom says. "It was lovely to see you up there tonight."

Victoria nods before focusing on me again. "How long have you been dancing?"

"Since I was seven—"

"She placed in YAPG a few years ago and trained at the Western School of Ballet," Mom cuts in. "Honestly, the school she's at is a bit below her experience level. It's public."

Trying not to wince, I step out of her grasp.

Victoria raises her eyebrows. "Have you thought about auditioning for the National School? With your pre-professional background, I think you'd be a good fit for our company's apprenticeship program when you graduate."

"Uh . . ." I trail off as I try to process.

Canada's National Ballet School is the number one school in the country. It had been one of Neil's and my top choices after the School of American Ballet back when we were competing together. After giving up on the idea of ever getting an apprenticeship, I can't even picture that being a possibility for me again.

"I'll be having dinner with one of my old instructors in a few days," Victoria continues. "He's on the lookout for new, diverse talent in the city. I'll be sure to mention you."

My eyes widen. "Wow. Thank you!"

Is this happening? I haven't really heard of ballet schools looking for diverse students other than token poster kids that end up in brochures instead of leading roles. But with Victoria and Siphesihle here as principals, it seems like it might not be a disingenuous callout.

Mom's smile is ear to ear. "That's really lovely of you, Victoria. And thanks again for having us back here tonight."

Victoria reaches out to hug her. "Of course, Callie. Thanks so much for coming. How's everything going at your firm?"

My mom tells her about making partner, but I'm too excited to focus, imagining what could happen if Victoria actually puts in a good word for me with her old instructor.

"It was a pleasure meeting you, Aisha." Victoria's voice jars me out of my daze. I can only nod and grin before Mom and I head back to the lobby.

"That was so cool," I gush. "Thanks for introducing me."

"No worries," Mom says easily as we step through the front doors of the theater. The night is alive with a dizzying array of artificial light—from the towering buildings to the zooming traffic. "That was fun."

"My showcase is coming up in a few weeks, by the way," I find myself blurting out. "If you're free."

I almost rescind the invitation when I imagine my dad finding out. Plus, I don't think I can handle her seeing me bomb. After what she said to Victoria about my school basically being awful, I'm sure she doesn't want to go. My ballet solo rehearsals have been going well, but my piece with Neil is still another story.

Before I can make sense of what's happening, she envelops me in a firm hug. The floral and chemical scent of her fancy perfume irritates my nose, making me want to sneeze, just like when I was little. I pat her back awkwardly before pulling away.

She smiles, her perfect teeth coming into view. "Of course I'll be there."

Damn it, I really wish I'd kept my mouth shut.

✳

The next day, after my free periods, I head straight to the ballet studio to get some more practice in during the lunch hour. With how badly the modern routine has been going, I can't risk my ballet solo being anything less than perfect. It has to be better than perfect. After watching Michaela a few more times, I get to work.

When I come to a stop after my third run-through, I find Ollie standing right inside the door. I freeze, my breath catching.

I haven't been able to stop thinking about what happened at his place on Tuesday. We only kissed for like fifteen minutes before he pulled back and then we cuddled for a long time, him asking before he gently ran his fingers through my hair. We ended up falling asleep for a few hours before he walked me home.

"Sorry to scare you," he says as he approaches.

I shake my head, a big grin taking over my face. "Hey."

"Hey." He's directly in front of me now, staring right at my mouth, and my pulse soars into my throat.

Leaning in, his lips feather over mine. Steadying my wobbling knees, I wrap my arms around his shoulders.

He pulls back a little, looking into my eyes. "Everything okay?"

"Uh-huh. Why?"

"I missed you at lunch yesterday," he murmurs, his arms tightening around me. "And since you didn't come today either . . ."

I pull his arms from my waist and take a seat on the floor. "Sorry. I just really had to rehearse."

He sits next to me and takes my hand. "Are you sure it doesn't have anything to do with avoiding Neil?"

"That's just an added bonus," I mutter. At home, things have been painfully silent between us whenever we run into each other.

"He hasn't been sitting with us all week anyway. He's been having lunch in the caf."

"Oh. Have you talked to him at all since . . . ?"

"No." Ollie sighs. "Last weekend was . . . you know. I really want him to be okay, but it's hard when he acts like that."

The door opens and Caroline, Tara, and Nina enter with a few of their friends. They all stare at us for a second before turning away.

I stand up quickly. "Class is about to start," I tell him.

He gets up and reaches into his backpack and pulls out a small paper bag. "Yeah, I gotta go, but here. You like carrot, right?"

I take the bag and look inside. It's a fresh muffin from the caf. "Thanks," I say, my voice quiet as I close the bag again.

"No prob. And, uh . . . Hope you're free later because I got these." He holds out two concert tickets.

I stare at the tickets in disbelief. "Midnight Cavalcade is playing downtown tonight?"

"So you'll come with me?"

"Obviously." Grinning, I lean into him but stop short when he tenses up. For a moment, I was completely unaware of the other girls in the room, but when I glance over, they're openly gawking.

"You okay?" I ask under my breath.

He nods, glancing briefly at my classmates. "They seem great."

"Yep. They're a fucking delight."

His brow furrows, and I force a soft laugh, rolling my eyes. "Meet me at my locker after the last bell?"

After he leaves, I take a seat on the floor again, pulling my head-phones out of my bag. Before I can turn on my music, the girls start talking about Ollie and me, not even attempting to mute their voices.

"Isn't he, like, into guys?" Tara asks.

"Well, she *is* pretty manly," Nina says with a snort. "I mean, look at her thighs."

Tara sniggers. "Right? They're *huge*. Caroline, didn't you say that she's . . . ?" She stops for a moment to make a disgusting gagging noise.

I freeze with my headphones halfway to my ears, unable to breathe. She must mean that Caroline said I'm bulimic.

Caroline shrugs. "She used to be. I swear, she looked like she belonged in one of those sad UNICEF commercials. But she's definitely let herself go."

"Hey, what's up?" Prasheetha nods at the girls as she walks in the door, heading toward them.

"Hey, Prashie." Tara shoots her a beaming grin. "Guess what?"

I force myself to move so I don't have to hear anymore, finally putting my headphones on.

I've never made myself throw up, but Caroline always had a knack for embellishing a good story. I don't know why I assumed Neil was the only one who noticed how thin I got at my old studio. Since I try to never think of the time right before I was sent away, it's hard to really remember.

Screw them. They're idiots. She's kind of right, though—I have let myself go. That moment in the department store dressing room pushes its way to the front of my brain, followed by my mom's eyes running the length of me, her face grim.

Stop it. Just stop. Ignoring the sharp stinging in my chest, I blast Midnight Cavalcade's latest album, pretending I'm already at the concert.

*
*

After school, Ollie and I take the bus to the subway station and head downtown on the train. We walk a few blocks to the venue, stopping in front of a little hole-in-the-wall concert theater. He leads the way downstairs to the basement record store where he works.

The narrow space is filled to the brim with vinyl, CDs, even stacks of old cassette tapes.

"Cheriet, you're late. You're lucky Brad isn't here," a stout guy with a beanie in his mid-twenties says from behind the counter.

"I'm not working today."

The guy looks up from counting the cash till and registers me standing beside Ollie. His eyes flash down to our joined hands.

"Ah, I see. This your girlfriend?"

Oh God. Since this is our first date, we definitely haven't labelled anything.

Ollie ducks his head. "Ben, Aisha. Aisha, Ben," he says, already leading me farther into the store. "We're gonna hang out for a bit before we check out the set upstairs."

"Nice to meet you," Ben says to me before nodding at Ollie. "Okay, cool."

We take our time going through the stacks. I've never seen him look more at ease as he excitedly points out his favorite albums.

Ollie leads me into a listening booth all the way in the back and we tuck ourselves into the tiny space.

"Hey." He waves a hand in front of my face, and I blink out of a daze to find him looking at me sideways. "Where'd you go?"

My pulse pounds when I realize I'd completely checked out without even noticing. "Nowhere," I say, scanning through the cycling albums in the booth player.

He frowns and I let out a sigh, scooting closer to him. With our legs pressed together, I can't help but notice how much wider my thighs are compared to his.

"It's fine, really. The girls in my Ballet class were being more annoying than usual after you left. They're probably just jealous."

"What did they do?" he asks quietly.

I shake my head. "It doesn't matter. It's stupid that I even let it get to me anymore."

Ollie glances at me like he's afraid I'm going to shut down. "I think you mentioned that people were assholes at your old school too?"

I know he means what I told him after he first sang for me on his roof that night.

"Yeah." It doesn't feel as embarrassing to talk to him about this since he gets how shitty people can be. "I always had Neil then, though," I say under my breath.

As annoyed as I am at Neil, not being able to talk to him anymore really, really blows.

Ollie squeezes my hand. I squeeze back and when I smile at him, I don't have to fake it.

I'm super aware in this moment of how incredibly lucky I am that I still have Ollie. How lucky I am that he understands exactly how hard things are with Neil.

Despite how crappy everything's been lately, it doesn't make being here tonight any less surreal. Sometimes it's still kind of hard to believe Ollie likes me back. But the way he's looking at me right now makes it impossible to deny just how much he does.

Remembering to breathe, I tear my eyes away from him. "Anyway, you never told me how it went."

He puts a giant old plush headphone to his ear. "How what went?"

"Your class performance yesterday?"

His arm circles my waist, pulling me closer to him so we can share the headphones. He avoids my gaze. "I, um, couldn't really do it, so my teacher let me send him a video instead for my grade."

I rub his arm, hoping he'll meet my eyes again. "That's cool of him to let you do that."

"Yeah, it was only a one-time thing, though. I don't know how I'm gonna get through the spring showcase."

When I fit my fingers through his, he looks up again. "Trust me, you're gonna kill it. And you know I'll be there."

He shakes his head but grins, biting down on his lip. "Thanks, Aisha."

Ugh, why is he so freaking cute? I literally can't take it. I lean into him, pulling back when I hear footsteps. Peeking out of the booth, I see it's just Ben headed into the supply room, focused on his phone.

Ollie starts to get up. "We should head upstairs before the line gets out of control."

When we get up to the front of the line, the bouncer nods us forward but then puts a hand out to block me from entering.

"ID?"

Ollie looks at him sideways. "It's all ages."

The bouncer ignores him, still staring at me expressionlessly. "ID."

"You didn't ask anyone else." Ollie's voice is sharp with annoyance.

I pull my wallet out of my backpack and fish it out to show him. He stares at it and back at me about five times. I stare back, my face carefully blank. He finally holds it out to me, and I snatch it back.

"Let me see your bag."

Resisting the urge to roll my eyes, I hand it over. He searches it before giving it back to me.

"I have to stamp you as underage, so you're not served drinks at the bar."

I hold my hand out for the stamp.

"You just let fourteen-year-olds in without a stamp a second ago," Ollie says. "And you didn't search anyone else's bags."

After the bouncer stamps my hand, he gestures for us to get out of the way.

Inside, Ollie is still visibly irritated.

"It's no big deal. Forget about it," I say, trying to shake it off even though there's a gross feeling in the pit of my stomach that's replaced the warmth that was there before.

He shakes his head. "That was messed up."

I'm silent. Looking around, I'm the only Black person in the entire venue. No one is outright staring, but I can feel the occasional side-eyed glance my way.

The opener is warming up, and I pull Ollie forward. "Come on, let's get up front."

When the band starts playing, the music booms through my bones. The amps next to us are so loud. After a few minutes, the noise pumping through me finally starts to feel good instead of jarring.

Our sour mood fades as the anticipation grows in the room. The energy is like a drug, and we can't stop grinning at each other.

When Midnight Cavalcade gets onstage, the crowd loses it—me and Ollie included. Their first notes start, and the crowd hushes. Ollie stands behind me with his arms wrapped around me, squeezing my hands. I relax into him and forget about everyone else pushed up shoulder to shoulder with us.

The energy stays at the same height for most of the show, the crowd and the band merging into one ecstatic entity. I turn in his arms to smile at him. He doesn't smile back, just stares so intently that I stop breathing. Ollie's eyes fall closed and then his mouth is on mine, slowly coaxing my lips apart. I know I should pull away after a bit, but I don't, forgetting to care what anyone else thinks.

19

The carefree bliss of the concert fades as soon as I step into Ballet the next day. Toward the end of class, Madame A. calls me up to the front. "Aisha, do you mind showing us what you have so far for the winter showcase?"

I'm not exactly psyched to be put on the spot in present company after how horrible Caroline and the rest of the girls were yesterday. But I focus on Madame as I nod and move into my first position, blocking out the other girls' bored faces.

When the music starts, my body slips into the choreo like a glove. I mirror the steps I've watched Michaela perform countless times—our movements identical. It's like some part of me has joined with her on a deep, energetic level even though she doesn't know I exist.

Madame nods when I finish but doesn't say anything. I suck in a breath, not letting my face fall.

I thought I nailed it. What's up with her? Maybe she's still annoyed I was short with her before when she tried to check in with me.

"All right, back to stretching, girls. Aisha, can I speak with you for a moment?" Madame asks when I start to head back toward my seat.

"Um, sure." *Crap, she's definitely upset with me.* "What's up?"

She speaks quietly so the other girls can't hear when I reach her desk. "That was beautiful. You've really captured Michaela DePrince's *Coppélia*."

"Thank you, Madame." I hold my breath, waiting for her to call me out for being a jerk to her.

"That being said, have you thought about putting your own spin on the routine?"

"Uh, not really. What do you mean?"

"I think incorporating some modern elements could really make this piece sing."

I resist the urge to roll my eyes. So much for this being my break from Modern. "What's wrong with doing it the classical way?"

"There's nothing wrong with it. I'd just love to see you tap into the magic of your first audition again."

"I don't really want to add any modern elements," I say, trying to keep my voice light.

Her face clouds with disappointment, and my stomach pinches.

I press on quickly. "I mean, if that's okay with you."

"Of course," she says after a second. "It's totally up to you. You'll be wonderful either way."

Obviously, she's backtracking to make me feel better. She wouldn't have brought it up otherwise.

I head back to my seat, and Nina looks me up and down before turning to her friends.

"God, what a teacher's pet," she mutters to Caroline. "She only got the solo because she's such a kiss ass. Your audition was better."

Caroline nods, letting out a heavy sigh. "Affirmative action strikes again."

Is she freaking serious? Nausea hits me in an unrelenting wave, but I swallow hard. If I puke, the bulimia rumors will get a million times worse. My shoulders drop thinking about solo auditions again, how, technically, Caroline's was better than mine.

They're all stifling laughter except for Prasheetha, whose face darkens at the comment. She narrows her eyes at Caroline for a moment but doesn't say anything.

You only messed up on your audition because Nina tripped you. Madame knows that. I try to calm myself down, but I'm losing sensation in my hands.

The bell rings and everyone starts to head out. I reach for my backpack, but my numb fingers slip, spilling the entire contents of my bag on the studio floor.

My insides writhe with humiliation.

Everyone stops to stare for a moment, their smirks barely concealed before they continue out the door. My fingers are still refusing to work properly, and it's taking me forever to get everything back in my bag.

Someone shoves my pencil case in my face, and I blink for a moment before focusing on Prasheetha. She gives me an odd look when I don't take the case, tossing it in my direction.

"Thanks," I manage to get out, my voice hollow.

"Uh-huh. I don't get why you always let them treat you like shit. You should stand up for yourself," she mutters before getting up and walking away.

Let them? I fight the urge to chuck my History textbook at the back of her head.

What a goddamn idiot. Like it's that easy. Does she honestly think if I said they were "hurting my wittle feewings" they'd just stop their bullshit? And being horrible right back would one-hundred-percent make it worse.

Sensation comes back into my body full force, my whole being trembling and on fire. I shove the rest of my stuff in my bag and sprint over to Modern so I'm not late.

Everyone is lined up by the door when I get there. I forgot about our field trip.

Hannah grins at me as she leads the way into the hallway. I fall in step beside Ebi, who's talking to Khadija.

Ebi nods at me. "Hey, where's Neil?"

"He's not here?" I ask, glancing around as the class heads toward the stairs.

"I guess he's skipping," Khadija says, her eyes on her phone.

"I guess." My shoulders start to tense up. I hope he's okay. I haven't seen him since last night. I left for school early for ballet rehearsal. I squint at Khadija. "Wait, you're not in Modern, are you? You're switching mid-semester?"

She glances up from her screen and gives me an odd look. "No, I'm not in Modern. Wow, those are some observational powers you've got there. Would you really not have noticed if I was in your class?"

I don't laugh. I'm not in the mood for any more jokes at my expense right now.

She bumps my shoulder and lowers her voice. "Relax. I just dropped Chem, so I have a spare this period. I really wanted to check out Pointe Noire and Ebi said you have one of those 'I'm-so-hip-with-the-kids, call-me-by-my-first-name' teachers. She's chill with me tagging along."

I nod as we head out the front doors and walk over to a waiting school bus.

"Wait a sec," Hannah says, glancing over the attendance sheet. "Aisha, have you seen Neil?"

I purse my lips, my mind whirring. "He has a stomach bug," I volunteer, think up on the spot.

He's never skipped this class before. I really hope he's not out somewhere with any of those idiots from the party.

We board the bus, and Ebi, Khadija, and I find some seats near the back.

"He's not actually sick, is he?" Ebi asks.

"Shh." I glance at Hannah up front talking to the bus driver. "I don't know. He didn't text me."

I kind of wish I'd skipped too. All I want to do is crawl into my bed. Or into Neil's couch, more accurately.

Khadija shakes her head. "What's up with you two? I feel like I haven't seen either of you in ages."

"Neil got wasted at Ollie's party, and now they're not talking," Ebi says. I glare at him and his eyes widen. "What? That wasn't a secret, was it? His sloppy hookup with Gwen is public knowledge."

I roll my eyes, resting my head against the window.

"You're not talking to him for getting drunk? But he always gets drunk at parties," she says.

Ebi raises an eyebrow at her as the bus rumbles to a start. "What's not clicking, hon? That's the point. You're one to talk about 'observational powers.'"

"Shut up." Khadija swats his shoulder before fixing me with a serious look. "Does he really get drunk *that* much?"

I hold in an exasperated sigh. Even though Neil and I aren't on good terms, I'm not going to go around telling people his business like that.

Ebi shakes his head at Khadija and mercifully changes the subject. "Anyways . . . How's ballet going?"

I immediately fall back into the humiliation of earlier, the girls' snickers ringing in my ears.

I don't get why you always let them treat you like shit. I imagine spitting directly in Prasheetha's face, but it doesn't make me feel any better. I move on to Caroline next and picture backhanding her so hard that she ends up on the ground. I kick her for good measure. I still feel nothing.

Ebi sucks in a breath, and I blink back onto the bus. "Wow. That bad, eh?"

I finally lift my head from the window to find them staring at each other worriedly.

"Everything okay?" Khadija asks, her voice gentler than normal.

Leaning forward, I cross my arms and plant my forehead on the back of the musty pleather seat in front of me. I try to suck in a breath, but my throat feels tight.

Ebi pats me on the back. "What's up?"

I don't look up, squeezing my eyes shut to stop the tears. "Nothing. Ballet's going great."

"It's fine if you don't want to talk to us about it, but we promise we won't, like, tell anyone," Khadija says.

"Surprisingly, we do know how to keep our mouths shut sometimes," Ebi says. "We've got you."

Swiping my eyes dry, I look up after a moment. I have to admit, it's a little touching they actually seem to care.

I think I was about ten when I gave up on attempting to make friends other than Neil. I don't really know why, but a lot of kids just decide they don't like me on the spot. The few girls who would actually talk to me over the years ended up icing me out when girls like Caroline would do their thing, saying whatever awful things they could to make sure no one ended up sticking by me.

I find myself blurting out what happened in Ballet with Caroline and Prasheetha, my voice clunky and robotic.

Ebi kisses his teeth. "That girl needs to keep her nose out of Black people's business. If you gave Caroline and them what they deserved, they'd *definitely* bring out the fake waterworks. And then guess who'd end up in the principal's office."

"Exactly," Khadija says. "Do you know how many times I've had to sit in class smiling like a fool at some racist idiot so I don't end up looking crazy? Too many."

"Yeah, but I hate that they think I'm so passive," I mutter. "I'm literally just trying to, like, survive."

Ebi nods. "I get that. Sorry you have to deal with them every day."

I smile a little before I put my head back on the window again and close my eyes.

It's nice having people validate that I'm not the problem because sometimes it really feels like I am. Like, there has to be something wrong with me because people consistently treat me badly.

Since I've always tried to be a decent person, I know that what so many people hate about me instantly is something I can't do anything about. I guess I'll have to figure out a way to come to terms with that.

"They just can't handle you winning," Khadija says. "You got the ballet solo, you got Ollie's cute ass—"

I open my eyes and turn to her. "Who told you about me and Ollie?" Caroline and her lackeys have probably been telling the entire school.

"Hello?" She raises an eyebrow. "Do you not remember how hardcore he was flirting with you at his party? That was wild."

A stupid grin takes over my face, and I relent, telling them about our concert date for the rest of the ride over.

When we arrive, the front hall of the massive Pointe Noire complex is lined in display cases with medals and awards of a vast array of Black dancers spanning decades.

I'm so focused on peering into the cases at the faces I don't recognize that I almost don't notice when Hannah stops us when we get to the auditorium door. "Best behavior, all right, guys? Please respect the performers and the space."

We all nod before we head inside. The large stage area is empty, and we take our seats in the first couple of rows.

"Eek, this is gonna be sick," Khadija whispers beside me as the lights dim. "Their production last year was so mind-blowing."

I didn't look up the company beforehand at all, so I really don't know what to expect. When the curtains lift, there are ten dancers onstage—the oldest might be in her fifties and the youngest in his early twenties.

The music that blasts through the speakers is a type of experimental, Pan-African beat I've never heard before. The dancers throw themselves around the stage in frantic, erratic turns and soaring leaps that leave me breathless. All of the choreo is unique for each dancer, timed in a way that makes the piece tick forward with a sense of growing, urgent intensity.

The music stops and so do the dancers, frozen in place before a young woman with dreads in her mid-twenties starts to slowly come back to life, the music gearing up again with her. Her expression isn't measured and pleasant like Victoria's and the rest of the dancers at the National Ballet. Her face is contorted with a visceral agony as the other dancers form a circle around her, their backs to her as she falls to the ground, moving in lightning-fast contractions before jumping up again and pushing through the circle to center stage. The other dancers grab hold of her arms and then her legs, trying to pull her backward. She fights against them, breaking free again for a moment only to be dragged back again, moving with the other dancers in a rhythmic, grappling undulation of limbs. The music reaches a fever pitch, the pounding drums vibrating through the hall before silence falls again once the lead dancer has finally broken free for good. Instead of looking triumphant, her exhaustion is palpable as she slowly gets to her feet.

Everyone claps around me, but I sit there frozen, still staring at her. My heart is pounding as hard as if I were up there.

The main dancer catches me staring and smiles before they all head offstage. There are a few more acts in a mix of genres: a pairs piece, a couple of solos, and then a final group performance. But the entire time, I can't stop thinking about that first piece, its unmitigated intensity awakening something primal in my bones.

After the final curtain, the dancers all come back out onstage.

"Thank you for joining us for our dress rehearsal," a regal sounding older man calls out. "I'm the company director of Pointe Noire, Juwon Igwe. Our company was founded as a reaction to the historical exclusion of dancers of the African diaspora in traditional spaces. It's our mission to keep alive the contributions of all the dancers whose names have been systemically erased from mainstream dance culture. We aim to reimagine the definitions of what is possible for our community both within and outside of the confines of white dance institutions."

He goes on, and I find myself thinking about all those dancers I didn't know in the display cases in the hall.

There were always so few Black dancers to look up to when I was growing up. Michaela DePrince was the first ballerina I saw with a complexion as deep as mine, since my mom is several shades lighter than me.

But Michaela, along with Misty Copeland, are basically the only Black ballerinas that most people ever talk about. It's awful to think about how there have been so many others whose legacies are just as important but are largely unrecorded because the dance world refuses to acknowledge them.

My eyes go to the lead dancer from the first piece again. For a brief moment, I imagine myself in her place, surrounded by dancers who look like me and can relate to my experiences. I'm still so terrified to go to the dark places these dancers tackle with ease, but I can't deny how liberating they made it look.

On the way back to school, I'm still thinking about the performance. I've always dreamed of a career at a traditional company . . . but the pure freedom of expression I witnessed today is something I've never seen in a classical space. I know that dancers don't stay with one company their entire careers, but I've never even considered myself ending up anywhere but a classical company.

I was utterly transfixed by my mom's old videos of her performances at NYCB when I was little. All I could imagine was being just like her. But, like the Pointe Noire director said earlier, ballet largely refuses to make room for people like us, forcing us to create our own spaces.

The thing is, though . . . maybe traditional ballet is finally changing. Like Victoria said, the National School is looking for more diverse students. It's hard to believe after so many generations of exclusion, but maybe the gates are finally budging. Maybe it's worth it to keep ignoring the girls in my class and do everything I can to push my way in the door.

I wish I could talk to Neil about this. I look at my phone and see that he finally texted me to tell me he was tired and headed home early.

Even though our Modern rehearsals have been a disaster this week, there's now a small but brightly burning spark of something inside me spurring me to keep at it.

I'm still going to put the bulk of my energy into nailing my solo. Even if I decide to take a different route one day, I'm not ready to give up on ballet. I'm resolved to do everything in my power to fight my way into the traditional world. I can't give it up after everything I've gone through. But at the same time, I know it's probably worth it to figure out our Modern piece together. Neil's really trying, and even though I'm not super happy with him, I know this means a lot to him even if he won't admit it.

I have to try and tap into the untethered truth and power I glimpsed today, no matter how scary and painful it gets.

20

The weekend ends up sucking pretty bad. Ollie's at work the whole time, and I'm stuck in the house with Neil and we still aren't talking. On Sunday, I spend most of the day doing laundry that's been piling up.

"What?" I grumble at Neil when he yanks open the laundry room door in the late afternoon.

"Are you almost done?" he snaps at me. "There's no hot water left."

I nod without glancing up from folding my clothes.

He sighs and bangs the door shut again. I blink hard before taking a deep breath. I really wish things could just go back to normal with us. I'm still hoping there's some way I can get through to him in rehearsals next week.

My phone buzzes, and my heart starts to palpitate. Every time Dad's called since I've seen my mom, I've felt awful for not telling him and terrified of him finding out.

I still feel like he's making too big a deal out of me being in contact with her. Yeah, it was difficult dealing with how strict she was about my training when I was younger, but that's what it takes in elite ballet. He always acts like she's some kind of monstrous villain when she was only pushing me to be my best.

I really don't know what he'd do if he found out. Send me back to ballet school? Make me uproot my whole life again to go live with him in Tokyo? I can't risk it either way.

I brace myself and pick up. "Hey, what's up?"

"Not too much," he says with a yawn. "How's everything at school going?"

I let out a silent breath. "Good. You know that field trip you signed my permission form for? It ended up being super cool. It was this Black dance company that does some awesome choreo in lots of different styles."

"That sounds great! I'm glad you enjoyed it. I'm sure you must be thinking about what types of companies you're interested in when you're finished school."

It's nice there's no pressure from him about that. He's always just wanted me to do what makes me happy.

When I came home from the clinic the summer before ninth grade, my dad asked if I wanted to move to Tokyo with him or go to the academy in Alberta. I couldn't believe that staying with my mom wasn't even an option. Before I was sent away, I'd overheard her threatening to try and get full custody, but my dad told her he'd involve my doctors. She never pushed for custody at all after that. I guess maybe she consulted with a lawyer and didn't think it would go well for her if they ended up going to court. So all of our original plans for me to follow in her footsteps at NYCB never ended up happening.

But now there's this possible National School opportunity. Maybe my mom won't think of my ballet career as a failure anymore if I get in. That's a big if, though.

"Yeah . . . Definitely thinking about it with senior year coming up."

I gnaw my lip as a sharp pang of guilt pinches at me. If I do end up getting an audition, I'll have to figure out a way to tell my dad. I'm having trouble thinking of any possible way I could spin it so it doesn't seem like I've been going behind his back.

He pauses at my stilted response. "How have you been feeling lately?"

The way he asks feels as if he's trying to gauge my level of sanity, afraid I'll go off the deep end again.

"Okay." My voice sounds squeaky, and I wince.

"Are you sure?"

My head starts to pound. "Yeah."

"All right . . . Remember if you *do* want to talk to someone, I can always set that up if you feel comfortable."

I take a steadying breath, trying to psych myself up. I should just tell him. Deep down I know he's not judging me. He just wants me to be okay.

"Well, um, I actually made an appointment to see the school counsellor because this thing's been happening where I . . . I, like, float away from my body. It's like I'm outside myself. It's kind of scary."

"What do you mean 'float away from your body?' And how long has this been happening?"

I squeeze my eyes shut. "I don't know. It started right before I left school. Sorry I didn't say anything. I just . . . I didn't really know how to describe what was going on because it felt so weird."

He sighs sadly. "I know talking about your mental health has been difficult for you in the past, but I'm proud of you for reaching out to a counsellor at school, hon."

"Thanks," I mutter.

"Let me know how it goes. Love you."

"Okay, love you too."

After we hang up, I let out a long breath before slowly inhaling the scent of fresh fabric softener lingering in the air. I feel a little lighter now that I told him. I thought he'd make a bigger deal out of it, but honestly it wasn't too bad.

I can't even imagine having the same conversation with my mom. Talking to her again is one thing, but I can't say I'll ever really feel as comfortable with her as I do with my dad even if things continue going well with us. The guilt returns, but I force myself to shake it off as I grab the laundry basket and head back upstairs.

*
*

On Monday after school, I stop by Ollie's place. I've still been rehearsing a ton, so I didn't get a chance to see him at lunch earlier.

"Hey." He kisses me on his back porch before he takes hold of my hand and opens the back door.

His mom grins at us as we enter. "Aisha!" She walks over and gives me an unexpected hug.

"Uh, hi, Anissa. How are you?"

Ollie shoots me an apologetic look. "Mom, give her some space. We'll see you later—"

"Not so fast." She gives Ollie a stern look as she pulls away from me. "Why don't you two help me with dinner?"

"Uh, we have a test tomorrow," Ollie lies. "We have to study—"

"I just need help with the vegetables," she says, shoving a cutting board into his hands.

"Of course," I say, taking the board from Ollie before he can protest further. Even though the prospect of sitting down for dinner with Ollie's family makes panic immediately rush through me, I know I need to try and make a better impression. Anissa has always been nice to me, so this is the least I can do.

Ollie's mom puts him on veggie cutting duty while I'm tasked with working on the rice for the dolma. She checks on the lamb in the oven and then takes the wooden spoon from me, tasting a bit of rice from the pot.

She lets out a happy exclamation as she chews. "Great job! Do you do a lot of cooking?"

I shake my head. "I used to make jollof, this Ghanaian rice dish, with my dad."

"Used to? You don't anymore?"

I stiffen a little. "My dad works overseas now."

"Where does he work?"

Ollie shakes his head at his mom as he brings some cored sweet peppers over to us from the sink.

"What?" she asks, looking confused at his grim expression. "Is it so wrong I want to know about the girl you're seeing? You hardly tell me anything."

Ollie rolls his eyes.

"No, that's okay," I say quickly, my face warming. These are pretty standard questions. It's just weird because I haven't even told Ollie that much about my family. "He lives in Japan; he's a stockbroker."

"And your mom?" Anissa starts stuffing the rice into the peppers, and Ollie and I follow her lead.

"She's a corporate lawyer," I say.

Anissa lays a grape leaf flat on the cutting board and puts a dollop of rice in the center before she deftly rolls it up, her fingers flying. I watch her hands carefully as I grab a leaf.

"Oh," Anissa says after a moment of silence. "She must be at work a lot then."

"Uh, I guess." I keep my eyes on the task at hand, but I can feel Ollie next to me shooting his mom another look. I'm guessing he didn't tell her I'm staying at Neil's, and I'm definitely not about to offer up that information and bring on a whole other painful line of questioning.

"Okay, Mom." Ollie takes hold of my hand again. "Do you need any more help or . . . ?"

Anissa shakes her head. "I can get Sophie to help me finish up. Dinner should be ready in an hour or so," she calls out as he leads me out of the kitchen. "Thanks again!"

Ollie winces at me once we get to his room. "Sorry. I know you don't like talking about, um . . . your parents."

I shrug as I take a seat next to him on the couch.

He puts an arm around me and studies my face. "What's up?"

"I saw my mom," I blurt out.

He blinks at me. "You did? When?"

"The day after your birthday she invited me for coffee. And then last week she took me to see a ballet downtown."

"Oh." I know he's wondering why I'm only mentioning this now. "I thought you didn't get along with her?"

"It's not that. It's . . . My dad's the one who doesn't want me to see her. He'd be pissed if he found out," I mutter, looking away from him.

"Why doesn't he want you to see her?" he asks quietly.

I let out a sigh as I lean my head against his shoulder, avoiding his gaze.

It shouldn't be this difficult for me to talk about this. I know I can trust him, but that doesn't make it any easier to say the words.

"Basically, before I moved to Alberta, Neil and I were prepping for this really big ballet competition in New York where kids compete internationally for scholarships at top ballet schools. It was a really intensive process getting ready for it . . . and my dad thought my mom was pushing me too hard or whatever."

He tilts his head and looks at me carefully. "Pushing you how?"

"Our training was extremely demanding. And, um, my mom was just helping me stick with it, but my dad didn't get that."

He waits for me to continue, but I can't bring myself to mention the super strict meal plan Madame D. and my mom had me on and how upset my dad got about it. And there's no way in hell I'm telling him about what Neil did and what happened after. Hot, bitter anger rises within me before I choke it down. Professional ballet is all about sacrifices, and I've always been willing to make the hardest ones. No matter what.

Ollie doesn't respond, but he looks concerned. Thankfully, he doesn't ask me to explain further.

"Anyways, at the ballet she introduced me to this principal dancer who said she'd mention me to her old instructor at the National Ballet School. She said they're looking for, like, more diverse dancers, so if that works out—"

"Wait, you'd be leaving again?"

"I wouldn't have to move—the school's downtown."

"Oh." His voice drops. "That's cool."

Why does he sound so sad? I'd miss seeing him at school every day, but it wouldn't be that big of a deal, would it?

"Yeah, so if I get into the National School, after I graduate, I might be able to get an apprenticeship at the National Ballet of Canada. I didn't get into the apprenticeship program at my old school, so this would kinda be huge for me."

He plants a kiss on my temple. "I know you'll get in."

It's sweet that he sounds so sure, but being passed over for so many opportunities really makes me question myself sometimes.

"Thanks. So where are you applying next year?"

He shrugs. "This music engineering program downtown probably. But my dad is pretty set on thinking music is a waste of my time. Music engineering is definitely *not* the type of engineering program he wants me to apply for."

"You'll probably be too busy on a big tour to do a music engineering program."

He laughs. "Okay, sure."

"I'm not joking," I murmur as I climb into his lap and wrap my arms around his neck.

His arms circle my waist and he leans in, his lips colliding with mine.

A while later, I pull his hands away from my hips, interlocking my fingers with his. I tighten my grip when I realize he's shaking.

"Hey. You okay?"

Ollie nods, but he's breathing strangely.

"Do you want some water?"

He nods again, leaning away from me and rubbing his face.

I jump up and grab the glass of water sitting on his desk. When I get back to the couch, he looks worse, his breathing quick and shallow.

"What's wrong?"

"I can't really breathe," he barely gets out.

"What should I do?" I'm getting so freaked out my own hands start shaking, and I almost spill the water as I set the glass on the coffee table.

"Nothing." Ollie leans back and squeezes his eyes shut. "It's okay, I'll be—I should be fine in a sec."

There's a loud knock at his bedroom door, and we both jump.

"Dinner's ready!" Sophie calls out before her footsteps bound noisily down the stairs.

Ollie rubs his forehead and starts to get up. "We don't have to have dinner with them, but I can grab you something . . ."

I shake my head, swallowing my relief that I don't have to eat in front of everyone. I pull him back down beside me.

"I'm good. Are you sure you're okay?"

He closes his eyes and does that thing I've seen him do before where he breathes really slowly for a few minutes.

"Yeah." He opens his eyes but won't look at me.

I wait for him to glance my way, but he doesn't take his eyes off the coffee table.

I move my hand to his shoulder. "Hey . . . What was that?"

Ollie shrugs as he reaches for the water. "Panic attack."

"Okay . . ." He says it like it's something we've discussed, but it isn't. I know he has anxiety, but I had no clue it could get that bad.

My stomach starts to squeeze horribly. "Did I . . ."

"It's not you. You didn't do anything," he assures me.

My stomach refuses to unclench.

"We don't have to talk about it if you don't want to," I start slowly. "But am I the only one you've told about what happened to you?"

Ollie shakes his head, still avoiding my gaze as he puts the glass down.

"You're not the first person I've told," he mutters.

"Your family knows?"

"God, no," he says quickly, finally glancing at me. "Just my therapist. When . . . When I was in the hospital after I got beat up, that scared them enough. I can't imagine how much worse they'd feel if they knew about . . ."

He trails off, and it's quiet for a long moment. I try to swallow down the queasiness in my gut. I really wish I knew how to help.

"If you ever want to talk about it . . . I mean, with someone besides your therapist, just let me know," I say quietly.

Ollie nods mutely before gathering me in his arms. We stay like that for a long while.

A bit later, he walks me downstairs.

"Hi, Aisha." Ollie's dad smiles at me as he passes us on the stairs. "Have a good night."

I smile back. "Night, Mr. Cheriet."

"You're leaving already?" Anissa calls from the living room. "Come in here for a bit first."

Ollie groans quietly as he leads us into the living room. I haven't really been in here for more than a few minutes before. There are a few pieces of traditional Algerian art on the walls and beside the TV there's a big antique record player. Anissa and Sophie are seated on the large couch. Sophie's totally absorbed in her sketchbook.

Anissa eyes Ollie. "Come sit down."

He plops down beside her. "What, Mom?"

"Why didn't you two come down for dinner earlier?"

I cringe and quickly turn away, focusing on the large collection of albums next to the turntable.

"I told you, we have our History test tomorrow," Ollie says without hesitation, and I let out my breath.

I examine the albums' sleeves. They all look well-worn, lots of older rock and folk, some adorned with text in French, Arabic, and some other languages I'm not familiar with.

There's a folk song playing on the record player—the singer's voice is incredibly warm and delicate. I pick up the empty sleeve and squint at it for a moment.

"Anissa, is this you? Your voice is so gorgeous."

She waves a hand dismissively and chuckles. "I recorded that ages ago before Sophie and Olia were born."

"That's so cool," I say. "Ollie didn't tell me you sing."

"I don't really. It's nothing special."

"What do you mean? You have a really great voice, Mom," Ollie says.

"Aw, sweetie." Anissa pulls him into a crushing hug.

"Ugh, stop," he complains but doesn't pull away from her.

Sophie finally looks up from her sketchbook and laughs a little. "Remember when we used to sing this together all the time when we were little?"

Grinning, Anissa starts singing along to the record. She gives Ollie a pointed look, and he rolls his eyes but starts to sing along. Their voices are so harmoniously tranquil that all the tension left inside me begins to settle.

Sophie laughs again and starts singing, too, before she waves me over to the couch. I sit between her and Ollie. Smiling at me, Sophie squeezes my shoulder for a moment before she flips her sketchbook open again.

I lean in and see she's drawing her mom and Ollie on the other end of the couch. When I glance at him, he's nodding along to something his mom is telling him in a mix of Arabic and French.

"Sophie?"

She looks up at me again. "Yeah?"

I lower my voice to a whisper. "Do you think I could see that drawing? You know, the one you did of me on the roof?"

She scrunches up her nose for a second and then grins again. "Okay, fine, sure."

I watch her flip through her sketchbook. Pages whizz by featuring self-portraits, some more of her family, some of her friends I recognize from school. And then toward the end there are quite a few drawings of Neil. Like, a lot of Neil.

Sophie realizes I'm looking over her shoulder and reddens. "Don't tell him," she murmurs.

I gawk at her for a second. Okay, so she *does* like Neil. Why doesn't she want me to say anything? I'm pretty sure he likes her too. Maybe because he and Ollie are friends? I wonder if Ollie told her anything about what happened with Neil on his birthday.

"I won't tell," I assure her. Even if Neil and I were on speaking terms, I wouldn't blow her cover like that.

She looks me over carefully before she nods and rips out a page. "Thanks. Here, you can keep it."

The drawing's not just of me—Ollie's in it too. She's captured me shooting him a blatantly smitten look while he was laughing at something Sophie said.

"What's that?" Ollie asks, having escaped his mom's grasp. He leans over and takes the drawing from me before I can object.

He doesn't say anything, just slowly breaks into a grin, and I can't help grinning back. He hands the drawing back to me and puts an arm around my shoulders.

I close my eyes as I relax against him. I try my best to memorize this feeling. What it's like being part of a functional family.

It used to be easier to stop myself from thinking about not having that. But that was back when Neil and I were okay. I could kind of forget sometimes how much I ached for my dad to be here instead of halfway across the world. And even though my mom is here, there's always going to be distance between us. Even on her best days, she's always so formal and closed off.

Now that everything's gone to shit with Neil, sometimes the loneliness is so suffocating it's like it's swallowing me whole.

I'd give everything to go back to how things were before my parents divorced, even just for a day. Before they started fighting about money and everything I ate. Before dance was work. Back when dancing was just what I loved doing most in the enchanted little realm of our backyard.

"You okay?" Ollie breathes near my ear, and I snap back into the living room.

Nodding, I squeeze his hand, not opening my misting eyes.

He squeezes back, and I try my best to focus on the pure warmth of this moment again, savoring every second before I'm all alone at Neil's again.

21

After a long run the next morning, I head over to school early. It's always a little eerie when the halls are abandoned. The staircase to the studio is mostly dark as the sun meanders its way upward, lighting the purple sky in a pink and orange haze.

I go through my solo a few times. Ever since the Pointe Noire trip, I've been playing around with adding some modern elements like Madame A. suggested. I feel like I'm getting somewhere with it, letting my body breathe into small moments where new additions feel natural. The original choreo is grounded in staccato, wind-up-doll-inspired movements, and I've sprinkled in some joint-locking isolations that exaggerate the mechanical feel of the piece. I'm excited that I've had a breakthrough with the solo, but now I have to up my practice schedule to make sure I have all of these new steps down.

Twirling around the studio, I let my body sway like my limbs are attached to invisible strings. The push and pull of my movements mirrors how torn I feel between exploring these new moves and staying in my comfort zone. How torn I feel between wanting to be accepted in traditional ballet and my curiosity about spaces like Pointe Noire.

The door to the studio opens, and I stop abruptly as Neil walks in.

My brow scrunches up. "What're you doing here so early?"

He rubs at his eyes as he shuffles toward me. "Looking for you. The showcase is coming up. We really need to get our piece worked out."

"All right." I do want to keep at it with my solo, but since he made the time to show up, I can take a little break to work on our modern piece. I'm just glad he's decided not to give up on this either. "Let's get to it then."

The beginning of the piece goes a bit smoother than last week, but the ending is still completely off. When I end facing away from him, he improvises by taking my shoulders and turning me back toward him. He's staring me square in the face, his eyes full of something desperate and pleading.

I wrench myself away from him. "Look, I already told you. I think we should end it facing apart," I croak out, staring at the floor.

When I look up, my mouth falls open. Instead of being closed off again, his eyes are tearing up. "What's wrong?"

He wipes at them violently before taking a hard seat on the floor, burying his face in his hands.

I drop beside him and put a hesitant hand on his shoulder.

"You're never going to forgive me, are you?" he grinds out.

"Neil . . . I just want you to admit you have a problem and try not to drink. Did you go to your counselling appointment?"

"Yeah. I went."

I let out a breath. "Okay. That's great, I'm glad you did." I wish he'd say something about how it went. Mine's at lunch today, and I'm still super nervous.

"I didn't mean forgiving me about drinking at the party," he mutters.

I blink at him. "What did you mean then?"

He looks up at that, his eyes dark. "You know. About telling your dad when you were sick."

I flinch, retracting my hand from his shoulder as bitterness starts to bubble up inside me. "It doesn't matter anymore. That was years ago."

"It does matter," he snaps. "You're always going to hate me for it."

"Well, you ruined everything!" I explode at him. "If you kept your mouth shut, I wouldn't have had to leave! We could have won at YAPG and gotten into SAB together."

"If I kept my mouth shut, you'd be dead," he shoots back.

"What are you even talking about?!" I scream at him. "You're being so ridiculous! Things were never that bad."

Caroline's gross comment about how I used to look like a UNICEF kid pops into my head, but I bury it quickly.

"It *was* that bad," he says, his voice dropping to a raw whisper. "You still don't get it, do you? How messed up it was what you were doing. What you're *still* doing."

Shit. My heart slams painfully against my ribs. God, why did he have to say it out loud? It's bad enough feeling his eyes on me whenever we cross paths in the kitchen. Giving me dark looks when he sees me leave food on my plate.

I lean away from him, squinting at the sun making its way above the golden yellow leaves of the trees lining the back field. "I'm not doing anything. I'm totally fine."

"You're losing weight again."

My eyes snap back to him. "How would you know?"

"Maybe lifting you in rehearsals all the time? Ish . . . Please don't do this."

I shake my head, looking at the floor. "You know I've been practicing a ton. I'm—"

"Totally fine. Right." Neil's face hardens before he yanks his bag off the floor and stalks off, slamming the door behind him. Looking at my hands, I become aware that I'm shaking.

"Fuck!" I yell out before kicking my gym bag. Crouching down, I struggle to swallow my sobs. I strangle down all my horrific thoughts until they go limp and subside.

After a moment, I get to my feet again. When I start moving, I shut everything out, not letting myself think about anything except for perfecting my routine.

＊

At lunch, Ollie finds me at my locker.

His eyes brighten when I don't head toward the studio like I usually do. "You're eating with us today?"

I shake my head. "I have my appointment at the counsellor's office. Do you wanna . . . ?"

"Yeah, I'll head over with you," he says, taking my hand and running his thumb over mine.

"Thanks. So, I talked to Neil. He said he actually went to his appointment."

"He did? That's cool."

"I know. I wasn't sure if he would." I try in vain to push the rest of my conversation with Neil out of my mind. I do my best to focus on the warmth of Ollie's hand in mine.

"Did he say how it went?"

"Not really."

"But you guys are talking again?"

I shake my head, avoiding his gaze as we step into the office.

"Oh. Is something else still up with you guys then?"

We sit down, and I stare at the flyers on the messy bulletin board in front of us. I shrug even as my heart starts to palpitate.

"Have you been talking to him at all?" I wonder if Neil would tell Ollie about his suspicions about me.

"Nope, haven't really seen him," he says, and I nod, exhaling.

We're quiet for a little bit.

When I finally speak again, my tongue feels oddly thick. "So, um, I've actually, you know, seen someone before, and it pretty much sucked ass," I mutter, unable to look at him. I'm too embarrassed to mention it was at that dumb clinic. "It feels weird telling a stranger about how screwed up I am."

"You're not." He bumps his leg against mine. "Once you get to know them, it doesn't feel as weird."

The receptionist looks over at us.

I stand up and head toward the door before I look back at Ollie. "Thanks. See you later."

"Okay, good luck." He nods encouragingly.

The counsellor, Ms. Vacik, is a small woman who looks like she has an Eastern European background. Her slight accent confirms it.

"Aisha Bimi?" She butchers my last name.

I sit across from her in the tiny, blank-walled, windowless room. She's looking down at some forms. "How old are you?"

"Sixteen."

She doesn't look up. "Do you do drugs?"

I blink. "What?"

"Do you do drugs?"

"Nope."

Finally, she lifts her head and focuses on me. "That includes cannabis." She pauses like she expects me to change my answer.

I glare at her. I don't have to wonder why, without knowing me at all, she's instantly suspicious of me partaking in the Devil's lettuce. "I don't do drugs."

"Do you drink?"

"No."

She looks back down at her sheet. "Are you sexually active?"

How is this any of her damn business? Shaking my head, I stare at the clock on the wall behind her. In a flash, I'm staring down at myself sitting in the chair. A moment later, I'm back in my body again.

"No."

"Hmm." She makes more notes. "Have you ever been pregnant?"

I barely manage not to roll my eyes. "I just said I'm not sexually active."

"That doesn't mean you've never been in the past."

"Well, I've never been pregnant." Annoyance comes through in my voice. "Also don't have any children, FYI."

"I have to ask these questions to start your file."

I take a slow breath and try to relax.

Ms. Vacik sighs audibly. "What seems to be the problem?"

Resisting the urge to narrow my eyes, I don't say anything. This really doesn't seem like a good career choice for her.

Folding her hands together on her desk, she just waits. I'm the one who came here, so I guess I have to say something if I want to function like a normal human being again.

I make my mouth move as I look back up at the clock. "Um . . . This thing's been happening lately where it feels like I completely leave my body. And then sometimes I have these really vivid memories I get trapped in."

"Hmm," she says as she writes this all down. "Do you feel like you lose time when that happens?"

"Sometimes, yeah."

"I can't diagnose you, but the symptoms you've described sound a lot like depersonalization, which is a kind of dissociative disorder."

I finally look at her again. "So what can I do to, like, stop it?"

"It's usually caused by trauma, so moving through it with talk therapy often helps."

"Can you just give me something to make it stop?" As much fun as talking to this woman again sounds, I think I'll have to pass.

"I don't prescribe medication. Besides that, talk therapy is still necessary. Can you tell me about those memories you felt trapped in? What were they about?"

I shrug, focusing on my nails.

"Well. We can get more into that next time. Make an appointment at reception."

I stand quickly. She must know there's no way in hell I'll be coming back here.

My eyes soften when I find Ollie still in the reception area with his earphones in. "Oll, you didn't have to wait for me."

"It's cool," he says, getting up. "How did it go?"

I rub a hand over my face as we exit the office. "Not great."

Ollie frowns. "What happened?"

"She was kind of rude," I say, shrugging. "Like, she wasn't that sympathetic or whatever."

He takes my hand again, weaving his fingers through mine. "That sucks, Aisha. Maybe it'll be better next time—"

"I'm not subjecting myself to that again," I mutter.

"Okay . . . Would you think about trying a therapist outside of school then?"

I close my eyes for a brief second. Every single time I've talked to a so-called professional, it's pretty much been a nightmare. I guess I have to keep trying, though.

"Yeah. My dad said he could help me out with that." As annoying as this whole thing is, I do need to find a way to stop leaving my body at the worst times, especially right after I dance. Hopefully, my dad can help me find someone not awful.

*
*

When I get home from a tense rehearsal, my mom calls to tell me she scored some last-minute tickets to the *Billy Elliot* musical tonight. I'm super excited for the opportunity to see it, so I push away the guilt about seeing her behind my dad's back yet again.

It takes me some time to figure out what to put on. Wearing the same blue dress again would be a bit weird, but I don't really have much else that's formal. I settle on some dark pants and a white collared shirt that I wore as a jazz routine costume a few years ago.

My mom grins when she sees me approaching her in front of the theater.

"Wow, I remember getting you that outfit. I can't believe you still fit into it."

A sick mix of nausea and elation flips over in my stomach. Maybe I have actually lost some weight? Weighing myself can make me spiral, so I try to avoid it. I thought Neil was being dramatic since my hips and thighs still look as gargantuan as ever. "Uh, yeah. Thanks for inviting me. I'm so excited."

"I know you used to love the movie," she says.

The elation takes over—I'm glad she remembered that.

Neil used to hate getting teased about being a boy in ballet when we were little, but after we first saw the movie, he didn't let it get to him anymore. It feels so wrong to be here without him. I didn't even tell him I was coming here tonight.

As amazing as the show is, I can't manage to fully enjoy it the way I would have if Neil was here with us. Afterward, my mom insists on going out for dinner, even though I tell her I already ate.

"I have some news," she says after we order. "Victoria's old instructor from the National School wants to come see you perform at your showcase."

"Oh my God!" I almost choke on my water. "Really?"

She nods, grinning again.

I can't contain my own smile. I can't believe it's really happening, that I finally have a chance to get my ballet career back on track. "Wow, thanks so much for talking to Victoria, Mom."

"No problem." Her face sobers a bit. "I did want to ask you something, though."

I stop pushing around the risotto on my plate. "Yeah?"

"If you feel comfortable, I was hoping you'd consider moving back in."

Looking down, I stare unseeingly at my plate. "Uh . . ."

I have no idea what to say. My last memories of living at home are so awful that it makes it hard to go back there, even just for Christmas. It feels like some type of sick museum of all my broken childhood dreams.

On the other hand, having a home again—even if it is a broken one—does sound tempting. Things are so terrible between Neil and me that it's been beyond grating to be around each other practically 24/7.

"Take your time thinking about it," she says quickly. "I just wanted you to know I'd really like you back home."

"Okay," I say, still unable to meet her eyes. I can't imagine living at my old house without my dad there. And I one-hundred-percent know he'll freak if I ask him about this. But I have to talk to him now—I can't keep this from him anymore. "I'll let you know."

When my mom and I finish dinner, she glances at my mostly untouched plate but doesn't say anything about it. She offers to drive me to Neil's, but I don't take her up on it.

Ollie said he was working tonight, and the record store is only a few blocks away. Zipping my jacket up as high as possible against the harsh wind, I tuck my chin into my collar.

I call my dad on the walk over, knowing I'll just obsess until I get it over with.

"Hey, honey," he says when he answers. "Good to hear from you. How did your counselling appointment go?"

I rub hard at my forehead. "It wasn't great. The counsellor kinda . . . made me uncomfortable. Can you still help me find someone else?"

"I'm sorry it didn't go well. For sure, we'll find you someone you like."

"Thanks." I squeeze my eyes shut for a moment, swearing silently. I have no clue how to start this conversation. "So, um, there's something else I need to talk to you about."

"Yes?"

"Well, first off, I have some good news. One of the instructors at the National Ballet School is coming to check me out at my school's showcase."

"That's amazing, Aisha! How did that happen? Did they contact you through your school?"

I navigate my way through the crowds on the sidewalk and wince. "Please don't get mad . . . It was through Mom, actually."

Dad never yells at me, but if he did, I know he'd be yelling right now. "Aisha . . ." He takes a deep breath before he continues. "I'm really disappointed you spoke with your mother without telling me."

I grimace. "I'm really sorry, but honestly, it wasn't a big deal. I know you were worried before, but it's different now. I promise, she's not as uptight. I was thinking of maybe, um, moving back in with her—"

"Absolutely not," he says with finality.

"But—"

"Aisha. That's not happening," he says, his voice low. "Even if it seems like she's changed, trust me. She hasn't."

Annoyance flares up inside me. I can't believe he's refusing to even consider it.

"Well, isn't it my decision? I'm basically an adult. I know you'll never see her any differently, but I think she's really trying to help me get where I want to go with my ballet career."

"I'm not worried about your career, Aisha. I'm worried about you.

This isn't a good idea."

"It would be better than staying at Neil's." I squeeze my eyes shut and swear internally after the words slip out of my mouth.

"Is something up with you two?"

At least Neil hasn't already gone running to tell my dad again. The thought of that happening again makes me freeze, my blood instantly chilling in my veins.

I bite my tongue for a minute then force the words out. "Neil's been drinking. And it's kind of bad sometimes. I'm pretty worried about him."

I know Neil will be pissed at me for telling on him, but it's not the same as what he did.

Isn't it, though?

I shake my head against the intrusive thought. It isn't the same. *I* have everything under control. He doesn't, and I obviously have no idea how to get through to him anymore.

"He's been drinking? What about you, have you been—"

"No, he has, like, a problem. I got him to see the school counsellor, too, but I don't know if that helped."

"Does his dad know about this?"

"Yeah. He isn't really doing anything about it, though. He said something messed up about Neil being weak and comparing him to his mom."

My stomach revolts, thinking about that night in his room after the party. Neil probably doesn't even remember what he said about his mom. It terrifies me to think about what he was implying, considering that him landing in the hospital might not have been a total accident.

"Jesus," Dad mutters. "I'll talk to his dad."

"You know how old school Mr. Roi is. I don't think he's gonna wanna hear it."

My dad just sighs.

"But yeah, considering everything . . . I think moving in with Mom might be a good idea. I promise, I'll keep doing my best to manage my mental health and everything," I say, my nearly empty stomach rebelling against me.

I reach Ollie's work and lean against the barren venue storefront.

My dad heaves out another sigh. "Honey, I gotta go take care of some work stuff, but I'll call you back in a bit so we can talk more about this. Love you."

For a fleeting moment, I consider asking him if he can make it to the showcase next week. I don't want to make him feel bad, though, since he already told me he can't get work off until the holidays. "You too."

I hang up and head down the steps to the record store. Ben and Ollie are the only ones there.

Ollie shoots me a stunning grin as he walks out from behind the front counter. "Hey. What're you doing here?"

"Just thought I'd surprise you," I say, managing a weak smile. "I saw a show with my mom earlier."

His smile starts to fade. He can tell something is up.

"You can take off early if you want," Ben says.

"You sure?"

"Yep, I'll close up."

"Thanks, man." Ollie grabs his coat and backpack from behind the counter.

He slides an arm around me when we get outside. We huddle

together against the wind. "Everything go okay with your mom tonight?"

"Yeah. She said for sure that instructor is coming to the showcase."

"That's great," he says slowly. "What's going on with you then?"

"She asked me about moving back in with her. I just called my dad about it, and he wasn't thrilled."

He raises his eyebrows. "Wait, you wanna move in with her?"

"I don't know." I drop my shoulders, realizing they're up around my ears. "It's weird to think about living there again. But you know how things are with Neil right now. Anyway, I did ask my dad about finding a therapist, and he said he'd help me get one."

He plants his lips briefly on top of my head, and I look up at him to find him smiling a bit now.

"Really glad to hear that. Did you wanna grab some food before we head home?" he asks as we reach the subway station entrance.

My stomach growls at the mention of food, but luckily, it's too noisy outside for him to hear it. "I just had dinner with my mom. Let's just go."

On the train, Ollie stares at me. Like a lot. Not at my outfit or anything, just at my face, which I haven't even done anything to.

I laugh. "Uh, is there something on my face?"

He shakes his head, snapping out of it. "Sorry. It's just . . . Are you okay?"

I close my eyes and lean my head against his shoulder. "Yeah. Sorry if I've been a bummer lately. You know I just have a lot going on right now."

"I know." I can feel his gaze firmly on me again. "But . . ."

My eyes snap open. "What is it?"

Did Neil say something to him? Or maybe he heard the rumor Caroline's been spreading about me being bulimic. My pulse starts to zoom, making me lightheaded.

He's really looking at me strangely now, his eyes drilling into me like he's trying to steal my thoughts from my brain.

"I don't know. Nothing," he finally says, exhaling as he leans forward, resting his head against mine.

I wrap my arms around him, barely containing my relief. "I'm okay. Thanks for being here."

He kisses me then, distracting me from all the unspeakable shame that's been slowly going bad inside me.

22

The morning of the winter showcase, Ollie meets me at my locker.

"Hey." After he hugs me, he hands over a paper bag. "It's blueberry—sorry they didn't have any carrot."

I manage to contain a grimace as I stick it in my bag. "Thanks."

He raises his eyebrows. "Did you already have breakfast?"

"Yeah, I had some eggs after my run this morning." It's technically true. I picked a little at the eggs Neil made before we headed to school for our dress rehearsal first thing, ignoring his annoyed looks. "I'll eat it later."

He shakes his head as we head toward the stairwell. "Can we talk for a sec?"

My pulse starts to jackhammer. "Uh, sure."

He guides me by the arm down the stairs and out the back doors. Leaning against the school's faded red brick wall, he reaches for me, wrapping his arms around my waist.

"How're you feeling about tonight?"

My shoulders unclench. This isn't about how little I've been eating, thank God.

"Pretty stressed, honestly." I push out a short laugh as my arms circle his shoulders. "This is it, you know? The National School instructor will be at the showcase and everything."

"Are you sure you're okay to do this?"

I nod. "Yeah, I think I've got it," I say with way more confidence than I actually feel. If I think too much about tonight, I might psych myself out of it.

"It's just, after your last performance . . . I'm worried about you dissociating like that again."

I avoid his gaze as my breath starts to shorten. I know he just wants to make sure I'm going to be okay, but talking about this isn't really helping me relax.

Making myself meet his gaze again, I search his eyes. "You'll be there tonight, right?"

He softly brushes his thumb over my temple and trails it down to my chin, making me shiver. "Of course I will."

"Then I'll be okay," I assure him, smiling a little.

The way he looks at me after I say it makes my heart quicken to an absolutely dizzying pace. I've never even imagined feeling this way about anyone. It's so incredibly bizarre that I'm pretty sure he feels whatever this is too.

His arms tighten around me, and I bury my face in his shoulder, trying to block out how truly petrified I am about tonight. Between handling my solo, my routine with Neil, and my mom attending with the National School instructor, I have no idea how I'm going to keep it together later.

*

I almost throw up on the spot when I get backstage after school. The auditorium is just as packed as for the fall showcase. I catch sight of my mom in the fifth row, beside a man with dark hair who must be from the National School. The instructor looks away from her, focusing right on me, and I snap the curtain closed, my heart racing.

"Aisha." I hear Hannah right behind me, her voice light and bubbly. "There's someone here to see you."

I turn, and my mouth drops open.

"Dad!" Squealing, I jump into his arms, and he laughs his deep laugh that travels right through me. "What are you doing here?"

"Heard you have a big night tonight," he says, grinning his megawatt grin as I let go of him. "Didn't want to miss it."

"I'm so glad you're here. You got work off?"

"Actually, I'm switching back to the Toronto office," he says. "Money isn't as tight as it was when I had to transfer to Tokyo. I can afford the pay cut. I wanted to surprise you."

I shake my head, unable to even begin to process.

"For how long?" I ask, careful to keep my voice neutral.

He tilts his head when I don't sound excited. "I mean permanently, hon."

"Really?" I ask, my voice cracking.

He nods, and I throw my arms around him again. Blinking hard, I manage to stave off the tears forming behind my eyes.

"I have something for you," he says, handing me a plain black shopping bag.

I give him a puzzled look as I reach beneath the tissue paper and pull out a shoe box.

When I open it, I'm unable to keep my eyes from welling over. It's a pair of glossy satin pointe shoes that match my skin tone.

I've always had to cake my shoes in foundation. A few companies started making shoes for dancers of color in different shades a couple of years ago, but they were way too expensive to ask my dad to pay for when I could just get pink ones and cheap makeup.

"They're gorgeous," I breathe out. "Thank you."

"No problem, sweetie. I'd better grab a seat—I'll see you out there."

I set to work breaking in and quickly sewing the new shoes. After I get them on, I look down at myself in my blush-tinted *Coppélia* doll costume. It reminds me of the sparkling, delicately jewelled fairy costumes I loved spinning around in when I was little. The shoes perfectly complete the look, elongating the lines of my legs, making my thighs look less chunky.

Madame A. cues me with a reassuring grin, and I run out to center stage.

My eyes immediately go to Ollie sitting in the third row. He breaks into that unbearable smile and my brain ceases to function like it always does.

"*You look beautiful,*" he mouths.

My breath halts altogether for a long moment. I can't stop thinking about how brave Ollie is with his performances, going to places that are so viscerally honest. Hopefully, I can channel a little bit of that tonight.

When my music starts, I immediately fall into the clockwork ticking rhythm as I do a few *chassés* and *tendus*, keeping my posture poised and elegant. As I begin a series of pirouettes, I spin faster and faster until the room is nothing but a smear of lights and colors.

I fall into the push-and-pull sensation of my routine, expressing all my fears and swirling questions about what lies ahead for me in my dance career. If I'll even have one. The feeling transitions into the back-and-forth tug between what my parents want for me. I drop into all the times before their divorce when it felt like I was about to be torn apart.

I told my dad I thought my mom had changed. But what if I'm so desperate for some type of normalcy with her that I made myself believe that things are different now. Maybe . . . Maybe I've been pushing down just how unworthy I feel around her sometimes.

Losing my point of focus, for a moment I think I'm going to be sick again. Breathing through it, I keep moving, not skipping a beat. My face stays placid even as my brain beats against my skull, shaking the whole auditorium.

When the routine ends, I come to a stop, my chest heaving as the crowd claps. Squinting at the pain behind my eyes, I can't make out anyone's face under all the lights. I head backstage and find Neil there waiting for me.

"I just saw your dad," he says instead of congratulating me on my performance. From his stony face, I'm guessing my dad must have told Mr. Roi that Neil's still been drinking.

"Not now." I walk past him, peeling off my tutu as I go. "Let's just get this over with."

Neither of us say another word after I change into my modern costume and we get some last-minute practice in. Like the last few days, we go through it in total silence, not fully moving into the emotionally fraught place we need to for our performance. But it's now or never. I have to push myself to the absolute limit of what I can stand.

What Ollie said earlier echoes in my brain. *If I do totally lose it afterwards . . . at least I won't be alone.*

Blocking out all the noise around us, I focus only on our movements, making sure we mirror each other perfectly.

Before I know it, we're up.

"You ready?" Neil walks out onstage, glancing back at me still in the wings.

Not even close. I force my feet forward and take my first position next to him. My hands start shaking, and I clench and flex them a few times, focusing on steadying my breath.

The music starts, and I make my brain turn off. Neil's eyes are dark as he executes a sharp-angled back bend, moving into a forceful roll at the exact same time as me. I realize he was saving something unnameable that he's putting into this, just for this moment. Going there with him, I let go of all my pretence and reservations. Hannah's voice plays in my brain, telling me to take that leap, revealing all that's inside me.

We take the piece somewhere I didn't know it could go, our emotions blending until I don't know where he ends and I begin. Our limbs twine together as if we're magnetically connected. Everything I've had trouble gleaning from his performance becomes crystal clear. No matter how angry we are, it doesn't change the fact that we'll always be a part of each other, bonded in a way that's stronger than blood.

Neil hoists me into an overhead lift, and I stare up at the stage lights. When he sets me back down, I slip and lose my footing.

Shit. Shit. Shit.

I can't believe that just happened. That I fucked everything up. I want to die. It's hardly a beat before I'm moving again, but it feels like forever. When my gaze shoots to my mom, her brow is tightly knotted, her mouth downturned.

Damn it, I *knew* I was going to let her down. I want to disappear on the spot, but I have to keep going.

I turn away from Neil toward the end of the routine, and when he spins me back around to face him, I don't pull away like in rehearsal. I meet his urgent gaze head on. Now that I've stopped avoiding it, I can see perfectly clear in his eyes that he's felt just as helpless about me not eating as I've felt about his drinking. There's no way for me to keep denying it now, keep acting like it's different.

I finally release my grip on my buried resentment toward him, and my eyes start to water in relief. I find myself nodding at him, and he lets out a breath when he realizes what I'm trying to say. That I get why he's upset and I know what I've been doing isn't okay.

It was so awful when he told my dad and we were separated. But I have to let that go if I want things to ever be okay between us again. From his face, I think he might forgive me for telling my dad about his drinking too. He gathers me in a tight hug as the music fades out and the crowd explodes in noise.

I pull away when I feel my whole body begin to shake. After taking our bow, we head off to the wings.

"Sorry about the lift. You okay?" His voice sounds like he's across the room, even though he's right next to me. My gaze moves back up to the lights of their own volition. They tremble wildly before they all go out at once, enveloping me in complete darkness.

23

When I wake up, my head pulses with a sharp, stabbing pain. I squint against the fluorescent lights as the room comes into focus.

My dad is sitting by the hospital bed I'm lying in. He looks horrible. I know I must have really scared him.

"Do you remember what happened?" he asks.

I start to rub my temple but stop and hiss when the stinging pain gets even worse.

My brain brings up half-formed memories of my head slamming against the backstage floor, of my dad yelling at my mom, blaming her and demanding that she leave. When I came to, all I could do was retch while I tried not to blubber and scream, the pain was so breathtaking.

I hate that my unconscious hasn't swallowed the hot tears of shame that formed in my eyes when I opened them and discovered Neil calling 911 and Ollie lying next to me, squeezing my hand, looking as vacant as when I first met him at the hospital.

"I remember." Picking at my nails, I stare down at my sad, powder-blue hospital gown.

"Neil told me you haven't been eating enough again."

I hang my head, unable to face him.

After laying everything out in the open during our performance and then terrifying everyone like that, I know this is over. I have to stop doing this to myself.

Right then, a doctor walks in and glances at his chart. "Okay, kiddo, how are we doing?"

He shines a tiny light in my eyes before I can say anything. He asks me to follow it.

"Good. Now let's look at that cut."

He pulls off a bandage on my right temple, and I wince at the acidic jolt of pain. "You're lucky—in a few ways, actually. It's great that you don't need stitches. And if you hit your head in a slightly different spot . . . we might not be here talking right now."

Shivering, I picture how awful it would have been for everyone if I hadn't woken up. All of the air leaves my lungs at once. *God, I'm such an idiot for thinking I had a handle on everything.*

"Thankfully you only have a moderate concussion," he continues. "You'll need to rest, take a bit of time off from school. And cool it on physical activity for a few weeks."

I nod, looking at my hands. I'm too choked up to respond.

The doctor gives me a sober look. "We've ruled out most of the possible causes for fainting, but a few of your test results are concerning. Have you been skipping any meals lately?"

All I can do is nod again, biting the inside of my cheek.

"Have you been doing that regularly?" He looks down at his

clipboard. "Your file says you were admitted to an eating disorders clinic a few years ago, but I'm not seeing any updates since then."

I freeze, unable to stop the tears from running down my face before I burst into silent sobs. My dad reaches out and wraps his arms around me. "Can you give us a moment?"

"I'll be back after I finish my rounds," the doctor says before he exits the room.

"Please don't send me away again," I sob into his shoulder. "I don't want to go to another clinic . . . Please don't—"

"Aisha, I'm not going to send you away."

"You promise?" I ask as I pull away from him.

Dad nods. "I'm so proud of you that you're willing to try therapy. I think that's a really good idea for you—not just for your dissociation, but to deal with your eating issues."

Nodding, I close my eyes as I let out a wavering breath.

He plants a kiss on my forehead.

"I'm so glad you're okay. I love you."

My eyes are so soaked with tears that I give up on wiping them dry. My dad hands me the tissue box on the table and I blow my nose.

"Love you too. Um, where's . . ." I want to ask where my mom is, but I'm afraid to bring her up. I guess she knew my dad would take care of me, so she didn't come along to the hospital after he yelled at her to leave the showcase. She must have been so embarrassed if the National School instructor was still around while my dad freaked out on her. "Are Neil and Ollie here?"

"Neil didn't come along," he says, frowning.

Why didn't he want to come? Despite what happened during our performance, I guess he's still mad at me after all.

"And your boyfriend you've never told me about? I sent him home."

"Oh." My face begins to boil as my dad stares me down. "Sorry I didn't mention him. It's just, uh, new."

Dad shakes his head. "Uh-huh. Well, they were both really worried. You might want to check in with them. I'm gonna grab a coffee and see if I can snag you something to eat from the cafeteria, okay?"

After he leaves, I reach for my phone on the bedside table. I have about twenty missed calls from Ollie, so I give him a call back.

"Thank God. You scared the shit out of me." His voice is so hoarse he sounds like a different person. "Are you okay?"

"I'm okay," I breathe. My shame feels like it's about to crush me, compacting me against the dirty white linoleum.

"Are you sure? You hit your head so hard—"

"I have a concussion, but it's not too severe."

"Your dad asked me if I'd seen you skipping meals. I forget to eat sometimes when I'm stressed too but I didn't realize you were doing it on purpose. I mean, how could you think that you weren't thin enough—" He cuts himself off. "I'm sorry, that was a really stupid thing to say. I didn't mean that."

"It's not just about my weight . . ." I trail off, too choked up to continue.

"Is it about feeling in control?" His voice is a gentle murmur.

"Yeah," I mutter as I think about how overwhelming everything has been lately. With showcase rehearsals, Neil, everything with my mom, and the horrible girls in my Ballet class, it felt like what I ate— or didn't eat—was the only aspect of my life I truly had control over. "I just kept telling myself I was okay. I convinced myself I was."

"Sometimes it's hard to know when you're lying to yourself. I get it."

I let out a sigh. It's kind of ridiculous how many things I've been lying to myself about. Forcing myself not to think about. I'm not sure how to even start unpacking all of it.

"You were amazing tonight, by the way," he says quietly. "I'm really proud of you."

"Thanks." I wish I could tell him that I wouldn't have had the courage to be so open with my feelings onstage if it weren't for him, but it feels too embarrassing to say out loud.

I look up as my dad walks back in.

"I gotta go now," I say quickly.

"Call me tomorrow?"

"I'll call you. I—" I stop short just before the words fall out of my mouth. My heartbeat thunders in my ears. I'm utterly unable to comprehend what I almost said. "Uh, bye."

When I hang up, a voicemail pops up from Mom. I dismiss it, trying my best not to think about the potentially life-changing opportunity I just royally screwed up. She's probably beyond pissed.

My dad comes over and sets a sad little turkey sandwich on the bedside table. "This is all I could scrounge up."

"Thanks." I make myself take a bite.

"I ran into that doctor again," he says as he sits beside me. "He told me about an eating disorders therapy group."

I nod but say nothing, chewing the bland meat and stale bread. At the clinic, they had a group therapy thing, but I refused to speak the whole week I was there. I felt like I didn't really belong in that place, like I didn't have a problem. I know I'll have to actually try this time, if I want to get better.

He hugs me again, and I close my eyes, too tired to even cry anymore.

*

My dad is Airbnb-ing a cozy little condo that isn't too far from my school while he looks for a permanent place for us. It's weird having my own room with a bed after being so used to sleeping on Neil's couch.

I picked up my stuff from Neil's place the morning after the hospital, but he was at school. It's four days later, and he still hasn't called or texted me. I haven't tried him at all, scared he won't respond. I really thought he forgave me during our performance . . . but I guess it's not going to be that easy for him to completely get over what happened.

My mom's been calling me a few times a day, but I haven't picked up or listened to any of her messages yet. I don't know what I even would say to her. I can't stop thinking about her face after I stumbled.

Now that I have lots of time to sit around and think, it's becoming more and more clear to me that obsessing about being a failure in my mom's eyes is pretty messed up when I should be focused on getting better. I know Mom does care about me, but I can't help thinking about the fact that Dad never makes me feel the way that she does. I've always known that how I'm feeling matters more to him than anything else.

I'm finally feeling some of the anger that he's had for her so long. It rumbles uncomfortably in my core, making me queasy. I'm not sure I want to entirely stop seeing her. But I don't know how to move forward with our relationship either.

It's just after dinner and I'm lying in bed, staring at my phone. I'm debating if I should listen to her messages. I look out my patio window at the bare, spindly trees in the little grove below, the dull gray sky not helping my mood at all. The first two days I was home, I was hardly able to stand for more than a few minutes without getting dizzy. But today I've just stayed in bed because I have nothing to do while I'm off from school.

I throw my phone onto the covers and look over at the plate of jollof my dad made me. I remember when I first learned how to make it with him and my grandparents. We would cram together in their tiny kitchen as we cooked, chatting in Twi. My grandmother's recipe was amazing—I used to always go for seconds. My dad nailed it today, but it was hard to finish my plate. I've been doing okay with fighting off the little voice in my head telling me not to eat carbs, but I'm still feeling sick from my concussion.

The doorbell rings. I sit up on my elbows, straining to hear my dad talking to someone at the door.

"Callie, when I gave you this address, I didn't mean you should come by."

Mom's here? I jump out of bed and press my ear up against the door, exactly like I used to do when my parents fought before the divorce.

"Aisha hasn't been answering my calls—"

"Why should she?" Dad spits at her.

"Look, I know you think this was my fault, but it wasn't. I didn't tell her that she shouldn't be eating as much."

She didn't tell me to eat less, but all her scrutiny and backhanded comments spoke for themselves. My nausea swells, and I cover my hand with my mouth as I try to force it down.

"You need to go."

"I have the right to see my daughter. You can't keep her from me—"

"You just said she's not answering your calls—obviously she doesn't want to see you. I can't believe you went behind my back to contact her, bribing her with your connections."

"You're being ridiculous, Dan. You know I just wanted to help her succeed after everything we've put into her dance career."

"Callie, I'm not joking. Please leave."

"How come I'm always the bad guy?!" she explodes at him. Her volume makes me start to shake, and a moment later the numbness overtakes me, blinding me—

"You don't understand the ballet world at all!" I hear Mom shouting from my parents' bedroom. "This is what it takes. It doesn't matter what that incompetent GP said about her being underweight. She needs to keep at it if she's going to get ahead, Dan."

"You're disgusting," my dad yells at her. "She's been fainting in her rehearsals. This can't continue. Stop acting like this isn't about your failed career—"

Snapping out of the memory, I realize I'm on the verge of hyperventilating. My parents are still yelling as I back away from the door.

I chug a tall glass of water to quell my stomach before I force myself to get down the rest of the jollof. Looking in my dresser mirror briefly, I pull my braids back into a haphazard bun and put on my coat and shoes.

I push open my patio door and close it as quietly as possible. Leaving their incensed voices behind, I make my way out of the small, frostbitten backyard.

24

Ollie's waiting on his back porch when I get to his place. He rushes over to meet me in the middle of the yard, folding me into his arms. I bite my tongue as I try not to lose it, but I can't help but sniffle when I feel his wet cheek against the side of my neck. He finally pulls back a few minutes later.

"Glad you called," he says as he wipes his face. "You're feeling better?"

I nod. We've talked on the phone every night since I left the hospital, so it's weird how great it is to see him. I clear my throat. "Mostly, yeah."

"Did you stop by Neil's?"

"No. Pretty sure he still kinda hates me." I'd mentioned to Ollie that I told my dad about Neil's drinking. "Have you talked to him?"

"Yeah. He doesn't hate you. I think he just needs some time."

I hope that's all it is. That he'll eventually reach out when he's ready. I don't say anything, and it's quiet for a second before he takes hold of my hand. "Come on, let's go for a walk."

In the park behind his house, he turns onto an overgrown hiking trail. The trail twists and winds so much I worry he's getting us lost. Then we emerge in a tiny clearing in the woods by a frozen stream.

Ollie sits next to the water, and I take a seat beside him. "Is this your thinking spot?"

"I guess you could say that," he says as he pulls me into his arms. "I come here to write sometimes."

I lean back against him as I watch the sunset reflect off the glittering surface.

"So what happened today?" he murmurs.

I close my eyes as I tell him about my mom dropping by and my parents fighting.

"When I was younger, they used to argue over what I ate all the time. When I heard them yelling today, I started dissociating. And I had to get out of there."

"I'm sorry." He squeezes my hand. "You said your mom used to push you pretty hard for your training. Did she pressure you about what you ate too?"

I nod, unable to look at him. "I ended up getting sick, and then Neil told my dad that I passed out during practice a few times. I was so pissed at him for telling because I had to move away, and it messed up our plan to win competition scholarships for this prestigious ballet school in New York. And that was kind of the last straw before my dad left my mom. I was just . . . completely in denial about why he was so upset, and I think part of me blamed Neil for everything falling apart. I didn't realize until all this stuff with the showcase that I was still kind of mad at him after all this time. But now I get why he told."

I finally look at Ollie again. He's studying me super closely, but I can tell he's not judging me.

Taking a deep breath, I continue.

"My dad . . . He sent me to an eating disorders clinic. I *hated* it there. All the doctors were so patronizing and would watch us like we were criminals." Even though I know I can trust Ollie, it's so awful saying what happened. I've never talked to anyone about this before. "I was doing better at ballet school, and even when I first got to Huntley, but when I started seeing my mom again, she made comments about my weight. Then those girls in my Ballet class started saying stuff about my body too. It was just a lot and I started eating less again."

That's not the full truth, though. All their comments did make it worse recently, but I still obsessed about food at ballet school and when I first got back here. I cringe internally, remembering all the times I avoided eating at Ollie's and Neil's before my mom even contacted me.

I never cared that much about what I ate until Madame D. and my mom put me on that diet when my hips and thighs started to balloon up when I was twelve. I felt so awful for disappointing them, but I'm realizing now it didn't really make any sense for me to think that I could somehow reverse the effects of puberty. That anger from earlier rises in me again and I stew over how truly messed up it is that my mom and Madame D. warped my brain this badly. I feel so stupid for always being so willing to make excuses for my mom and for telling myself again and again that her strictness was for my own good.

"I hate that your mom and the girls in your Ballet class treated you like that," Ollie says quietly. "I'm so sorry."

"I'm really sorry too. I know how much I scared you and Neil."

We fall silent for a while.

Saying it all out loud has clued me into the fact that I need to reevaluate how dance is affecting me. Both of my showcase performances were cathartic . . . But I can't deny how obsessive I've been about ballet and how much that contributed to what I was doing to myself.

"I can't do this anymore," I find myself whispering. "I have to actually take a step back and figure out what's going on with me."

His face pales. "Do you mean you wanna take a step back from us?"

"No, I mean a step back from ballet."

"Oh. That makes sense."

I search Ollie's eyes. "Wait, do *you* wanna take a step back from us?" I can't breathe for a moment, the thought sucking all the air out of my lungs at once.

He shakes his head and tightens his grip on my hand. "I don't want that either."

"Good," I manage to say, my relief almost overwhelming me.

I suddenly become aware my face is wet. I swipe my coat sleeve over my eyes before he reaches out and takes my face in his hands, wiping my tears with his thumbs.

"Aisha . . ." He doesn't say anything else, but it's there. I can see how he feels so perfectly clearly, blooming in the space between us. And I know he can see the same thing in my eyes.

Genuine terror overtakes me. How could this possibly be happening so soon?

I pull away from him and lie back, trying to curb my panic and catch my breath. Ollie lies back next to me and closes his eyes. His face is serene while his shoulders rise and fall slowly.

"When you breathe like that . . . Are you meditating or something?"

"Yeah. I know it's stupid." He shrugs sheepishly.

I shake my head. "No, it just sounds impossible. How do you not *think?*"

Hannah's emotion exercises were hard enough. Trying to clear my mind altogether sounds even more difficult.

"It took me a while to get it. I try to see myself as just watching my thoughts, not seeing them as me. And then they start to slow down a bit."

"But aren't your thoughts you? 'I think, therefore I am' and all that?"

"There's a me behind my thoughts that just watches them without getting all attached. Does that make any sense?"

"Um, not really."

"There's this thing that helps. Instead of thinking about what everything actually is when I look at stuff, I try to see things without putting a label on them."

Taking a deep breath, I let my thoughts drift as the sun sinks below the tall trees around us. I'm aware of the sound of their turning leaves brushing gently against each other, the crispness of the winter wind whooshing over my face, the cool ground beneath me, and Ollie's warm, always warm, hand in mine. All of these things are one singular thing that encompasses me, every inch of separation completely washed away.

Ollie's eyes open and he smiles a little.

I smile back before I let myself drift back into everything again. My mind gets further away, and I don't miss it. I wonder who the "I" is that remains so present, the true presence of everything. The I that doesn't care about all the things my mind does. All the things that make up my identity, all the roles that I play.

I'm not a dancer. I'm not a girl with dissociation and an eating disorder. I'm not the color of my skin. Who I am at my core is beyond definition.

I let out a quick breath as the realization fully hits me.

"You okay?" he asks.

"Uh-huh, I'm just . . ." I can't describe it. I don't even try to reduce everything down as eloquently as he can. "I'm okay."

He smiles again before he gently brushes his lips against mine, torturing me until I can't take it anymore, kissing him in earnest.

I pull back a while later when his hands start shaking. The sun is gone—it's almost completely dark now.

I look at him closely. "Are you good?"

"Yeah. It's just freezing," Ollie says as he stands up and pulls me to my feet.

Once we get back to his house, he helps me up the tree and through his window, setting me down gently.

He still has his arms around me, and I can't look away from him.

"I missed you," I find myself saying. "I've, uh, been thinking about you . . . A lot."

He stares at me unblinkingly, and my face burns as I realize how that sounded. He says nothing, but from how he leans in and kisses me deeper than he's ever kissed me before, I know he missed me too.

We shuffle backward until we bump into the end of his bed. I move away from him to take my jacket off, and he does the same. His eyes are weighted and impossibly dark in the low light of his room.

There's no way to hide what I'm thinking right now. All my shyness melts because I know he's thinking it too. My hands don't shake at all as I take in a breath and peel off my shirt, not looking away from him for a second. His eyes slowly trace across my skin, his gaze leaving a trail of heat in its wake.

He pulls me into his arms, and I can't think for a long moment. I lean away from him and gently tug at the bottom of his shirt. "This okay?"

Ollie nods, his eyes only half present.

I wait for him to meet my gaze. "You sure?"

After a second, he catches his breath, focusing all of his attention on me.

"I'm sure." His voice and body are steady now.

After I get his shirt off, Ollie wraps his comforter around us, and my thoughts abandon me again. At his touch, my blood starts to simmer inside my veins. When his hands finally stray from the neutral areas of my body for the first time, he shoots me a questioning look. I nod and then I'm only feeling again but so much more intensely than I ever have.

Then he's seeing me like no one has ever seen me. It isn't perfectly seamless like I imagined alone, but it's honest and that's somehow even better. All the awkward fumbling and regrettable noises stop mattering in the little sliver of space that makes up this moment of us together.

Ollie squeezes my fingers tight as he pulls away from my face to watch me. My mind melts into nothing and my body follows suit, my bones going liquid.

When I can focus again, he's looking at me in that way that cuts right into me, laying everything bare.

"Was that okay?" he murmurs.

"That was great." I can't stop the dopey grin that takes over my face. Ollie grins back before burying his face in my shoulder.

I close my eyes and catch my breath. "Um, did you want me to . . . ?"

He shakes his head as he pulls his face away from the crook of my neck and wraps an arm around me.

It's quiet for a really long time, but it isn't natural and relaxed. I can tell something's wrong.

I sit up to look at him. "What's up?"

"Nothing. It's just . . ." Ollie sighs deeply and closes his eyes. "What if I can't . . . you know."

"Uh . . ." I almost stop breathing. We haven't ever talked about this and I'm not sure how to. We'd been taking things pretty slow up until now and I thought he'd already sensed that I wanted to wait and that he wanted to hold off too. "I'm not really ready to—"

"I don't mean now," he says quickly, and oxygen enters my body again. "I know we're not in a rush or anything. But what if I never can? Would you be okay with that?"

What just happened was overwhelming enough; I'm fine with not going much further beyond that.

I squeeze his hand. "Of course that's okay with me."

"Okay." He gets quiet again.

"What are you thinking?" I murmur into his shoulder.

"I don't know. I've gone over it with my therapist so many times and I get that what happened isn't my fault. But sometimes—" Ollie cuts himself off, and when I pull back to study him, he's squeezing his eyes shut.

I tighten my grip on his hand. "Sometimes what?"

He's silent for so long, I think he's not going to answer, but finally he does. "Sometimes I think there might be a part of me . . . that likes guys. And that he knew it, that's why he . . ."

I run a hand through his hair, pushing it off his face. He keeps his eyes shut.

"You know, liking guys doesn't make it your fault," I say quietly.

Ollie finally opens his eyes, and I can see that he doesn't fully believe me. It's physically painful seeing him like this. I'm glad he trusts me enough to talk to me about it, but I really wish he didn't feel this way . . . like he's done something wrong, like there's something wrong with who he is when there isn't.

"Did you think . . ." I stop and wait until I can speak without my voice breaking. "Did you think you being bi would change how I feel about you or something?"

"It might have. Even if you didn't want it to," Ollie mutters, not meeting my gaze.

I wrap my arms around his neck, and he looks at me again. "It's okay. Nothing would change how I feel."

The weight of my words fill the room, and he searches my eyes for an airless moment.

"How do you feel about me?" he whispers.

I shift away from him a bit, worrying he might have already felt the frantic thrumming in my chest.

The way we're staring at each other is just like how we looked at each other by the stream earlier. I'm just as terrified now as I was then, but there's no escaping it anymore.

"Ollie, come on. You know exactly how I feel."

His face softens, his eyes lighting me up before he's too close to see.

I can only feel him as he brushes those three tiny words against my mouth without a sound. I say them silently back before I part his lips with mine. Everything he feels rushes into me, filling me up until I almost overflow.

*

I'm awoken by loud knocking at Ollie's door. "Aisha's dad is here looking for her!" Sophie calls out.

"Oh shit." I jump up and pull my shirt back on.

Ollie sits up, blinking for a second before he processes what's happening. "Crap." He flies out of bed as well.

I give him a quick kiss before I head for the door.

"Do you want me to come down with you?" he asks.

"No," I say quickly. "Stay here. I'll call you later."

I race down the stairs way too fast and I have to stop on the middle landing and lean against the wall when everything starts to tilt and whirl around me. After a few breaths, I continue down at a much slower speed.

"Aisha!" Ollie's mom says from the door, standing next to my dad. "You're here. I wasn't sure. You should have come down for dinner."

"Hi, Anissa," I say as brightly as possible, even as my dad's eyes dig sharply into me. I brush carefully past him at the door. "Sorry, I'll stop by for dinner soon. Bye."

"Um, I guess Neil told you where Ollie's place was?" I ask my dad once we're outside.

He only points at the car, gesturing for me to get in.

"Are you not gonna say anything?" I ask once we've been driving for a while.

"Do you have any idea how much you scared me?" he shoots back, his voice low. He's still focused on the road.

"I'm sorry."

"Why would you take off without telling me?"

"You were busy fighting with Mom," I say quietly.

"You should have at least texted," he snaps at me before taking a deep inhale. "You're grounded."

Grounded? I do my best to keep from laughing. He hasn't been here for years and now he's acting like some type of helicopter parent. "Okay then."

"Watch your tone." He shoots me an unamused look. "Aisha, you're still recovering. Why would you think going out on your own was a good idea?"

"I wasn't on my own."

"I'm aware. Do I even want to know what you two were doing?"

My face explodes in heat as I quickly turn away from him. I stare out my window, not saying anything else for the rest of the ride home.

25

The drive to my first therapy session the next morning is almost as awkward as the ride home from Ollie's. As much as I'm not looking forward to the appointment, it'll still be a relief to be away from my dad for a bit, given how tense things have been since last night. The only noise the entire way is the sound of the windshield wipers squeaking across the wet front window. After waiting a while at reception, I'm led to the doctor's office.

When I sit down, I stare up at the bookshelf of psychology books above the sleet-streaked window, reading over the long, wordy titles.

Dr. Maheshwari introduces himself but doesn't ask a bunch of intrusive questions since I filled out a form earlier. All he says is that we can talk about whatever, whether I prefer to talk about what's been going on with my day or get into deeper stuff.

I start by telling him a bit about my time away from school.

"It's been super boring. I don't really know what to do with myself."

He studies me. "Does the idea of doing nothing scare you?"

"Not really. I just don't like lying around wasting time."

"Letting yourself relax and not feeling like you have to be doing anything productive might be worth exploring."

Is he telling me to be lazier? "I guess that's a doable thing to try."

"So why are you taking time off school?"

I tell him about falling and my concussion and everything. It's easier to talk about than I thought it would be. There isn't any visible judgment on his face at least.

"You're not returning your mom's calls because you're upset with her?"

I nod, focusing on the bookshelf again. "At first, I was mostly worried she was mad about me messing up my performance after she helped me get that opportunity with that ballet school instructor. But since I've been away from school, I've been thinking I'm pretty upset with her too. Like, I wonder if she cares more about the performance than how I'm actually doing."

"Do you think it's possible she realizes how much pressure she was putting on you and is trying to get in contact to apologize?"

I bite my tongue, too embarrassed to admit that I don't think she's really sorry. From what she said to my dad about not believing any of this is her fault, I don't think she really gets how screwed up everything she's done truly is.

It seems blindingly obvious now, all the ways in which my relationship with my mom and my relationship with ballet are mirror images of each other. How I've always molded myself to live up to their standards. Ignoring my pain, forcing myself into impossible positions. Refusing to acknowledge when I began to bend and break, shoving the pieces of myself back into the shape I thought I had to be.

As hard as it is to think and talk about this, I know it's what I need to make sense of things for myself and finally figure out what I need to do to get better.

*

When I get home, I head to my room and collapse on my bed, staring blankly out the patio door at the rain assaulting the barren trees in the yard. I can feel the building pressure of tears behind my eyes, but nothing actually happens. Rolling over on my back, I take a few deep breaths before I put my phone to my ear.

"Aisha." Mom picks up almost immediately. "Thank you for calling me back. How are you?"

"My concussion's a little better," I mutter.

"Glad to hear that," she says. "Don't worry about your performance. I talked to Victoria's instructor, and he said you can audition at the National School in January."

My heart thrums with excitement for a moment before I force the feeling away.

What would Michaela do? For once, I don't have a concrete answer to that. It's all on me now. I'm the only one who can make this decision.

I take a steadying breath. "I don't think that's a good idea."

"What do you mean?"

My mouth goes dry. "I need to take a break from ballet."

"Of course. I meant after you're all healed up—"

"I don't mean because of my concussion. I mean because of my eating disorder."

This is the first time I've said it out loud. It's not a relief exactly, but something loosens in my throat after I've said the words.

"I know your father is making a big deal out of this, but it's really not as serious as all that. You don't have a *disorder.* You just have to be a little more careful—"

"Mom, stop." My voice breaks. "Look, I just need to get better. Dad was right. I feel like this is more about you than it is about me."

"Aisha, how can you say that? Everything I've done is for you," she says, her voice strained and tight. "All the sacrifices your father and I have made. All the money we've spent . . ."

"You think I don't know that?" I blurt out. "I get how much you and Dad invested in me all these years. I worked so hard to be everything you've wanted me to be. But I have to figure out what *I* want now."

"You want this. You've always loved dancing. That's why we put you in classes."

"I do love dancing. But I feel like doing ballet isn't the right thing for me right now."

"So you're going to keep doing modern?" she asks, her voice flat. Since she was there for Neil's and my performance, I'm sure she saw how deeply modern has affected me.

I think about the Pointe Noire performance again, and how I'd never tell my mom how much it inspired me because she doesn't take modern as seriously as ballet. She sees everything in such a binary way, like both forms can't have value—completely discounting mixed forms like contemporary ballet because they don't have the same historical prestige as classical.

Even though modern has been so emotionally taxing, I think sticking with it might help me continue to sort out everything that's been lying dormant in me for so long.

I suck in a deep breath before finally responding. "Yeah. I'm going to stay in modern when I get back to school."

"Aisha—"

"I gotta go." Hanging up, I bury my face in my pillow. Still, no tears come.

I'm not giving up ballet forever. I do still love it, even though a lot of the time it hasn't loved me back.

Maybe there will be a place for me in ballet when I'm ready. Madame A. was definitely right about contemporary ballet being something for me to explore—it's already unlocked a lot for me.

Classical will always be my first love, but I know going back to a ballet-dedicated school wouldn't be healthy for me. Still, it's hard to believe I'm passing up a National Ballet School audition after everything I've been through. My throat constricts as I start to second guess myself. What if I never get an opportunity like this again?

I quickly grab my headphones, putting on one of the playlists Ollie sent me this week to distract myself from the thought. I focus on the calming tones until my mind gets fuzzy and I doze off.

✳

My dad has the week off work, so it's impossible to avoid him. When he finally stops giving me the silent treatment the next day, I help him make fufu and plantain for dinner.

I'm going stir crazy, so I convince him to let me go out for a run after we eat, but he insists on tagging along.

An old lady walking her ugly little crusty-eyed dog stops in her tracks as we jog by. She says nothing when we greet her.

"Well, isn't this just delightful," I mutter after we pass her.

"Yeah, just great," my dad grumbles through his sharp intakes of breath. We run a little farther before he says, "Just wanted to check in with you about that eating disorders therapy group. It's coming up next Monday. Are you still willing to check it out?"

I nod at him briefly. I'm not excited about it or anything, but I know I should give it a chance.

I stop, letting him catch up. He wraps an arm around my shoulders but I lean away from him. "You're kinda stinky."

"Rude," he says as he pulls away and turns around to start back toward our place. "And here I was thinking when we got home I was going to give you some of the sugar bread I picked up."

My grandmother used to make sugar bread all the time, giving me a huge hunk of it to dunk in my hot chocolate on cold evenings.

"Wait, you got sugar bread?" I call after him as I start moving again.

*
*

One of the plus sides of having a couple of weeks off school is that I have more than enough time to take out my braids and redo them. I've had them in for a while. After I'm done, I start working on thread instead of my hair, weaving together some bracelets. I'm thankful for something to keep my hands busy at least.

Ebi and Khadija text me to check in, and I let them know I'm doing okay. I appreciate that they don't push me to tell them everything. It's nice to have some normal, not super heavy conversations.

Ollie keeps sending me playlists while I'm stuck at home. One night when I'm looking up some obscure band from one of them, I come across a video of him on YouTube, doing a cover of the song I was looking up.

When I click on his channel, I can't believe it. He's posted a ton of covers and original songs. I click on the earliest post, and it's the song he wrote about me. It must be the video he handed in for his class.

It's so strange seeing him singing on a screen instead of right in front of me, close enough to touch. He doesn't seem very comfortable with recording himself. As he introduces the song, he stutters way more than he usually does. When he starts singing, though, his voice is completely steady. I replay it way too many times, like an obsessive freak.

Eventually, I stop and go back to his channel, clicking on his latest video. To my surprise, it's a full Q&A instead of a cover. He seems a little more comfortable on camera now than in his first video, but he still flubs his words quite a bit more than he does in person.

"Uh, not really sure why you guys want this. But you kept asking so here it is," he says as he stares down at his phone. "I guess I'll just answer the questions I got the most. I would say my biggest songwriting inspiration is probably Leonard Cohen, I guess? Bob Dylan, Alex Turner . . ."

He goes on, but I get distracted when I take a look at the view count. It has over five thousand views. The video was posted yesterday.

What in the living hell? Why didn't he tell me about this? I guess he wanted it to be his own thing. But this is wild that he wouldn't mention how much attention he's been getting.

"Oh, this was a popular one—Am I dating anyone?"

Checking back in at that, I find him biting down on a brilliant smile. "Yes. I have a girlfriend."

I'm grinning like a total dope. We've never actually said out loud that we're boyfriend/girlfriend, which is kind of funny considering everything we've been through and what we said to each other the other night. I spend the rest of the evening listening to all the songs he's posted, way too many times, letting his voice lull me to sleep.

*

When Neil spots me in the cafeteria at school the following week, he comes over and traps me in a bone-crushing hug. I squeeze back just as hard.

"I'm sorry," I say as I pull away from him, "for telling my dad what was going on with you."

He shrugs as we move along the lunch line. "It's cool. My dad did force me to start going to this sponsor program thing. But it's not too bad."

"That's great, Neil." I wish I knew how to bring up that I'm still worried about what he said when he was blacked out at Ollie's party. Hopefully his sponsor can help him get to the root of his drinking. "I'm so glad you're doing that."

"I'm really sorry about everything. I promise, I'm gonna try to stick with this program, okay?"

I nod, breaking into a smile. "Okay. Hey, let's see your hand for a sec?"

He holds out his arm, and I quickly tie a friendship bracelet around his wrist, just like the ones we had when we were kids. I hold out my wrist to show him mine.

He shoots me a surprised look. "You made these?"

I shrug. "I had a lot of time on my hands. Neil . . . You know that I get why you told my dad about my eating stuff and everything, right? I'm not pissed at you."

He searches my eyes for a moment, and I can tell he's glad I've actually taken to heart what we said without words at the showcase.

"Thanks." He lets out a big breath as we finish grabbing our food and head to the caf doors. "I thought you might still be mad. So are you going to be in Modern later?"

"Yeah. I'm taking a little bit of a break from ballet, but I'm still gonna stick with Hannah's class."

Thankfully, Madame A. said I can do some online work to make up the credits for my Ballet class.

"Cool. She's gonna be really happy to have you back."

I nod, biting at my lip. "Even though Modern's not always easy, I'm glad I get to do it with you. You were great at the showcase, and, um, you really helped me figure some stuff out."

He shrugs, his face reddening. "No prob."

I take a deep breath before continuing. "I know you said you might not apply to college . . . But I really hope you think about it next year. Maybe we can apply to schools together?"

"Yeah." He squeezes my hand for a second, and I squeeze back. "That might be cool."

When we get to our little theater group, everyone else is too busy talking about their upcoming *Chicago* debut night to say hi, but Ollie grins at me as I sit down next to him.

He pulls me into his lap and starts to lean into me. "Hey, you."

"Hey, yourself," I say, pulling back a bit. "Is there something you wanted to tell me?"

Ollie frowns. "What do you mean?"

I look over at Neil, but he's busy talking to Ebi and Khadija.

"I found your channel," I murmur. I don't think he wants me

advertising it to everyone.

He stares at the hallway floor. "Oh."

"Sorry if you wanted it to be your own thing," I say quickly. "It just felt weird not telling you I found it."

Ollie rubs his eyes. "It's okay. Yeah, I guess I wanted some feedback from people who don't know me. You basically have to say I'm good because you're my . . ."

I raise my eyebrows. "Because I'm your what?"

His eyes widen, and I see the exact moment he remembers what he said about me in his Q&A. He opens his mouth but then freezes, not saying anything.

I get that saying it to a camera was probably easier for him than this is. Things have been so unbelievably intense between us since that day I snuck out, but we've still only been dating for a relatively short amount of time.

I let him off the hook for now. "I mean, I don't have to say you're good. I wouldn't lie and say you were if you actually sucked."

"That's sweet of you," he deadpans, rolling his eyes.

I fix him with a stubborn look. "Now you have to admit how talented you are since so many people like your stuff."

Ollie shrugs, glancing away from me again.

"Come on. You have, like, thousands of views. Oll, that's *amazing*."

He winces. "It kind of freaks me out when you say it like that."

I wrap my arms around his neck. "I think it's really cool that you're putting yourself out there," I say before moving in and pressing my lips to his.

"Hey, you two like a nice, steamy free show, right?" Ebi asks loudly.

I break away from Ollie, grinning sheepishly, while Neil snorts at us.

Khadija laughs. "We've got some free tickets to our show next week if you want them."

"Thanks. Wouldn't miss it," I say.

Ollie's brow furrows. "Aren't you still grounded?"

"Well, I'm actually ungrounded under the condition that you come over for dinner at my place this weekend."

"Uh, doesn't your dad want me dead? Might have to pass on that."

"Neil's coming too," I say. "We'll protect you if he tries anything."

Blinking, Neil looks up from his phone. "I'm going where?"

Ollie shakes his head. "Well, that's reassuring."

⁂

In the Modern studio later, Hannah takes me aside before class starts.

"I just wanted to check in with you about your recovery."

I suck in a deep breath. "I'm doing okay. Like, I'm getting help with stuff. Thanks for having me back to class."

"Of course. Please let me know if you ever need anything, okay?"

Madame A. basically said the same thing when I told her I needed to take a break from ballet. She was so understanding, I almost teared up when I saw her this morning, but I managed to keep it together.

When I left the Ballet studio, I ignored the girls' whispers. Madame A. has always tried to be in my corner when she's noticed them being awful, but I know there's not much she can really do. I bet she realizes that getting their parents involved would only make them dislike me more. I'm sure she's been there herself.

Prasheetha was the only one who came up to ask me if I was okay. I said I was fine and left it at that. I think being away from all of their petty toxicity for a bit is really going to do me some good.

I know I really need to work on getting myself together to avoid becoming obsessive about ballet again. As much as I wish getting better was something I could set a date to be done with, deep down I know it's going to be an ongoing thing I just have to deal with. The same thing applies to Neil's recovery, so I'm going to do my best to be patient with both of us.

Sometimes I still get the overwhelming feeling that I've made the wrong decision, that I'm ruining my life, just like my mom thinks. But that's been happening less and less lately. Since Madame A. isn't writing me off for taking a break, I guess I don't have to, either. Whether it's later this year, or in twelfth grade, I know I do want to go back to ballet again. I just want to be totally sure I'm ready.

Toward the end of class, Hannah has us do some freestyle solos. When it's my turn, I let myself go to the place I did during my first week here. That unfiltered world of joy that existed when I was a kid, completely swept away by a spellbinding fairy kingdom of my own making. That place where I'm not thinking about anything besides how amazing it feels to move with limitless freedom and abandon.

Everyone claps when I finish, and I don't feel super embarrassed when I have to wipe my eyes. Neil smiles and wraps an arm around me as I take my seat. Taking a deep breath, I let myself sit in how fully grounded I am in this moment. I know I'm exactly where I need to be.

A Few Months Later

I'm sitting at my desk, the early sunlight streaming in through my window as I finish off the letter I'm writing to my mom. Dr. Maheshwari suggested I start writing to her, even if I never actually give her the letters.

We haven't spoken since I told her I didn't want to audition for the National School. When I first started writing, I knew I was upset with her, but all the rage that poured onto the page was a shock. The letters I've written recently have been a little more measured and possibly something I could send her at some point in the future. It's still a bit terrifying to think about how she might respond.

I hear a honk and glance outside. Sophie's car is pulling into the driveway. Stuffing the letter in my desk drawer with all the others, I run down the stairs.

"Dad, I'm heading out now. Call you when I get there!" I yell over to him as I slip on my shoes.

"Aisha, can you come in here for a moment?" my dad calls from the kitchen.

"But they're waiting outside."

"Just a moment," he says, and I stifle a sigh. I'm lucky he even agreed to let me camp overnight at a music festival, so I head into the kitchen without further protest.

"Honey, I really want you to have fun with your friends. But please promise me you'll be careful." From his dark expression, I get that he means that in every sense of the word.

"I will."

He looks relieved. I think he can tell that I mean it.

It's been a gradual adjustment, having him around all the time. At first, I kept telling myself it wouldn't really be permanent. When he was in Tokyo, I'd always forced myself to keep him at arm's length to protect myself from how much I hated that he wasn't here. I'd wished for him to be around more for so long, I think I'd kind of given up on it ever really happening.

Getting used to being completely honest with him about how I'm doing with my recovery and everything has been difficult. Dr. M. and I have talked at length about all my trust issues. Letting the people who care about me know when I'm not okay, instead of pretending it's not happening, has been a huge challenge, but I've been getting a lot better with actually opening up when it matters.

"And don't take any drugs from strangers. I know what goes on at these things."

I nod, containing another sigh. He can't really think I'm dumb enough to take mystery drugs from randoms. "Okay. Anything else?"

"That's it, sweetie." He reaches over to give me a tight hug.

"Dad, you're crushing me," I say, laughing as I pull away.

"Have a good time. I love you so much."

I hear Sophie's car horn blare again out front.

"Love you too. Gotta go."

I fly down the driveway and hop in the back seat next to Ollie. He throws his arm around me and grins, practically humming with excitement. He's been talking about this festival for weeks, breaking down every single band we have to catch and the exact times we have to get to each stage, in excruciating detail.

"You're so lucky we didn't take off without you," Sophie says as she pulls onto the street.

Neil grins at Sophie before looking back at me from the passenger seat. "Everything go okay with your dad?"

I shrug. "He was pretty much shitting himself about all of the drugs, sex, and rock and roll I'm about to be exposed to."

Neil snorts. "Poor Dan."

I shake my head, laughing. "He'll get through it."

Ollie reaches over the console, connects his phone to the sound system, and then settles back next to me, wrapping an arm around me again. Music floods the car, and I let my brain float off, syncing completely into the now. I lean back against him before I turn to watch out the window as the road endlessly zooms up and disappears behind us.

Acknowledgments

Thank you to my family for your support throughout the years and being so generous with your time when I forced you to read all my bad first drafts. And to my mother, Loretta—thank you for instilling a deep appreciation of literature in me from the start. For filling my childhood home with the work of Black authors like my namesake, Maya Angelou. For nurturing a love of reading within me and my sisters while we spent countless hours in our living room taking turns reading entire novels to each other.

Eternal gratitude to my agents, Lesley Sabga and Julie Gwinn, as well as my editor, Claire Caldwell. Thank you for believing in this story and working so hard to get it into the hands of those who need it most. Many thanks to the Annick Press team, including Amanda Olson, Bailey Hoffman, Stephanie Strachan, Serah-Marie McMahon, Sarah Dunn, Kaela Cadieux, Katie Hearn, Khary Mathurin, Monica Charny, Rivka Cranley, Yousra Medhkour, Asiya Awale, Brendan Ouellette, Diana Itseleva, Gayna Theophilus, Heather Davies, Jieun Lee, David Caron, and Rick Wilks. A big thank you to consultant editor Ameerah Holliday, copy editor Debbie Innes, and proofreader

Mary Ann Blair. And thank you to the people involved with my beautiful cover, PeachPod and Zainab's Echo.

Community is a huge part of my writing process, so many thanks to all the people at InkWell Workshops and Kathy Friedman for cultivating such a vibrant group of talented writers. Shout out to Louisa Onomé for being for a great mentor through my querying journey and fielding my millions of questions with patience. Thanks to Eli Matilda for the countless hours spent talking through this story and your unwavering support. Thanks to the 2023 debuts group, the Toronto Writers Crew, and all of my incredible writing buddies. Thanks to freelance editor Natalie Crown and my fabulous beta readers: Danielle Davis, Davona Mapp, and Chelsea La Vecchia.

Also, a huge thanks to authors Jonny Garza Villa, Joya Goffney, Gabriela Martins, Joy L. Smith, Cheryl Rainfield, Ryan Douglass, Debbie Rigaud, Kayla Ancrum, Mariko Turk, Vanessa L. Torres, Liselle Sambury, Britney S. Lewis, Kristin Dwyer, Kristina Forest, and Courtney Summers for your support. <3

About the Author

Maya Ameyaw is a Toronto-based community arts writing instructor and a former bookseller. She has edited several mental-health-themed anthologies, and her writing was included in *Brilliance is the Clothing I Wear*, which was featured in *Quill & Quire*. Maya also runs a YouTube series and blog where she interviews debut authors about their journeys to publication.

🐦 @MayaAmeyaw